THE QUEEN OF ALL POISONS

The Queen of all Poisons

A Dr. Lily Robinson Novel

BJ Magnani

Encircle Publications, LLC
Farmington, Maine, U.S.A.

Editor: Cynthia Brackett-Vincent
Book design: Eddie Vincent
Cover design by Deirdre Wait
Cover photographs © Getty Images

Published by: Encircle Publications, LLC
PO Box 187
Farmington, ME 04930

Visit: http://encirclepub.com

Sign up for Encircle Publications newsletter and specials
http://eepurl.com/cs8taP

Printed in U.S.A.

DEDICATION

To all mothers and daughters.
May they always find each other—on earth, and in heaven.

ACKNOWLEDGMENTS

Many thanks to my friends and colleagues whose superb feedback enriched Lily's story, and my life.

And to my patients, who provide inspiration every single day.

PROLOGUE

COLOMBIA, SOUTH AMERICA, MANY YEARS AGO

The little girl felt a soft hand push her head down.

"Get under the cot now and stay down," Maggie shouted.

There were many earsplitting noises, like a pop, no it was a pop, pop, pop in quick succession. The child could hear men, not just Maggie, shouting in loud, angry voices and her tiny body felt that wave of tingles spread outward in a fan pattern across her tummy. It always appeared when something scared her and she started to cry. As Maggie peered out from between the nylon zippered ends of the tent, she was crying too, and waved her hand behind her trying to indicate shush. There were bodies everywhere oozing small pieces of themselves onto the jungle floor. Maggie swung her head when she heard the swoosh of a machete.

"Oh God, no. Please don't hurt me, please," Maggie pleaded as a hand thrust through the split zipper and grabbed her by the hair, yanking her out through the opening. Maggie screamed as loud as she could while trying to free her head from his hands and scratch her way back towards the nylon. She howled one last time and then there was quiet.

There was a momentary lull within the tent and the terrified child dared not move from under the cot. A very faint patter, like an insect scurrying across the ground, was the only sound she could hear. "Mommy, mommy?" she whimpered. "Where's mommy?" Her eyes finally opened. The basket of tiny frogs had tipped over, the lid off to one side, and one small yellow dot hopped toward the cot and jumped under a box. The little girl knew she wasn't supposed to touch it. Mommy had said so. Then there were voices again. Men's voices.

One came closer. A huge figure entered the tent and looked around. He kicked the grass basket and the rest of the frogs jumped out. She tried to

1

hide deeper under the cot, but his hand grabbed the child and pulled her free.

He said something to her in a language she didn't understand. The air seemed trapped in her lungs. It wasn't that she didn't want to breathe, she wasn't sure if she could breathe. The man took the bandana from around his neck and fastened it over her tear-filled green eyes. Everything went black. She felt herself being lifted and then carried over his shoulder. The sun was hot on the back of her head and the steam in the air filled her nostrils. It was heavy air, air weighted with the smells of death.

Although her eyes were covered, she squeezed the lids tightly together, and felt the tears stream down her cheeks. *Angel, angel please come to me; take me up into heaven and keep me safe,* she prayed. Her small body could no longer hold the tension and her hands fell to her sides. She let go of her consciousness, drifting into the blackness as they moved into the jungle and disappeared into the emerald forest.

Part 1

The Asphalt Jungle (the present)

CHAPTER 1

BOSTON

Just between beats. There's a 20-millisecond window of vulnerability to create chaos, just before the heart squeezes out its next beat. I keep thinking about the assassination while I'm sitting in my office. He was just another threat with a bad heart. My poison incurs sudden death, like a physical blow to the heart delivered at the right time. I try not to rationalize these deaths anymore or allow my emotions to creep in. Years of denial have trained my clinical mind to focus only on the target. I do whatever I must to get the job done. It's about mastering control, yet letting go.

About a month ago, the Agency asked me to assassinate a terrorist infiltrator quickly and quietly in New York City. I waited for him at a coffee shop he frequented. It always amazes me how we are such creatures of habit. Routines—we eat the same breakfast, walk or drive the same way home, and visit our same favorite little café, every day. Even the terrorists. My target took two sugars with his French dark roast—the waitress brought him the two packets when she served him. They don't leave the sugar bowls at the tables anymore in this neighborhood.

She poured the coffee while standing behind the counter, and when she turned back to put the pot on the burner, I swapped out the packets. Coffee, delivered with steam rising from the brim, waited patiently as he tore open the sugars, dumped the contents into the abyss, and stirred the dark mixture with a cheap spoon. After drinking only half a cup he began to gasp for air and had difficulty breathing. He turned blue and slid off his chair, seizing as he hit the ground. Several people jumped up in alarm, including me. "Call 911!" While everyone surrounded the man on the floor, I picked up the empty sugar packets from the table and used my napkin to replace them with ones I had used.

5

I killed him with cyanide.

Not exotic, I know, but reliable on short notice. Most people think they can smell the bitter almond scent, but only a small percentage of the population can reliably detect any odor. Luckily, I've got that gene. Potassium cyanide crystals can't be distinguished from common sugar crystals. White crystals look like, well, all other white crystals. I always carry packets of sugar—and even packets of artificial sweetener—laced with enough potassium cyanide to produce death within minutes. Once you ingest the poison, the acid in your stomach converts it to hydrogen cyanide, and death will soon follow. Within minutes it delivers a knockout punch to the powerhouses of your body via the respiratory electron transport chain—the mitochondrial workhorses of your cells that generate ATP, which gives you the energy you need to live. Cyanide blocks all that, and without oxygen your cells die of chemical asphyxiation.

I exited the café during the commotion, having already paid for my cup of coffee. Another fatal blow, just between beats. With the collar turned up on my coat, I inhaled the wind and felt the oxygen fill my lungs, as my own mitochondria powered my disappearance into the crowded street.

*   *   *

I hear a knock at my office door, bringing my mind into focus. It must be Lisa. Best administrative assistant I've ever had, who anticipates my every professional need. Lisa knows I'm a physician with expertise in toxicology—that's *all* she knows. Her job is to keep my calendar and sort out when I'm at the hospital, or at the medical school. Her biggest challenge is how to account for the days when I'm at neither.

"Hi, Dr. Lily. Just reminding you that you have a lecture at the medical school you have to prepare for. Do you have everything you need?"

"Thanks, Lisa. I'm all set. Everything for the students is on the internal network."

"Okay," she says, rolling her eyes just a little as she spots my stilettos. "Here's your itinerary for the day. You also have some meetings scheduled this afternoon. One with the Dean, and a last-minute meeting with Chad."

A meeting with Chad. The acid in my stomach begins to rise like a tide during a full moon. The pH of my entire gastric contents drops precipitously, and I find myself reaching around to the back of my desk for antacids.

Chad is Pixie Dust's replacement. That was her code name. A woman with a pink streak in her hair met me in my office years ago and begged me to help. She told me I would be serving my country. All I had to do was poison one man, an enemy of the State, and make it look like he died from natural causes. I was at a low point in my life, when post-traumatic stress had hijacked my brain after a devastating incident on the job. I never really recovered. At the moment Pixie Dust asked, I probably could have been talked into anything. It's been years now. The Agency has taught me well, and I hide behind their cloak of invisibility.

My medical work keeps me in the city of Boston where I take the T as our subway is known, between the hospital and a small condo central to the buzz of the Hub. Yet the truth is, my home, and my heart, reside at a seaside cottage on the coast of Massachusetts where I escape this life, and that life. It's there where I keep a poison garden, nurtured by the moist sea air and ready to yield the natural killers I need.

There've been many bodies.

My conscience still screams, but my ears have turned deaf. Pavlov would call it conditioning. I take solace in the realization that I am not alone. A band of highly trained specialists, sworn to protect this country and other democratic nations, have fought by my side for many years. We are a team, subtly shaping the politics of the world by wiping out the bad and the ugly. Protecting global freedom from the terror that swells beneath our feet. This is our mission, and I'm all in.

The acid content of my stomach has reached epic proportions. When I see Chad this afternoon, I'll swallow the bitter pill that has become my treatment for unimaginable loss.

*   *   *

I expect him here any minute. When he visits me in my office he does a 360 review of the walls and shelves, scanning for any new mementos of toxins or other drug paraphernalia I may have acquired since the last time he saw me. There's noise outside my door. He must be here.

"Hi Chad, come on in and have a seat," I say, pointing to a chair in front of the table that stands in for my desk.

"Doctor, so good to see you again." He grabs my hand and places his other hand on top of it, as if to weld us together. "I want to give you an update on the NYC case, you know, the lone wolf from the coffee shop." He sees my surprise. "Robinson, I know this is always hard for you, and coming so soon after the last case. We sort of left you on your own for that one, and I know you need some time to…to, catch your breath. We've learned quite a lot in the last several weeks, and it turns out our lone wolf wasn't such a lone wolf after all. We knew he had ties to Russia, but we didn't know how extensive they were—are. Every day in the news, the American public hears how the Russians are disrupting our way of life. They've hacked our computers, they put out fake news using bots and Internet trolls who obscure the truth; and we know they've meddled in our elections. Oh, and they're moving illegal drugs into the US."

"I know about the drugs, Chad. Don't forget—when I'm not working for the Agency, I'm working here, at the hospital, trying to save lives."

"Well, this time it's something big. You've seen what's been happening internationally. They're targeting the French, the Brits, and of course, us. It's chaos. We're busy tying our shoelaces and they're about to punch us in the gut. We need you."

I choke up and feel my stomach churn. I've done this long enough to know I want to help, but there's always that part of me that holds back. It's the oath I took to do no harm. Now I'm a killer. But it doesn't matter. Each life I take will save so many more.

"What's the plan, Chad?" My voice is almost shaking.

And then he lays it all out for me.

CHAPTER 2

NEW YORK CITY

Beth Winslow finished putting on her face powder at her dressing table. She walked back into her bedroom and caught a glimpse of herself in the mirror over her dresser. *Hmm, wrinkled.* She pulled down hard on the bottom edges of her suit jacket to straighten it out. Across the room, her husband Bill fixed his tie in front of the full-length mirror. When they'd completed their preening, Beth and her husband walked out of their apartment on the upper West Side of Manhattan and caught a taxi to Penn Station.

"I've just got some last-minute stuff to do before my meeting on Monday," he said apologetically. "Really appreciate you coming to Newark with me on a Saturday." Bill leaned over and took her hand from her purse, gave it a squeeze, and brushed his thumb across the nail polish decorating her fingertips.

"No problem, honey. I'll manage to keep myself busy."

When they parted after the train ride, Bill met with a few colleagues at his office while Beth occupied her time shopping at the outlet stores. After she'd been out for only two hours, she began to feel fatigued and a little nauseous. She looked into one store window filled with women's designer suits and started to cough. She stepped in to look at an outfit from the display.

"Good afternoon, miss," said the older woman behind the counter. Beth started to unbutton her coat.

"Boy, it's crazy. It's so cold outside, but I feel so hot. Must be all the walking around in this giant coat." Beth's voice sounded congested.

"Miss, would you like to sit down for a minute?" inquired the saleswoman. She moved out from behind the counter, wondering if her customer was old enough to be suffering from hot flashes. She certainly knew how that felt. It was like someone had set you on fire.

"You know," said Beth, buttoning her coat back up with a shaking hand, "I think I better get going. Thank you for your help." She let out another cough.

Beth found a taxi down the block and caught up with her husband back at his office. It was getting to be early afternoon and the lunch hour had long passed.

"Bill, I really don't feel well. I think I need to go home." By now she was wheezing slightly and rubbing her eyes. She couldn't decide if her stomach discomfort was from lack of food, but she was nervous about eating anything for fear of throwing it all back up.

"What's wrong, honey? You were fine when we left the apartment this morning." There was a note of concern in Bill's voice, but he was more preoccupied with the papers in front of him than with his wife. Then, recognizing he had been a little selfish and noticing his wife's tired appearance, he added, "I guess I could wrap it up. Can you give me about a half hour, babe?" Beth nodded and sat in a chair in the corner of Bill's office, flipping through a magazine.

They left the office about forty-five minutes later and got a train back to the city without much waiting. When they reached Manhattan, Beth suddenly felt a squeeze in her chest, as if someone's hand had slipped beneath her blouse and grabbed her heart through her rib cage. Desperate to catch her breath, she struggled to call out to her husband, but the sound was muffled. She grabbed his arm instead, her polished nails digging hard into his wrist.

Bill turned toward his wife, looked into her red eyes, and could see a trickle of blood at the corner of her mouth. Now she had his full attention.

"Beth!" he said with alarm.

Beth clutched her chest, mouthed something that Bill could not quite understand, and fell forward into his arms.

"Someone call 911 NOW!" Bill shouted, his voice and his body trembling.

*　　*　　*

Jim Cassidy was an Emergency Medical Technician-paramedic who still lived with his parents, conservative Christians residing in Brooklyn. He kept his blond hair short so it wouldn't get in his eyes while leaning over his patients, starting an IV, or putting on EKG leads. The days were long between work and school, but he hoped he could make the transition from paramedic to physician with ease. All he needed were a few more courses before he could send in his medical school application. As a paramedic he had many more hours of training than a basic EMT, but regardless of training, all the members of his emergency medical services team referred to themselves as EMTs—the first responders to 911 calls for chest pain, building explosions, traffic accidents, gun shots, drug overdoses, and jet planes crashing into skyscrapers.

Jim's additional skills—airway management to help stabilize a patient's breathing, starting an intravenous line, reading an electrocardiogram, and giving medications to patients in the ambulance en route to the hospital—allowed him a certain independence that basic EMTs did not possess. He was confident his paramedic training would be an advantage to getting into medical school, and he wanted a career in Emergency Medicine anyway. He liked shift work and the idea of having only a brief relationship with a patient.

Jim's ambulance was dispatched from the bay to pick up a woman who was feeling tightness in her chest and having acute respiratory distress. She was accompanied by her husband, who told the EMT they had left Penn Station for New Jersey in the morning and had returned later that day when his wife felt sick.

"I called 911 right when she collapsed," her husband said. His voice was trembling as he fidgeted with his tie. "I don't know what happened. She was fine when we left the house this morning."

His wife's condition deteriorating, Jim pushed the husband to the back of the ambulance. He started an IV and put the oxygen mask over her nose and mouth. The husband overheard Jim on the phone with ED staff at the hospital.

"This is Jim Cassidy. Yeah, we got a 40-year-old woman, well this morning, now in severe respiratory distress, chest pain. We got the IV in, she's on oxygen but she's dropping her O2 sat. No, doesn't look good. Probably going to need intubation. Uh huh, uh huh. Yup, got it. Uh huh, yeah, husband's riding with us."

When they reached the hospital, the doors to the ED flew open as the stretcher emerged from the ambulance like a thoroughbred out of the gate. Emergency Department doctors and nurses triaged her to acuity level one and she was immediately moved into one of the open rooms. The ED team simultaneously intubated Beth, started another IV, and hooked up cardiac monitors, while Jim Cassidy relayed the vital information. After he completed his hand-off, Jim retreated quietly from the organized chaos to give the doctors their space. He decided now might be a good time to follow up on some other cases that had come in earlier in the week.

Jim went to the clinical laboratory and asked to speak with the pathologist. The only pathologist available was relatively junior and had just recently been hired into the practice as a locum tenens, a temporary fill-in, to cover another physician's maternity leave. Jim found the physician-temp sequestered in the cutting room in the front of the Pathology Department, where all human tissue removed from the body was handled. The cutting room contained stainless steel tables with small hoods above to capture any errant chemical fumes. The doctor was grossing a lung specimen presumably filled with cancer. Jim watched the dissection, wincing a little when he realized there were pieces of body parts being cut up on the table.

"Excuse me, are you the pathologist?" he asked as he looked around. The room was surrounded by white subway tile walls with steel shelving to the ceiling, and filled with strange and unfamiliar equipment. Occupying every inch of the long line of shelves were jars filled with fluid and floating pieces of human tissue, stacked up high and into corners and displayed as if a prized collection. The smell of formalin confronted his uninitiated senses and brought back memories of some pickled frog he had dissected during a science class long ago.

"Can I help you? Kind of busy. I've gotta finish grossing and then have an autopsy to do. We're really backed up today." The pathologist put down the scalpel and waited for a reply.

"Oh, sorry. Look, one of my buddies brought in a woman about a week ago with severe respiratory distress. She was maybe mid-thirties, died in the ED. Not sure if she had an autopsy. I asked the nurses in the ED, but wrong shift. They didn't know. Thought I'd check in with Path."

Jim told the pathologist about several patients he had recently transported to the hospital who had similar histories.

"What's odd is that the cases we're picking up tend to be younger people in their twenties and thirties, some forties. I'm still seeing some older patients, but not as many as the younger ones. I checked with a few other EMTs and several have seen an uptick in respiratory illnesses with similar symptoms. What do you think?"

The pathologist was not all that interested and was feeling quite tired. His mind heard only selective parts of the EMT's story. "Well you're right, it's unusual," he said with some impatience. He removed his gloves and plastic apron, scratched his receding hairline, and unbuttoned his lab coat. He still had an autopsy to do and he was waiting for his assistant to arrive. "Any chance you could come back in the morning? I've really got to finish grossing and do this autopsy, and I've got a pile of paperwork. Not to put you off," said the doctor pressing his case. He was preoccupied with planning a special evening for himself and his wife for their one-year anniversary—dinner and a concert at the Garden. Tickets had been purchased earlier that morning to go with the heart necklace he'd bought the previous week. Now he needed to get the autopsy over with and get some rest.

The EMT looked at his watch. "Geez, I've gotta get going. I'll check with you in the morning. By the way, what's your name?"

"It's Bajian. Dr. Avy Bajian."

Jim ran down the hall from Pathology, up the stairs, and right through the ED to his ambulance without even stopping. The woman he had brought in only minutes earlier, intubated and unresponsive, had an unexpected seizure. Her EKG monitor went from steady intermittent beeps to continuous alarm as her pulse slowed, and finally went flat. A code was called, but attempts to resuscitate the patient were unsuccessful. Time of death was called at 6:07 pm. The ED physician pulled open the curtain and went to find the husband. In the waiting room was a middle-aged, smartly dressed businessman, pacing across the floor with his tie loosed. The ED doctor caught his eye.

"What the hell is going on with my wife? She was fine this morning. When can I see her?"

"Please sit down. Look, your wife came in here with serious respiratory symptoms, um, she had trouble breathing, chest pain. She also had a seizure, and we tried everything to bring her back, but whatever it was, we just couldn't save her. I'm sorry, I really am."

The husband stared in disbelief. He was trembling.

"I, I can't believe it. This is not happening. I don't believe you. She was fine this morning. We just took a train ride to Jersey. I want to see her now." The ED physician dropped his eyes and stared at the floor. He always hated this part of his job.

"Uh, will you please come this way," the doctor said in his softest tone. "By the way, I'm Stu Greene, one of the ED attending physicians."

Stu Greene pulled the curtain aside, and on the stretcher was a woman's body partially covered by a sheet. The IV was still hung and the monitors were hooked up, but silenced. All her fingernails were red except one, which was naked and exposed. This had been the initial contact point of the pulse oximeter used to check her oxygen level. The nail polish interfered with the transmittance of the wavelengths, so it had to be removed.

The unpolished fingernail caught the husband's eye and he started to cry. Stu Greene shifted his weight from one foot to the other, cleared his throat, and hesitantly put his arm on the husband's shoulder. "I'm so sorry."

"I don't understand it. She was fine. There's nothing wrong with her."

"Mr. Winslow, from your story of your wife's illness, it seemed like a very sudden onset of respiratory symptoms. Any unusual travel, any sick pets in the home, or anyone with flu-like symptoms that you or your wife has been in contact with?"

"NO, no, nothing. We took a cab ride to Penn Station this morning, we got on the train. I went to my office and she did a little shopping. There's nothing, nothing. She's fine!"

"Would you mind if I looked in her handbag?" Dr. Greene asked, knowing it sounded like an odd request.

"Sure…Fine…I…I need to make a few phone calls." The husband handed the doctor his dead wife's purse, tears streaming down his face.

Stu Greene opened Beth Winslow's large handbag, unsure of what he was looking for aside from a potential pattern. He had seen the contents of another handbag from a young woman with similar symptoms, who had also died inexplicably. The friend who had brought her to the hospital had dumped out the patient's handbag to look for her friend's keys. Beth's handbag looked to have similar contents: loose tissues, a brush, her wallet with several credit cards, receipts from recent shopping, and a small makeup case. He unzipped the case and peered inside; lipstick, a compact with pressed powder, an eye liner pencil, a bottle of ruby red nail polish, and a small vial containing a fine white powder. The only item of interest to the doctor was the vial of white powder. He wasn't sure what it was. Plastic bags with pills or vials filled with powders wouldn't be uncommon to find on patients with drug overdoses. But Stu Greene was fairly certain this case was not a routine drug overdose. The initial symptoms just didn't fit.

"Would you mind if I kept this?" Dr. Greene asked the husband. He held up the vial.

Without a question as to what it was, the husband nodded his head confirming his consent. He was distracted and distraught.

The doctor zipped up the case. The only other items in her handbag were some perfume cards, some wrapped in cellophane and some not, and a flyer advertising current Broadway shows. He closed the pocketbook and handed it back to the broken man standing in front of him.

The ED doctor tried his best to console the husband, who wasn't certain how to take the next steps in his life. The medical examiner had been called to pick up the case, as the patient had died unexpectedly after arriving in the ED. This wasn't the first occasion in the past few weeks when Stu Greene had made such a call, but this time the medical examiner declined because of a backlog of autopsies. Instead, they requested that the hospital pathologist handle the case and report the findings back to the ME.

After all the paperwork was completed for the autopsy and the hospital staff were assured family members could be with the distressed husband, the ED nurses finally prepared the body and rolled her down to the morgue. The autopsy would be scheduled for the morning. When they reached the morgue, Dr. Bajian, dressed in scrubs, emerged from the autopsy suite.

"You're here late," said one of the nurses.

"Yeah, I'm on call tonight and wanted to get this autopsy out of the way. I'm not feeling all that well," he said with a slight cough, rubbing his irritated eyes.

"You look a little feverish. Why don't you come up to the ED and I'll take your temp."

"No, I'm okay, probably just coming down with a cold. It's winter— everyone's got a little runny nose or something. Anyway, I'm going home now. I've got to get some rest. Big date tomorrow," he said with a tired grin. "That case you just wheeled in will be done tomorrow. Chief of Service will be on then—Dr. Becker." He picked up the chart and glanced over it quickly, realizing this was the case the EMT had discussed with him earlier that evening. Dr. Bajian made a note to review the autopsy results with Dr. Becker after the case was completed.

*   *   *

The Chief of Service woke up early the next morning after a restless sleep. Troubling dreams and a deep pain in his back had kept him tossing and turning throughout the night. His right foot was numb as he swung his legs out of bed and placed his feet on the floor. He cursed his years in the army, which had sent him home with leg wounds filled with shrapnel and a mind filled with unforgivable images. He craved the morning caffeine that would jump start his day and help him face the case load he knew was waiting for him.

Dr. Becker was a man north of sixty years who had grown up in West Texas, but who had come east for college and most of his medical training. Though he had a high level of integrity and was extremely knowledgeable about many things, he was a man who kept his feelings to himself and drove through life in the passenger seat, letting others define his path. Francis Becker was a relatively happy man, but lately felt that his life was wanting, was missing something he yearned for—something he had once had in his younger days, or maybe never had at all. When he reached the hospital that morning, he embraced the escape of his vocation, ready to bury his own feelings and begin his day giving a voice to the dead.

*　　*　　*

"Good morning, Dr. Becker," said the administrative assistant when he stopped in the office to grab his cases. Francis Becker looked down at her from underneath the halo of gray hair that capped his six-foot-two frame. A black bolo tie stood in sharp contrast to his starched white shirt, the silver buckle on his belt engraved by a master silversmith.

"Did you get your coffee this morning? You know your patients like you perky," she giggled. "Oh, I see you're wearing your cowboy boots today. What are they? Lizard, ostrich, cowhide?"

Dr. Becker looked straight into the admin's eyes. "Ma'am, these are black Tezu lizard," he answered with a slight twang to his voice. Some days the twang seemed more pronounced depending on how strong his longing was to return home to his native Texas. He walked over to the shelf labeled with each doctor's name and, finding his, removed the chart on the middle-aged woman who had died the night before. He started reading.

"Dr. Becker, oh, Dr. Becker, thank God you're here!" shouted the clinical manager from the ED as she burst into the Pathology administrative offices. "We need you in the ED right now. It's Dr. Bajian. He was brought in about an hour ago. I'm so sorry; he didn't make it. We also got a call from the Medical Examiner's Office. The Chief said she wants to speak with you. Says the whole city is going crazy."

Francis Becker choked back disbelief, and feeling the heat creep into his face, followed the clinical manager up the stairs and into the ED. He entered one of the exam rooms and saw the body of his colleague on the gurney. He paused for a moment and turned as a portly physician in a lab coat approached him.

"Dr. Becker?" said Stu Greene. "I'm sorry to meet you under these circumstances. I understand this doc was one of your staff. I called the ME's office and they said that their Chief would call us back. Apparently, she knows you. I figured I better give you a heads up. We've had several of these acute respiratory cases in the last week. Mostly women, but some men, maybe in their twenties, thirties, some forties. Normally we see these illnesses in older people this time of year. Last one was the woman I sent down to you last night. I looked through her handbag—something I've been doing lately, with all the drug overdose deaths. Anyway, I found a small vial with some powder in it and asked the husband if I could keep it. I was hoping the lab could tell me what was in it."

Stu Greene's cell phone rang. "Hello, yeah, this is Dr. Greene. Oh, thanks for getting back to me. Yeah, like the one we had yesterday, except this one is from Dr. Becker's staff. Yeah, we got ahold of him. Sure, I'll put him on. Dr. Becker," he said, "it's the Chief ME. She wants to talk with you." He handed the phone to the pathologist.

"Howdy, Marie. How ya been?"

"Francis, so good to connect with you. Like the old days, in Boston. Listen, we've got unexplained deaths happening all over the city. My shop has been inundated with cases. I need your help doing some of the autopsies since you're a deputy ME. Can you handle a few extra at your place?"

"No problem, Marie. We can oblige." Francis Becker buried his feelings even deeper, unsettled about having to perform an autopsy on a colleague, and felt the ache creep into his back and right leg. *Goddamn army.*

"One more thing. We're working on the assumption that this could be an emerging virus. Take all necessary precautions during the autopsy. I've contacted the CDC for some help. But one of my docs, who's a very smart young guy, thinks this could be toxin related. Francis, remember that pathologist we trained with, the poison expert in high heels?"

"You mean Lily Robinson? Yeah, I have a couple of her toxicology books. She's still in Boston."

"Yes, her. I was wondering if you might give her a call. She and I were never very friendly, so I thought it might be better if you called and asked for her help. Frankly, I found her detached and frosty, but she's got a pretty rare skill set and we need all the help we can get."

"Will do, Marie. I'll be in touch."

He hadn't thought about her in a long time. Francis Becker headed back down to the morgue to prepare for the autopsies, and to call Lily Robinson.

Chapter 3

BOSTON

Chad is gone. I'm sitting alone in my office figuring how I'm going to plan the next few weeks of my life. Lisa opens the door slightly after a gentle knock and reminds me I have another meeting this afternoon, but I have some cases I have to finish first. I walk out of the office and go into the lab to find Dr. Kelley who is my Fellow, a sort of advanced doctor in training. Kelley is over by the automated instruments that analyze blood electrolytes and enzymes. I try and catch his eye and wave my hand up in the air.

"Kelley," I call out, "Are we going to see that case in the North Tower?"

"Hey doc," he responds, "Great case. You're gonna love it. Cool shoes today," he adds glancing at my feet.

I have a real thing for shoes. An elderly woman I met once looked at my shoes and said, "Wear them as long as you can, honey. They make you look sexy." So, I still do. Kelley likes to comment every day on my shoes. Today they are black and silver metallic with 3-inch heels.

"Thanks, Kelley," I answer. "What's the case?"

"We got a call from Dr. Stern, the resident on the medicine service. He's got a cyanotic looking 62-year-old male who's hypotensive and has persistent abdominal discomfort."

"What were the results of the arterial blood gas? I assume they ran one," I interject.

"Yes of course," Kelley says, "Results were surprisingly normal."

"Maybe not. Let's see." The elevator door opens and we spill into the hall on our way to the North Tower. Nurses and doctors are on the same path as we, all leading to the busy patient hub. We push through the swinging doors and head toward the core. I look at the display screen and find our patient's name and room number and then walk over. Kelley, looking shorter and

19

rounder than usual, is steps behind me even though I'm walking in stilettos and he's not. These slim-heeled shoes usually herald the image of a *femme fatale* and not a university Professor. The stem of the heel, reinforced with steel, makes them an attractive weapon and worthy of the long thin blade they were named for.

"Here we are," I say, as I pump the hand sanitizer dispenser before I enter the room.

"Hi, Mr. Garcia. My name is Dr. Robinson and I'm from the toxicology service. This is my associate, Dr. Kelley. How are you feeling today?" Before me is a man enveloped in bluish-gray flesh. He doesn't appear to be in respiratory distress of any kind and he shows us his yellow teeth as he parts his lips with a smile.

"Well I'm okay today. Just a bit tired. And I have pain in my stomach."

"Mr. Garcia, how long have you been this color?" Kelley asks.

"Can't remember, but maybe several years," he answers.

Then I add, "Do you use any special home remedies for your allergies? I read in your medical chart that you have severe year-round allergies with a frequent stuffy, drippy nose."

"Well, doctor, I get these special drops from a little bodega in my neighborhood. They have good stuff, you know, not stuff you can get from a drug store. I have the bottle with me."

He gets out of bed, this stooped bluc-gray man, and with Kelley holding him by one arm, walks over to the closet that contains his street clothes. He rifles through his bag and finds a small brown bottle that he hands over to me. I look at the label, *Argent Colloidal*. I hand it over to Kelley.

Mr. Garcia is now safely back in his bed. I glance at Kelley who has the look of someone who is in the know. He nods his head and hands me back the bottle.

Now I turn to our patient. "Mr. Garcia, the nose drops you have been using for several years contain colloidal silver. When the silver gets into your body it's deposited in the skin and causes an irreversible pigmentation of the skin. This is why you look blue. Unfortunately, the silver can also be deposited in other organs of your body giving you some of the symptoms you are experiencing. What you have is called argyria. There is no known treatment for this. However, I suggest you stop using the nose drops."

We reassure him he will be cared for by the rest of the medical team during his hospitalization and say our good days.

Kelley and I make our exit and take one pump of the hand sanitizer on the way out. We discuss our unusual patient, now shrouded in silver that is permanently complexed with his body's RNA and DNA. He bathed in sunlight forcing a chemical reaction in his skin and soluble silver became metallic silver. Now wide awake, his pigment producing skin cells upped their production of melanin and the end result is our bluish-gray man. He will remain this way for the rest of his life, his face radiating like an image on a silver dollar.

*   *   *

It's my cell phone. I'm not yet back to my office and Kelley is still by my side. I recognize the number; it's the Agency so it will be a secure line. Kelley and I part ways.

"Hello, this is Dr. Robinson."

"Robinson, get yourself to a TV. There's been a chemical attack in Syria. That's what it looks like. We're going to have our people on the ground as soon as we can get in safely and verify."

"I'm still at work. What's going on? We just saw each other a few hours ago."

When I hear the words "get yourself to a TV," déjà vu takes over and I'm transported back to the year 2001. I was in my office on that September day when staff knocked on my door and urged me to find a TV. There was news on the radio. A plane had just crashed into one of the World Trade Towers. The only TV available was in the patient waiting area adjacent to the operating room. We thought there had been an improbable accident, a plane tragically flown off course, until the second tower was hit. I remember I went back to my office where there was a large window that overlooks the Boston skyline. The Prudential Tower and the John Hancock building were still standing. But for how long? Thinking that patients might be triaged in New York and sent to Boston if the New York hospitals were overwhelmed, prompted my hospital to prepare for masses of wounded. Boston does trauma well. I went to the blood bank to check the inventory and the line was already starting to form. Everyone wanted to donate blood, even those who weren't eligible. In crisis, we all want to do something, anything, to help. At the time, no one knew that there would be no hosts for the hundreds of units of blood collected throughout the city. Living people need blood. Not the dead.

21

I shake my head as if to dislodge the thoughts of the past, and I'm back in the present. "What do you want from me?" I ask.

"We need to move up our time line. We need you back in New York as soon as you can get there. I'll call you later with further instructions."

By this time, I've reached my office. Kelley has retreated to the lab to draft the consult notes on our blue man. I call Lisa into my office and tell her that I've got to leave a day or two sooner than we originally planned. Emergency of some sort. Can she arrange coverage of my service? She gives me that look. The one where she knows something is up, and I'm just pretending otherwise. She never asks too many questions, only if there's anything she can do. I tell her to cancel my meetings for the rest of the week. I tell her that I'll try and take care of business tomorrow, but after that I'm not sure when I'll be back. Her face is blank. We've done this before.

"Dr. Lily," Lisa finally says, as if coming out of stupor, "I can cancel the rest of the week's meetings. But you missed the one with the Dean scheduled for today and he's not happy. I also put a folder on your desk with info to remind you that you have two book chapters pending, and the one on toxic plants is due in two weeks. I don't know how you're going to get it all done."

"I'm used to it," I tell her. "And the Dean will have to wait. Patients first."

*   *   *

I walk back into the laboratory to collect a few cases I left with Kelley. The laboratory is a distant destination for those on the patients' floors. Linked by a pneumatic tube or p-tube system where specimens can travel up to 18 miles per hour on their way to the lab, the core receives several hundred thousand specimens a year of blood, urine and other body fluids from floors all over the hospital. Few doctors and nurses ever visit the lab other than to occasionally drop off a specimen at the window if travel through the p-tube is deemed too dangerous. There's Kelley.

"Doc, you just got a call from the poison center," he says. "There's a 56-year-old woman in Cambridge with a spider bite. They're going to send you the pics. Want to see if you will confirm that it's a brown recluse."

"It's been a while since I had one of those cases," I tell him. Actually, I can use a little distraction right now. *Loxosceles reclusa* is only one of two spiders in North America with necrotic venom that's medically significant. The patient would have a deep black wound where the spider sank their fangs. Then, I ask Kelley if he knows the other poisonous spider whose reputation of sexual cannibalism earned her her name.

"The Black Widow," Kelley answers with confidence.

"Yes, exactly," I confirm. "Most people know of the black widow because of the red hour glass shape found on the abdomen. The rather dull little brown spider has only the shape of a violin marking the dorsal side of its cephalothorax. That's why they call it the brown fiddler or violin spider. Let me know when you get the pics, Kelley."

*   *   *

I can finally get back to my office to wrap things up. My desk is piled with folders left by efficient Lisa. My cell phone pings me to say I have messages. A news banner streams across the phone indicating a high rate of what are presumably flu cases in New York City. Officials are encouraging the public to have their flu shots and if they are feeling ill, to stay home. I got my vaccination several weeks ago. Looks like I'm going to need it if I'm going to New York. There are two messages on the phone; the first is an unknown number from yesterday I must have missed, and the second number has a NYC area code that must have come in today at some point. I hit the play button for the unknown number and listen to the message.

"Hey doc. Just want to stop by your office tomorrow and run a few things by you. We've done this dance many times. Please give me a call. Thanks."

I recognize Chad's voice and a little wave of acid hits my stomach again even though I've already met with him today. I turn off the phone, slip into my fur coat, grab my bag, and head for the car. As I slide onto the cold leather, I flip the seat warmer button, determined to survive Boston winters, and think some more about Chad and Pixie Dust. This woman with the colorful hair had been a special operative from the government, a top-secret division of the Agency that I had already encountered as part of an earlier clandestine drug operation. She sat in my office and told me about a traitor whose dealings had already resulted in the death of several Americans.

"Dr. Robinson," she said, "a few months ago, we learned that this man gave the names, the true identities, of some of our undercover agents to hostile foreign governments. He's been able to steal government secrets and sell them to the highest bidder in the foreign markets."

Apparently, he had been a gifted scientist at one time. But the brilliance of his younger days had given way to a thin bitter man with a wild mane of gray hair and untied shoelaces. The scientist's son had lost his life in what his father considered was an unjust and unnecessary war. He felt betrayed by his country and was propelled to return the favor.

"Yes, of course we tried to reason with him," I remember her telling me as she pushed the pink hair strands away from her eyes, "but he wouldn't listen."

Pixie Dust and company had arranged a dinner for the scientist and his colleagues later in the week purportedly to discuss grant money to support further research. They wanted me at the dinner as the guest of one of the other attendees, a French government operative who always worked with the United States. And then without a blink she said, "What we want you to do is to create a lethal tea for the dinner." Just like that she had asked me to commit murder. I felt a little nauseous, a little scared, and I tasted acid in my mouth. I can taste it now.

"Dr. Robinson, please consider this," she continued. "You'll be doing your country a great service. And the beauty of the plan will be that with your help, it will look like he died of natural causes."

Of course they would think that. They already knew I preferred natural toxins and venoms, those that nature packaged in perfect creatures: beautiful, colorful, scaly, exotic, or floating—and always deadly. Plant or animal, I know them all.

*   *   *

I'm now at the garage of my city condo, so I park the car and take the elevator up to the 12ᵗʰ floor. My stomach is now etched by the acid between Chad's visit and the car ride down memory lane. After that initial episode, I vowed never to kill again, even for my country, but the vow has been broken many times over the years. Like I said, I'm all in now. They teed me up for this covert life and I've been living a dual existence for almost twenty years now. Some of the deaths seemed easy and even rewarding, but some were unexpected and troubling. Like icicles dangling precariously from the edge of a roof, they are beautiful when catching the sunlight, but an unanticipated break in the hardened water conjures death for anything in its frozen path.

I exit the elevator, start down the hall, and unlock my front door. I throw the keys into the green ceramic bowl on the entryway table and head straight for the antacids, again. It never got any easier, despite what Pixie Dust told me. Code name Pixie Dust. She's dead now. I miss her.

I start thinking about dinner and look at the contents of the fridge. I'm not surprised, it's almost empty. One sad plastic container partially filled with wilted spring greens sitting alone on a cold glass shelf. I dump the contents down the drain and turn on the food grinder. The brown sticky leaves swirl the ring before disappearing into the blackness and I watch it all unfold like a premonition. The coat's back on and I go down to the street to get some dinner in the little market across the way. Bright yellow and orange peppers catch my eye, as does a tomato, a warm baguette, prosciutto, fresh mozzarella and basil. When I get back to the apartment it feels a little warmer than before. Good thing I turned up the heat the first time I came in. I remove the groceries from the paper bag one by one and set them on the counter. I make a nice sandwich and then curl up on the chenille sofa, with my plate set on the coffee table. The moon is rising over the historical skyline. Boston, a city of revolution, medical and scientific innovation, education, and paved cow paths had been a constitutional breeding ground from the start of this country. Poisoning has always been an ancient art used over centuries to shape both political outcomes and personal fortunes. My patriotic beginnings had started with the beautiful flower Monkshood, the origin of the toxin aconite. I'd used it to poison tea. It had seemed so easy that I had convinced myself that with this single act, my life would once again have direction, and my pain would be quieted.

*   *   *

The next morning at 10, Lisa quietly knocks on my office door.

"Dr. Lily, I didn't see this appointment on your calendar, but he says he has a meeting with you. It's Chad."

"That's fine, Lisa. Show him in please."

"Sorry doc for barging in again," he says, "but I've got that update I promised you. Decided I didn't want to do it by phone."

I'm listening to every word he says. For me to see him two days in a row is unusual. He starts talking about all the latest Internet chatter generated by the recent chemical attacks in Syria. They believe something is going to happen within the next few weeks in the U.S. There's going to be a conference in New York City for international bankers and their guests. They're going to hold a special dinner during the conference at the History of Science Museum on the West Side.

I ask Chad what is it that they want me to do.

"We want you to join the curator to host the event; you even know him," he says. "About twenty exclusive tickets for the affair have been purchased. It's not just a dinner, but also a tour by that flashy curator of the hot new exhibits."

I'm thinking, that's it? Way too easy. I know there's more. "Come on, Chad, don't bullshit me, who do you want assassinated at the dinner?" I ask.

This is as hard for Chad as it is for me. It's not like I assassinate people every week. Sure, the government has these special covert teams that train together and are at the ready. You occasionally hear about them in the news, but only after they penetrate some impenetrable foreign country and whisk out an American captive or kill the head of a terrorist group. But my group doesn't go out on a very regular basis. There is some restraint here. So, I put it to Chad again.

"Who am I to kill?"

His eyes look away from mine. Then he says, "We think a key operative will attend the dinner disguised as one of the bankers. Not only is this group supplying the chemical warfare agents we've just seen being used in the Middle East, but they also make some of the most innovative improvised explosive devices or IEDs on today's market."

I feel the acid swirling in my stomach. I ask Chad for more details.

"We don't actually have a specific ID yet, but when we do, we'll get that information to you. We know this is a Russian operation and we believe they may try to launch a chemical attack on U.S. soil. You know the Russians have a tender spot for poison, Robinson. Anyone who speaks out as a political dissident runs the risk of death. Vladimir Kara-Murza, an opposition activist who lived in Virginia was poisoned twice. Viktor Yushenenko was poisoned with dioxin, Alexander Litvinenko died from polonium poisoning, and Alexander Perepilichny was poisoned with that plant from China."

"Yes," I add quickly. "*Gelsemium elegans*, also known as *heartbreak grass*, grows in Asia. If you ingest it, you can get very sick—dizziness, nausea, blurred vision, seizures, paralysis, and finally death. Did you know Arthur Conan Doyle, a physician and creator of Sherlock Holmes, experimented on himself with a tincture of gelsemium? He took about 9mL, that's not much and got a headache, and diarrhea. When he upped the dose, the symptoms got worse, so he stopped the experiment."

"There's more, Robinson. You already know the Georgi Markov story from the days of the Cold War. I've heard you tell it. He was poisoned with a ricin-filled pellet delivered into his thigh from the tip of an umbrella."

"Of course," I said.

"And we can go way back in history, if you like. In the 1400s the Grand Duke of Moscow, Dimetry Shemyaka was poisoned with arsenic in a chicken dinner, and in the 1600s the Russian General, Mikhail Skopin-Shuisky was poisoned on orders of the Tsar. They got his wife to doctor up his food. I think we have to be open to anything, Robinson. Ah, I see your face. Too much ancient history?"

My face, blank with wide-open eyes, is reflecting my inner feelings. I already tuned out the history lesson and started thinking about going back to Manhattan to assassinate someone whose identity is unknown at this point. I need more time between assignments for healing people, before I do more killing.

"We think the terrorist will be at the dinner looking to make contacts with wealthy influential men. Maybe a way to move his product through some legit businesses. I don't really know how he scored a ticket to this very élite event. Look, we do our best to vet everyone, but some people are just too deep under cover. If we can identify him, just take him out."

I sit quietly and think about what Chad said. Another mission in the service of my country. For me, I spend most of my life saving lives, not taking lives. Then Chad says, "Robinson, I know it's short notice, but you've got to come down to the Big Apple tomorrow and meet with the curator. We want to put the plan in motion, sooner rather than later."

I ask Chad if he's sure about the museum, the bombs and the chemical weapons. It's not like the intelligence hasn't been wrong before. And then the evil score invades my brain. Is this guy bad enough to kill without due process? Just who is the scorekeeper who decides who lives or who dies? Is he like the Roman emperor overseeing the rousing crowd in the Coliseum debating whether he gives a thumbs-up or thumbs-down to the gladiator sprawled almost lifeless in the dirt with blood oozing from everywhere? My own instincts were honed to preserve life, but these must be tamed with large doses of patriotism and blind obedience.

"Lily," Chad says, waking me from my introspection—he doesn't usually call me by my first name. "We don't have his name yet, but we have seen his work. He's at our doorstep."

I tell Chad that I have to drive up to my cottage first to take care of a few things, and then I'll head down to the city.

"Okay, then," he says, "we'll catch up with you at the museum."

Chad walks out and the door closes behind him. My mind races. I'll have to focus. Finish the cases, go to the cottage and head to the Big Apple.

*   *   *

Before New York, I'll need to collect the perfect poison for the mission. I keep most of my poisons at my cottage, that clandestine ocean home along the Massachusetts coast. It's a small place with weather-worn cedar shingles and trim outlined in robin's egg blue. The front porch is made of mahogany and I surround it fully in white drapes to close out the world around me. It's my quiet shelter, my perfect escape. When I'm up there, I take long walks on the beach to clear my mind, skirting the occasional burst of frothy water from the sea. The undulations of debris and foam across the sand remind me of cluttered brain waves, but it's just the tide washing up the jumbled remains of sea life and human hope. I always find myself gazing out over the depths, longing for that part of me that had been swept away by my twisted and uncertain past.

The cottage is a chameleon and blends with the seasons. In winter, it's nestled within tapestries of mint green reindeer lichens intermixed with beach heather and rose-gold grass-covered beach dunes. But in the summer, low clouds shroud the horizon and steam from the sun-kissed waters rise to meet the sky above. It's paradise. Behind the little house there are lush grasses of *Miscanthus* and *Pennisetum* which conceal my most favorite retreat for solitude and thought-rejuvenation: my garden—or should I say my "extreme garden." This is where I grow my prized flowers and plants that hide nature's poisons within their green foliage, small fruits, or in the fibrous structures buried beneath the ground. I have an appreciation and love for almost all flowers and plants, not just those that are poisonous. Plants are immortal if they are cared for. Not true of human life. There's only one flower I won't plant in my garden and it's ironic that it's my namesake flower. The scent of that beautiful blossom hijacks my immune system so histamine shuts down my airway. It could be lethal, so I take precautions. But anything

28

else that can grow in New England for the summer and have roots deep in the brown and sandy earth for all seasons is out there. The rest I pot and bring in for the winter. Berries, seeds, leaves and roots can be harvested and frozen for future projects, as needed. I'm thinking about what I want to use for this museum banquet. I've got something in mind. It might be more of a summer dish, but in my mind, I see the deep gray-blue waters of the New England summer coast, spring rains that soak the rivers to their edge, and the hot sunny days that follow. It's then, when the ocean surface temperatures warm and nutrient-rich water flows into the sea, that green blooms into red. Yes, I'll find my poison there, floating in the summer waters of the Atlantic.

*   *   *

Now I've got to get back to my clinical cases before I make the transition to assassin. I know, you find it difficult, maybe even unbelievable that a doctor might also be a killer in a parallel life. But know this. The government does what it's got to do. And yes, people who have unique skills can be recruited for the unbelievable if it's for a greater good. I beg you to keep in mind that the good of the many outweighs the good of the one. Don't judge me.

I find Kelley and we head off to the 6th floor to see a cocaine addict who's here because he has necrosis of the tip of his nose, and the helix and lobes of his ears. When we enter the room, he's lying in his bed and I can see his legs are covered in bandages. His face has blackened patches of skin.

"Hi, Mr. Moore," I say to him, "I'm Dr. Robinson and this is my associate, Dr. Kelley. We're from the toxicology service. You want to tell us what's been going on?" I like to hear from the patient's point of view before I start with my questions.

"Doc, I swear I'm not doin' heroin," he starts out defensively. "Just cocaine. Been living at the shelter, but that last batch of coke messed me up. See, I got these sores all over my legs and now my nose is falling off." He pushes aside one of the bandages on his leg and we can see a big gaping wound.

"Mr. Moore, are you getting your cocaine from the same dealer?"

"No ma'am. Had to go to someone new this time."

I'm always surprised when patients think their drug dealers are Eagle Scouts. Dealers want to make money, so they'll tell you, and sell you, what you want to hear. Pure cocaine, best shit around.

29

I look away from my patient and turn to Kelley. "What's your diagnosis?" I ask. Kelley's smart and doesn't hesitate because he's already figured it out.

"His white blood cell count is low and the skin biopsy they took yesterday shows vasculitis. It's levamisole induced vasculitis."

Now I turn back around to my patient and say, "Mr. Moore, the cocaine you're using has been cut with another drug called levamisole. This drug causes inflammation in the vessels that supply blood to the skin. When the skin can't get the blood it needs, it dies and causes all these blackened patches on your face, and the ulcers on your legs. We're going to do a few more tests and then report back to the doctor who is treating you."

"Doc, I'm not doin' heroin."

"I know. The morphine we found in your urine is from the medication they're giving you for pain. Nice to meet you, Mr. Moore."

"That's a horrible case," Kelley says as we approach the elevator.

"They're all horrible to me," I tell Kelley. "Drug addiction, or substance use disorder, chains its victims to a life they don't want, but can't escape. So many of these people are trapped. They can't even get good drugs any more. Most of the cocaine today is cut with levamisole which is a drug used to kill worms in animals. Funny thing though, at one time it was used in humans to treat some immune diseases, but was withdrawn from the market because of the fatal side effects. No worries, the illicit drug chemists came up with another use for levamisole. They add it to cocaine, reducing its purity and saving some bucks. But it turns out that its metabolite, aminorex, causes an amphetamine like high. When the cocaine fades, the aminorex kicks in keeping the high around a little longer. So even though the cocaine's not so pure, the addicts get a little boost with each hit. So much for chemistry. Levamisole is definitely in the cocaine in Massachusetts. I've seen this drug listed on a lot of toxicology reports from decedents from the medical examiner's office. Anyway, we should confirm there's levamisole in the urine for documentation in the record. Please make sure we have Mr. Moore's specimen analyzed."

When I finish my speech, my voice darkens and I say to Kelley, "Listen, I've got to go away for a few days on a consultation. We'll keep in contact on the service. You can call me anytime if you have questions on a case. Lisa knows the drill." I reach out and touch his forearm, and then head back to my office to prepare myself mentally and to take another antacid.

Chapter 4

NEW YORK CITY

Jim Cassidy's ambulance was dispatched from the bay to pick up a young woman who was unable to get herself to the hospital after returning to NYC having spent the weekend in Philadelphia. Jim assessed the patient's vital signs and saw that her blood pressure was low and that she had labored breathing as she drifted in and out of consciousness. He pulled out a bag of saline solution and gathered his equipment to start an IV. It was difficult to find a good vein on her right arm, but with a tight tourniquet and some coaxing he was able to insert the catheter, connect the tubing and open the roller clamp to let the saline flow. Once the patient had been stabilized, Jim opened her handbag in hopes of finding identification but was confronted with layers of a young woman's disorganization: loose tissues, keys, credit cards, flyers, a hair brush, a small bottle of ruby red nail polish, and stuck way at the bottom, her wallet. He opened the wallet and pulled out her license. Only twenty-two, he thought. He found an address for the Greenwich Village area and an ID card from one of the local universities where she was currently a graduate student. With her identity known, he was able to call in her case directly to the emergency department of a local hospital. She was severely ill, but he thought she would make it.

That same morning he transported a man in his seventies who had severe chest pain and was struggling to survive in the back of his ambulance. The patient was experiencing shortness of breath and was sweating profusely. The paramedic knew that if his patient were hooked up to an EKG machine his T waves would be elevated. That wave pattern of the heart's electrical signal was the sign of a myocardial infarction. The sirens were screaming overhead as the ambulance fought to move through the streets of Manhattan. Jim could hear his partner swearing in the cab upfront, as the ambulance battled its way through traffic.

"Goddamn assholes, why can't they move the f- out of the way. Jaa-sus, can't they hear our siren and see we're trying to get through? Morons."

Cassidy cringed at his partner's words but was used to it. He had been raised in a strict religious household where swearing was never used. But Jim had adjusted to the modern world, and in spite of the swearing he loved working with his partner.

The patient was oblivious to this rant, since he was barely conscious. Jim could see that the old man's hair was matted with sweat and his face was pale. He started an IV, and put an oxygen mask over his patient's face. The man tossed in the gurney, moving his head from side to side while Jim contacted the ED to let them know he was bringing in a patient having a heart attack.

"Yup, bringing in a 71-year-old male with a probable MI. BP stable and holding at 100 over 60. Pulse rapid at 113." Five minutes later he pulled into the drop-off bay at the hospital where he had been the night before. Additional shifts were tough, but necessary when one was young and needed extra cash. After wheeling in the old man, and transferring him to the ED staff, he asked the charge nurse about the patient he had brought in earlier in the week.

"You mean the woman around forty who came in the other day?"

"Yeah, did she get admitted? I wanted to ask her husband some questions."

"Let me check, but I think she went down to the morgue." She ran her finger down her clipboard and stopped. "Yes, here it is. Beth Winslow. She's down in the morgue."

The nurse could see the look of surprise on the EMT's face. He knew the patient had been in respiratory distress, but he hadn't expected she would die. Jim Cassidy moved quickly out through the double swinging doors and took the stairs down to the lab.

*   *   *

Francis Becker had spent many years doing autopsies, and cases of those dying before what seemed a reasonable length of time on earth had always made him sad. He rubbed his right leg and made a mental note to make certain to connect with the husband after he had determined the cause of death. Closure was something he always provided to the family. It was the best he could offer.

32

"Hey there, Chief," said the diener, a sprite thin man with an outgoing and cheerful personality despite spending his days with the dead. Billy was the best morgue attendant or autopsy technician Becker had ever worked with.

"Billy, glad you're here. We have two autopsies. Bajian and that middle-aged woman."

Billy could see the sadness in his eyes. He knew his Chief was tough, but not without emotion. There would always be some difficult days in the autopsy suite.

"Let's do the lady with the respiratory collapse. Shouldn't take us too long." He preferred to work with Billy rather than any other assistant since as an experienced diener he would anticipate his every need.

Becker changed into his protective equipment: scrubs, white zip-up disposable jump suit, shoe covers and a plastic apron. He double-gloved and put on a face shield. He was an exemplary role model for his staff in what type of personal protective equipment to wear during procedures that could expose the pathologist to contaminated blood and body fluids.

Francis Becker performed an external exam and noted nothing unusual. His patient was a woman who looked her stated age. He looked at the stark eyes before him and noted that just the day before they probably sparkled, and gazed at someone she loved. They were red and irritated. He then proceeded with the Y incision starting at the top of each shoulder and running down the front of the chest until he reached the lower sternum where he continued to cut to the pubic bone. Billy handed him the shears so Becker could cut the lateral sides of the chest cavity and remove the chest plate. Now the heart and lungs were exposed.

"Okay, Billy, everything looks good *in situ*, everythin' where it should be, in its place. Get me the pan please, would ya. Let's be careful here. We could be lookin' at some new viral strain or somethin' unknown. I understand from the ME's office that they've had quite a few of these respiratory cases lately. Make sure your N95 mask is tight, Billy." The organs were removed "en block" and placed in the pan.

Many of the organs, still together in the pan according to their anatomical relationship, looked congested and Becker noted that the lungs were heavy and filled with fluid. Each organ was weighed while Billy carefully detailed all the findings.

"Hey doc," Billy said. "This heart looks big too. It's about 325 grams."

"That is big. I'm surprised to see that in a woman this young."

This had been a fast onset of illness in a relatively young person with similar findings to those from Dr. Bajian's case. Becker was curious. He removed the lungs and placed them in fixative. After examining the organs grossly, Dr. Becker re-examined the external nares, the nostrils, and the airway to see if he had missed anything. When he was satisfied he had not, he left the autopsy suite. He doffed his protective gear, threw it in the hazardous waste trash, and sat down on the chair waiting for him outside the autopsy room. He moved his hand through his thinning hair while his brain grappled to understand his findings. After a few minutes, he headed back to his office to do what he loved best, "push glass." This was pathologist slang for reading the patterns in the tissues that were fixed to the glass slides. It's how the diagnosis was made and Becker was a superb diagnostician.

* * *

Jim Cassidy reached the administrative offices of the Pathology Department and looked around for Dr. Bajian.

"May I help you?" said the office receptionist.

"I'd like to speak with Dr. Bajian," he said anxiously to the young woman behind the desk.

Her eyes looked down at her desktop and she bit her lower lip.

"You can check with the Chief of Service, Dr. Becker, if you want. But I think he's doing an autopsy."

"Would that be a patient named Beth Winslow?" He could see the look of distrust on the receptionist's face. "It's okay, I brought her in."

"You're going to have to ask the administrator. I don't have the names of the patients."

Jim Cassidy rushed to the autopsy suite, but it was empty. He found Dr. Becker's office and knocked on the door, which was already partly open. He pushed it fully open, and saw Becker peering through his microscope. He glanced around the office and noted the catalogue-grade wood furniture with stacks of gray slide folders piled on both the desk, and on the floor.

"Can I help you, sir?" said the graying pathologist as he looked up from the scope and adjusted his round wire-rim eyeglasses.

"Excuse me, but did you just do an autopsy on that 40-year-old woman, Beth Winslow, that I brought in to the ED the other day? Apparently, she was in respiratory failure."

"I did indeed. Who 'ja say ya were?" said Dr. Becker with a bit of suspicion in his twangy voice.

He explained to Becker the events of the previous evening including his conversation with Dr. Bajian. Becker just listened.

"I've been thinking, some of the other EMTs have also had cases of relatively young people having acute respiratory difficulties, red irritated eyes, and possibly chest pain. It's unusual. I think this is the second one I brought here that's died. Have you checked with any of your other colleagues around town?"

Dr. Becker stood up from his chair. He felt his right leg buckle under him and he grabbed the microscope table.

"Can't say I have. You said you discussed this with Bajian the other night?"

"Yeah, is he around? The receptionist hadn't seen him when I asked her. He said he was feeling too tired to talk with me the other night. He said to check in with him in the morning. He did look a little under the weather, now that I think about it. Red eyes."

"You thought he didn't look like he was feelin' well. Red eyes? Did he say anything specific?"

Jim Cassidy thought about his other patients. Those who had red eyes and respiratory symptoms. "No, why?"

"Dr. Bajian passed away the morning after you brought in Beth Winslow. I'm about to do the autopsy on him in a bit. We're trying to figure out what the hell is goin' on."

"I, I didn't know." Cassidy was reeling. He hadn't expected this. "This is like the 5th or 6th case I've had with similar symptoms. Young or middle-aged people with what looks like a flu, but with some of them dying, and quickly too." He couldn't explain it to Becker. "You're the pathologist; shouldn't you know what's going on?"

"I'm workin' on it, young man. I'm workin' on it."

CHAPTER 5

THE COTTAGE

When I stare out of the window I can see the river pushing into the ocean like an angry broad-winged raptor swooping down on the coast. I feel myself fixating on the water, watching the waves pile up like notes one after another fringed with white froth as the wind blows in from the northeast. It's cold, very cold, and so I curl up by the fireplace, and struggle to keep my eyelids open. My cottage in the winter in some ways is better than in the summer. Deserted beachfront offers solitude that can never be found during the busy summer months. It's more peaceful now. I can see the houses on the distant shore outlined by an azure sky. They dot the coast with their snowcapped roofs and look like frosted cupcakes. I'm anxious thinking about this next assignment and coming up here allows me to escape the deafening sounds of the city, and collect my thoughts, my courage, and my poison. I sit on the couch and slowly my eyelids close and I drift off into a dream:

A woman with dark hair and wings, like an angel, floats through the woods. She speaks out loud but there is no one there: *I always had a passion for collecting—never for murder. My autumn walk through the New England woods, mixed with pine and oak, led me to small armies of fungi. Each soldier, standing tall with white gills and stems, bearing smooth pure white helmets, was ready to stealthily deliver death on command. This is me, what I've become—the Destroying Angel.*

The scene changes rapidly. Now I can see myself in the woods with a young man who is familiar to me.

"Dr. Robinson? Dr. Robinson? Ah, do you think we have enough specimens?"

I see myself looking up and into the face of one of the graduate students. He stands in front of me, young, with blond hair and brown eyes wearing khaki pants and a thick pile fleece parka. I say to him, *"I'm sorry, Stuart, what did you say?"*

"I wanted to know if you thought we had collected enough specimens, you know, for your next trip."

I watch the dream unfold before me, as if I were watching a movie. I see myself speaking with my graduate student and watch as the dream image of me pulls up the collar of my jacket as the wind nips at my neck.

"Yes, Stuart I believe we have enough," I answer him. *"Stuart, why don't you go ahead and get the car warmed up; I'll be there in a minute; I just want to look around a bit more."* I watch Stuart leave and move out of the scene and then I see myself sort through a few more fungi, but this time, I pick the Death Cap, *Amanita phalloides*.

*   *   *

My phone rings and startles me out of my dream. My heart's racing and there are tears in my eyes. I must have been crying. But, I'm home; I'm in the cottage, not in the woods. It was just a dream. I feel unsettled. I've had this dream many times before, and can never get to the ending. I pick up the phone and say hello.

A man speaks. He has a twang in his voice and he says, "Well, howdy, is this Lily Robinson?"

I say yes and then ask, "Who am I speaking with?" I try and recover my composure, still shaken by the dream. I can't quite place the voice on the phone. Then he answers.

"Lily, I hope you remember me. Francis Becker here. I left you a message on your phone the other day, but I thought I would give it a try again today when I didn't hear back from ya."

"Yes," I say cautiously.

"You remember those years back in Boston? We overlapped a bit in our training but mostly I was doin' research and you were runnin' the toxicology lab at what we used to call Man's Greatest Hospital," he says with a laugh. "Well ma'am, I've actually kept tabs on your career, since we trained together." He's trying to flatter me, and hopes I remember him. I do.

He may have been keeping tabs on me, but he doesn't know my career took one major deviation since my training days. Hidden under a cloak of legitimacy, I have been pressed to deliver extraordinary service for my country. It has been a successful ruse. A premium blend of dark deception with just an aroma of truth.

"Of course, I remember you Francis," I tell him. "You have brown eyes, a thick head of dark hair and are about six foot two." I let out a soft laugh and draw him in. He's probably wondering if I look the same: long dark hair, green eyes, an ample bosom and shapely legs. Then I say, "It's been a long time, Francis. How can I help you, or is this a social call?"

He answers defensively. I probably put him off with my clinical tone.

"No, actually it's about a case. A very odd case... or two."

He tells me this story about the respiratory cases flooding New York City and the autopsies of the woman in her forties and then of his locum tenens, Dr. Bajian. They think it could be an emerging virus. But someone raised the possibility of it being related to poisoning. Hence the call to me. Then he says, "I have to report back to Marie, Marie Washington. She's Chief ME now for New York. You do remember Marie, don't ya?"

"Ah Marie," I mumble. What a bitch. She and I had our moments during training. It's a wonder we didn't kill each other. But, that was years ago. I act like she and I didn't have a history and say, "Francis, I heard on the news that there were a lot of influenza cases in the city. What does Marie think? Does she think it's flu, an emerging virus or poison?" I sound even.

"Well, we're not sure. These are relatively young patients presenting with pulmonary edema. Look, Lily," he continues, "these cases all had a fast onset. I've got the lungs fixin' now on some of those cases, so when I get the microscopics, we can sit down and look at the slides together, if you're willin' to come on down to the city."

He doesn't know I'm on my way to New York in a day or so. Then he says to me, "Lily, an ED doc found a vial of white powder in one of the hand bags of a woman who died from this, whatever it is. Don't know that it means much, but probably should have it analyzed."

I feel intrigued. Yet, it's so common to find these bags and vials of pills and powders in drug overdose cases, I'm surprised he hadn't considered that. "A vial of white powder?" I respond. "Francis, I was planning on coming down to New York tomorrow anyway. Why don't I swing over to your place, you said you're at Mercy, right, later in the afternoon? Then you can give me all the details on the cases."

It occurs to me that while the government is working on detangling a terrorist plot regarding the bankers' gala at the museum, my colleague Becker is trying to understand the circumstances surrounding the deaths of healthy individuals in the city. Coincidence? Maybe, but I have to consider that chemical warfare isn't out of the question as the cause of the respiratory cases. Chad made a point of telling me the terrorists have a predilection for unconventional weapons. A museum filled with individuals who control the economic future of the global economy would be a nice target for someone wanting to destabilize democratic societies. It's entirely possible that New York City, the financial capital of the world, not just the museum, is the real target.

CHAPTER 6

NEW YORK CITY

I feel myself in motion on the high-speed train from Boston to New York City. It's deep winter and the northeast is battling subzero temperatures. The landscape streams by my window at a dizzying pace, and I think it looks more like the tundra than New England. Boats, shrink-wrapped in their winter white coats, are nestled in small pockets of the coast, and blocks of ice are heaped on one another at the water's edge like dominos after a push. I pull together the ends of my dense fox collar on my coat and wrap it tightly around me to keep out the cold. There's a chill in my bones that I can feel right down to the marrow and I'm craving something, anything at the moment, to warm my core. For me, winter is bittersweet. The cold temperatures are hard to endure, but with it comes joyful solitude, which I treasure. My therapist says that I insulate myself in fur as a way to protect myself from the world's unforgiving tangible and intangible elements: frigid air, harsh winds, loneliness, and thoughts of an impending assignment. He may be right.

* * *

The train rumbles along, swaying from side to side on the tracks, while the scenery out the window blends in a blur of grays and browns. The man on the seat next to me gets up to walk toward the dining car.

"Excuse me miss," he says as he tries to squeeze past me. I glance at his face and wonder who he is, what his reasons are for traveling to New York, and does he have a family. I look at people and try to figure out who they are. I once had a family. But that was a long time ago. Peace and sleep do not come easily for me these days. My dreams keep me from true rest as

I sometimes relive the assassinations our government demands in order to reset the baseline of good vs. evil. But the line always moves forward and I'm forever running faster just to stay in place.

I shut my eyes to close out the world and despite the cold, I can feel the steam of the jungle around me. Hot air plumes shoot into the sky, and a soft voice calls out to me. I reach out into space as if to caress a shadow, and my eyes well with tears. The train gives a jolt and jostles me. My eyes open.

"Mommy, mommy can't I get some food, I'm hungry," whines a small voice two rows up from my seat. "That man has food," she says pointing her finger in the air.

Discreetly, I wipe away a tear, and turn my head to look out the window. My thoughts trail off when the man who had gotten up to go to the dining car earlier returns carrying a box of food. He slides into the seat next to me and places the box on his tray table. I can smell the hot dog, and the pungent mustard. When he opens the bag of chips, I inhale just a few particles of fried potato. My stomach grumbles, triggered by the mixed messages that food gives me. It's life sustaining, but in my hands with a little additive, it can take life away.

Traveling on a train gives me too much time to think. Sometimes I use that time to work on a manuscript of an interesting case or toxin, but at other times my mind wanders in and out of all the years of painful losses and challenging cases to fill the empty space. I find my attention drifting to places I've been, and to colleagues and friends I've worked with in the past. Often, I think about Dr. John Chi Leigh, a superb chemist and toxicologist, unmatched in his ability to extract and identify any toxin known to man. His British father met his Chinese mother while he was in Hong Kong studying chemistry. Chemistry runs in John Chi's DNA, forming a double helix with a backbone of genius and base pairs of deception and cunning. He had been a formidable foe at one time, but switched to the side of the good to make restitution for his inevitable human frailty. We've worked on several cases together since the Agency uses him as a consultant. While working on one case with Leigh, I found a journal he kept hidden in his lab. I was startled by his feelings for me that spilled onto the page like a poetic chromatogram: "I'm drawn to her because of her intense focus, her single-mindedness and her simple beauty. Lily Robinson is a subtle force of nature with captivating emerald eyes and raven hair. She uses her ingenuity to dismantle her victims and make it appear they die of natural causes."

In reality, I've merely mastered the art of secret poisoning. I feel the train give another jolt as the wheels grind to a stop and so I close John's journal entry in my mind's eye.

*　　*　　*

I've reached my destination at Penn Station. When I step out onto the train platform, I feel the chilly morning creep in between my slightly parted coat, which reveals a sleek black leather pencil skirt, topped with a black and white striped tee, and tall leather boots with the feel of butter. I took some time to pick out this outfit to wear to the museum. Professional and fashionable. I put my hand to my head to secure my crystal fox headband while I head up the escalator to face the crush. Bodies move together as a single pod and I feel as if I'm being swept up to Seventh Avenue on a tide of humanity. On the streets above the train tracks are young men, working for little money, handing out flyers to travelers and tourists alike for Broadway shows, restaurant menus, and discount coupons for the stores. One young man hands me the schedule containing upcoming sports and media events at the Garden, another with menus for the surrounding restaurants, and a third young man, clearly college age and hungry, a small card wrapped in cellophane advertising a perfume. I must look like a tourist. No time to look at these, I stuff the advertorials into my bag and head for the stream of yellow taxi cabs waiting patiently to pop their trunks and welcome a visitor to New York City.

"Good afternoon, Miss," offers a turban-wrapped driver, "where to?"

I tell him to take me to the History of Science Museum, and pull around to the side entrance.

*　　*　　*

I love this museum. I loved it while growing up and I still love it. Probably most children love it, as well as the parents who bring them there. Families often sit together in front of dioramas of wild animals and sea creatures taking in the entire scene as if it were real. Sometimes you can overhear mothers soothing their children's fears when they look at some of the exhibits.

"I know it looks dark and scary in there, but it's just a make-believe fight between two enormous sea creatures." Or "No, the lions aren't alive, so they can't hurt you."

I'm going to meet the museum curator so I have the taxi pull up to the midtown side entrance where pink brownstone and granite tower ahead. I walk through the cavernous stone gallery and make my way to the curator's office, my heart pounding as I quicken my step through the office door. Then it happens. My body slowly relaxes, and my heart rate eases when I see the warm wooden bookcases overfilled with books, jars of worms, snails, and arthropods, and the sparkling strings of lights suspended from the ceiling. The large wooden desk is stacked with more books, and papers. I have to laugh, what is it little boys are made of? Snips and snails, and puppy dog's tails. It's welcoming and secure.

The museum curator was already known to the authorities before this assignment came up. The Agency always taps into local talent, particularly for background information. These niche specialists surprisingly store valuable obscure facts in their brains that appeal to different branches of the government.

"Ah, my friend, so good to see you," says the curator as he wraps his arms around me and gives me a big hug and a kiss. "I see you had no trouble making yourself comfortable."

I hug him back. Eric Vandermeer is a charming man, middle aged with wispy dark brown hair, graying at the temples. His horn-rimmed glasses give him a learned look and when he dons his brown corduroy jacket with the leather patches, he reminds me of the quintessential caricature of a university professor. I suppose that's his intent. I first met him several years ago at one of his lectures. I waited patiently in the lecture hall for him to finish his talk. Then after answering multiple questions from the audience, he moved right to me, linked his arm with mine, and walked me to his office, where we talked about all things poison, while sharing a bottle of wine. There was an unstated communication between us, a shared reverence for nature's miracles, a genuine joy in the appreciation of science and that undefined chemistry between a man and a woman. I could feel it. Our eyes met just at the moment there was a pause in the conversation, and I sensed that the curator felt he had been embraced by the petals of a Venus flytrap from which he could not escape. I can have that effect. But this connection paved the way for collaboration, and a shared sense of purpose.

"Eric, so good to see you again. I guess you've been briefed on the situation.

I did hear concerns that explosive devices may be hidden within the museum, particularly in the area of the special exhibits. Imagine the economic havoc you could create if you blew up the museum, and half the world's top bankers." I tell him this knowing that there's much more to the story. Eric is a little taken aback by my bluntness. It shows in his body language. He's tense.

All Eric knows is that Lily Robinson is a pathologist specializing in toxicology. My purpose at the museum is to help him entertain the guests with science and showmanship, and hopefully garner bigger donations. He knows there's a suspicion of a possible bomb. Both the local and national authorities are taking the threat seriously. Earlier in the week, there was a meeting with museum leadership to discuss whether the dinner should be cancelled. I confirmed as much. He wonders how I know all this and I'm sure he suspects there must be more to my own story. But those are the questions he's always too afraid to ask. So he makes a little small talk.

"Lily, I'm so glad you're here. Tell, me, how are things at the medical school, what's new with your cases, what have you been doing?"

"It's been very hectic at the medical center, Eric. The toxicology service has been flat out with all the synthetic drugs that have been flooding this country. However, I did take a short leave from the hospital this past summer and worked in Dr. Leigh's lab. I'm sure I've told you about John Chi Leigh. Haven't I?"

"Yes. What did you two work on? Something exciting I hope."

"It was pretty exciting for me. We were in his Hong Kong lab synthesizing toxins and extracting venoms to use for medical research. You might say, a little drug discovery. I know you have a lot of interest in these compounds too and are hoping to have an exhibit on poisons in the museum, what, maybe next year? Anyway, working with Leigh is an education. The man's a genius."

"Yes, you've told me that before. I think I'd like to meet him one day," Eric says.

"You'll find John Chi to be complicated, even at times intellectually intimidating, and he's always testing you," I tell him. At least he's always testing me.

"The next time he visits the U.S., I will get you two together. I promise."

While in Hong Kong, John Chi and I created a nice toxin that I'm going to use for this New York job.

Eric and I review the plans for the gala banquet and I make some special requests for the menu so my poison will fit in without notice.

44

"Always the cook, Lily," Eric says. "It's the chemist in you."

"Eric. I have to get over to Mercy Hospital to see a colleague of mine. He's had some unusual cases, and I promised to look at a couple of slides with him. I'll catch up with you later."

"Yeah, from what I hear, the docs in this town have been very busy. Apparently, this is the worst flu season ever. I think someone told me they've called in the CDC to see if it's some kind of mutant strain."

"That's what they're thinking," I say. I'm not about to tell him what the Agency has been throwing around. Visions of mass poisoning.

* * *

When I meet up with Francis Becker he has some preliminary tissue to review with me under the microscope. I haven't seen Becker in years, yet he's still a striking man, his hair a little thinner, and he's got that same warm smile. He had already prepared thin sections of fresh lung tissue that had been frozen, dropped onto a glass slide, stained and protected with a cover slip. The rest of the lung tissue was fixing in formalin to make it firm and suitable for permanent sections. The formalin fixed pieces of tissue would later be embedded with paraffin wax, cut ever so thinly, and then mounted permanently on a glass slide. We sit down at the double-headed microscope.

"Lily, you see this area here?" Becker says, moving the pointer in the microscopic field to a thin pink area on the slide.

"I do, it looks like increased alveolar-capillary permeability."

"Right, small leaky blood vessels in the lung. I saw the same thing in all the cases I reviewed. This patient also had myocardial hypertrophy. That right ventricular wall was thickened. If you look at these microscopic sections you can also see some focal drop out of the myocardial cells and some contraction band necrosis." He drives the slide of the heart muscle around on the stage so I can clearly see areas where useless fibrous tissue has replaced necessary cardiac tissue. The pointer lands on fine eosinophilic lines crossing the heart muscle.

"I see it, Francis, but contraction band necrosis can be a non-specific finding found with resuscitation as well as with any stimulant. I often find these in hearts of cocaine users."

"I know. I know, I'm going out on a limb here, but you don't think it's anthrax, do ya Lily? I'm askin' you first before I say something to the ME and set off city-wide alarms. You know how Marie is. She'll be on this quicker than flies on sh….." He stops abruptly when I interrupt him.

"Francis, do you think I could have some blood and urine specimens from a few of your patients? I have a colleague who has a highly sophisticated toxicology laboratory and I'd like to have him analyze some of these specimens in addition to the white powder. I need you to keep this just between the two of us for the time being. Do not call the ME with any specifics. Just tell Marie you're working on it. That should keep her satisfied for the time being." I pause for a moment, then quickly add, "Other than the symptoms, is there anything else connecting these cases?"

"Lily, I'm gonna have to check with that EMT fella. He said his colleagues have had other cases in the city, mostly picked them up near Penn Station, I think he said many of them had been traveling. I'll see what I can find out. As far as the specimens go, let's go down the hall and I'll have my staff prepare some for shippin' anywhere in the country you'd like."

Anywhere in the country? He doesn't know I want them shipped to Hong Kong.

*   *   *

John Chi Leigh lives in a city of seven million people located on China's south coast, but this time, instead of flying halfway around the world, I'm meeting with my brilliant ally via computer connection. John Chi's electronic image looks troubled.

"Hi my friend, are you okay?" I say. Sometimes I feel like I've known him forever, although this isn't the case.

"Everything is okay, Lily. I received the specimens you expedited from New York City. I should begin to work on them tomorrow," Leigh says in a soft voice, shifting his body as he sits in a wide brown leather chair.

Usually when I speak with him, I can gauge his mood. He sounds distant, almost uncomfortable, but I'm not sure I'm such a good judge of body language when looking at a computer screen. I need to feel it.

Then John just pops out with, "I know how you work Lily Robinson. You like to keep it simple and natural. It's the best way. Little evidence to follow."

I take in his face with my eyes. His straight black hair is cut short and barely touches his ears, and his black glasses sit distinctly on his small shallow nose framing his brown eyes.

46

When I look into those eyes, even through the monitor, I know what he means without actually saying it.

So yes, is all I have to say to him.

His eyes hold my gaze. He relishes the fact that he's much smarter than I. Years ago, he saved my life. I'd been sent by a government consortium to Hong Kong to eliminate one of the world's demons who also happened to be a diabetic. I didn't think that anyone would know that I had substituted the diabetic's vial of insulin with toxin from the box jellyfish, *Chironex fleckeri.* I'd used one of the most toxic sea creatures on the planet to kill a slave trafficker and murderer. But Leigh figured it all out.

I stopped in Hollywood, California on the way back to Boston to visit a producer friend on the set of his hit show, satisfied that everything had gone well in Hong Kong. But I was wrong. I had been followed by one of the trafficker's henchman who tried to kill me right there in the studio. Just at that moment, John Chi stepped out on the stage and killed the bastard. This genius that I'd never met, had created a toxin of his own, one with fangs that dropped its victim within a hundred paces of striking distance. A viper from southern China, the Chinese moccasin, had provided all the power he needed. I have forever since been in John Chi Leigh's debt.

I don't think John realizes that the Agency investigated him extensively after that incident. I was hoping we could use his skills in some of our operations if his background checked out. There were problems, like for one, we found out he had a history of serious gambling over many years. He'd gone to the equivalent of Gamblers Anonymous, but occasionally he'd relapse, losing large sums of money, and to pay for his losses, did unthinkable things. Originally, he'd been contracted to kill me to pay back a debt. This breach in the armor makes him vulnerable to temptation. We know he's a risk, and I'm fully aware that desperate men are capable of desperate things. I told the Agency I'd take that risk, just to be able to touch the hem of the lab coat worn by a genius.

"You just seem a little preoccupied, John," I say to him, maybe sounding a little too critical. He's sensitive.

He tries to make his voice sound stronger with his next entry into our conversation.

"Nothing is wrong," he says. "You mentioned earlier that you were working on another case. Anything interesting? Are you going to use one of the toxins we synthesized this summer?

"I can't really talk about it," I tell him. It's now getting a little awkward so I sit quietly and wait. Leigh looks back at me and says nothing.

I can't share with John that I'm thinking that there's a real hole in the information on the museum dinner and therefore considering that the poisoning cases from Becker may be related in some way to my original mission. It might be a stretch, but in medicine you look for the common denominator, the single disease to explain all the symptoms rather than multiple diseases. To make that leap, I have to push through my logical-mind, and head toward my feeling-gut. It's called intuition.

As if he's reading my mind he says, "Look for the common denominator."

It spooks me. It's as if he knows more than he lets on. My mind races. All the cases were from people who had traveled through the railway exchange at some point. That's what Becker had told me. They were all cases where people had crossed in and out of Penn Station. Except Bajian, the locum tenens pathologist. He hadn't traveled through Penn Station. He hadn't been to NJ, or Boston, or anywhere up or down the East coast. But I had, and just recently, yet I haven't been infected. At least not yet. What then is the connection?

"You're right, John. When I speak with Becker again, I'll see what I can find out. Meanwhile, let me know what you discover in the white powder, and the tissue and body fluids."

"When I find something, I'll call you."

I hit the end button on the computer screen hoping John Chi will find something soon.

CHAPTER 7

NEW YORK CITY

Dr. Leigh finished his teleconference with Lily feeling somewhat distracted. He looked at the black screen on his computer, closed the cover and pulled up the horse racing slip for the day's picks. He would get to the analysis a little later. New York would have to wait.

* * *

Francis Becker had remembered Lily Robinson quite well. Yes, she was older, but she had that same captivating smile, and although seemingly warm and engaging, had a sense of aloofness about her. He imagined that she was never close with anyone since she appeared to keep herself focused on business and little else. Not unlike Marie Washington, except Marie wasn't as disciplined or as smart. He made the call.

Becker updated the Chief ME on his findings regarding the autopsies he had conducted. "Hi, Marie, Becker here. Yep, still workin' on the cases. Looks like some respiratory process goin' on. I need to do a few more studies. Well the microscopics showed some congestion, but I'd like to do some IHCs. What?" he said with slight laugh, "Yup, I know you medical examiner types don't do those immunohistochemical stains, in fact you shy away from the microscope and just go by the gross for the most part, but I'm just an ol' surgical pathologist. We depend on 'um. Yup, I'll keep ya posted, okay, will do. Bye."

He didn't let her know that there had been similar lesions in the lungs in all his patients and when he compared notes with his colleagues across town, they had seen analogous results. He thought he should probably check in with Jim Cassidy and perhaps even with the ED physician, Stu Greene to see if there had been additional circumstances where the patient may have recovered.

Becker took the stairs up to the ED and looked to see if Greene was on duty and to ask if he had seen Jim Cassidy. Greene was sitting in the center bay checking lab results when Becker interrupted him.

"Dr. Greene, sorry to interrupt," said the Chief of Pathology. "Have you had any additional cases like the ones I did the autopsies on? I sent out that vial you found to be analyzed, along with some fluid and tissue samples. I imagine we should have the results back in a day or two."

"I did have one additional case, but she seemed to do alright after several hours in the ED. A kid in her twenties. Gave her supportive care and she came around. Weird, but she also had been down around the Garden the day before she got ill. I asked some of my coworkers around town and they've had similar incidences. Oh, and one other doc I talked to found some white powder in a plastic bag stuffed between his patient's butt cheeks. Who knows what that was since he didn't hang on to it. Anyway, if we're talking a viral illness of some kind, then it's not easily transmitted from one person to another. Or it has a very long incubation period. Let's hope you and I don't come down with something in a few weeks. God, I don't want to relive the Ebola scare and I don't want to be on your autopsy table."

They stopped talking when they saw a commotion at the entrance to the emergency department. A group of young girls, in their mid to late teens, were being wheeled in by several EMTs.

"This one's going down fast. I need some help here," shouted Jim Cassidy, pushing a stretcher with a lifeless form. She looked about fifteen, had long brown hair, a petite body with two IVs and a breathing tube. The other two girls were ill, but not intubated.

Stu Greene ran over to the group. "What cha got here, Jim? Looks like these kids are having respiratory difficulties, and hmm, red eyes too. Hey, we got one here we need to get on fast," he said in a loud voice. The triage nurse had already cleared one of the exam rooms.

They hooked up the girl who was intubated to a heart monitor and when her blood pressure dropped, they pushed in the drugs and the defibrillator was readied to deliver the counter shock. It whined as it charged, and then beep, beep, beep.

"Get that epi in the line stat. Shit, we're losing her." The EKG went flat. "Stand back. Watch the paddles," Greene said turning to the nurses.

"Ready, one two three." A loud zap was heard in the room as the instrument discharged. The voltage was dialed up both on the instrument, and within the doctor delivering the jolt. One of the girls who wasn't very sick began to sob loudly, and the nurse gave her a small dose of a sedative, midazolam, through her IV. She closed her wet eyes for a moment and quieted down with a look of relaxation on her face. They pulled the curtain between the rooms.

Jim Cassidy and Francis Becker watched the scene unfold.

"Are you thinking what I'm thinking?" said Cassidy.

"Yes sir," was the answer.

"Miss," said Dr. Becker in his very polite and twangy voice, "where are ya'll ladies comin' from?"

The girl with the midazolam peaceful look on her face opened her eyes and stared at the two of them.

"We were just, like, down in Times Square, ya know." She struggled to get the words past her oxygen mask.

"Take ya time miss. It's okay. We're here ta help ya. I'm Dr. Becker and this here is Mr. Cassidy."

"I don't know. Like, we were shopping, thinking of going to a concert. Our parents like let us go into the city for the day." She wheezed, rubbed her eyes and tried to sit up, but fell back into the bed.

"Miss would you mind if we took a look in your handbag?" said Jim Cassidy very gently.

"Um, like, I don't know. Um, I have some things in there I don't want my parents to see. Sometimes I have a cigarette. Uh, I guess it's okay, but please, can you not talk with my parents about this? They're really going to freak out."

Jim Cassidy took the handbag and opened the flap to expose the contents. He methodically took things out one by one. A brush, a comb, an iPhone in a pink case, a pack of Camels (which he put off to the side), a key chain with three keys on it, hand cream, a wallet, a flyer with the list of upcoming events at the Garden, a water bottle, and in the front pocket some cellophane wrapped perfume cards. There were no vials of white powder or anything else that he thought could remotely contain poison. He opened the privacy screen, and went to see how the other two patients were doing.

Stu Greene emerged from the next room and pulled the curtain behind him. He looked at Cassidy.

"This one's for Becker, or the ME, however they want to handle it. Christ, what the hell is going on? I got a teenager in my ED who just died of respiratory failure. Looks like severe pulmonary edema."

Jim Cassidy went into the cubicle and looked at the dead girl. She had a tube down her throat and lines coming out from both of her arms. She looked restful. Hands lying by her sides with fingertips adorned with ruby red nail polish. He thought she was too young to be at this kind of peace. He quickly searched the room for her handbag. When he saw it, he rummaged through to see if there were any vials or powders. Nothing of note. This handbag too had flyers for restaurants and concerts, a bottle of red nail polish, and the familiar perfume card. He decided this time to keep those items and not return them to the purse.

*   *   *

Becker went back to his office trying to understand what had just happened. He picked up the phone and called Lily. He hadn't heard back from her since delivery of the tissue and blood samples to her chemist friend. When he finally reached her on the phone he inquired as to the toxicology results, but she just apologized and said she hadn't heard back from Dr. Leigh. She wanted to know whether Becker had any additional information. Anything that could tie the cases together.

"Lily, let's not do this over the phone. Come on in, darlin'," I have a nice leather chair in my office, been crafted in Texas. You know, it's for those days that never end."

Lily took a taxi right over to Becker's office and when he saw her, he began to collect pieces of the puzzle for her review.

CHAPTER 8

NEW YORK CITY

I'm back at my hotel after a long day. The grand lobby is lined in marble and gold leaf with opulent chandeliers dropping from the embellished rotunda above. Large vases of flowers in stunning arrangements don tables located in the center of the entranceway. Although I feel agitated from all the stress, and I can still taste the acid in my mouth, there's always time to admire the beauty of the blooms. I like the way they're clustered in happy groups of color, blue puffy hydrangeas alternating with delicate white, baby's breath. A short pause at nature's best gives me hope, and I wish summer would come soon so I can work in my own garden that gives me peace. I pull up my fur around my shoulders as I move across the room and wait impatiently by the elevator. Waiting at elevators is not something I do well. I missed out on the gene for patience. So, I take those few minutes and think of all Becker has told me and carefully begin to finish assembling the puzzle in my mind. Francis Becker had neatly put the corner pieces in their place, those that came together with two smooth sides forming a right angle, but I need to take all the seemingly endless jagged parts and create the final reveal. The elevator finally opens and I ride to my floor all the way thinking about the case while I'm turning my hotel key in my fingers.

This historic grand hotel uses an old fashioned key to turn the lock. I have a special interest in keys, particularly ones that open secret boxes used to hide family heirlooms or personal papers of significance. The hotel key is a bit key, one with a bit that turns the lock, and a solid shaft that connects that piece to the bow, or the handle. It's the kind of basic key design used for more than 1,500 years. There's still charm in that. I put the key into the lock, and I can hear the click. The door is open. What's this? I can see as I enter the sitting room that on the desk is a bouquet of red roses. I approach cautiously and look around me for anything out of place. I'm not alarmed. Odd, there's no card. I lean down, close my eyes and breathe in the soft scent, curious as to the origin of the flowers. The air now stirs behind me, and I can sense the hairs on the back of my neck stand straight up. My heart begins to pound. I take a deep breath. How could I have missed someone in the room? I feel it now. I turn around quickly to see a dark-haired man standing directly in front of me. He reaches out, and pulls me into him.

"It's you," I say, my voice shaking, as I struggle to pull away. "You scared the life out of me." My fists are pounding at his chest. He grabs my wrists and I begin to soften, and then finally let my body relax. I look into his blue-green eyes, and move my hands up to his face and touch the gently worn creases in his skin. He pulls me into him, once again, and kisses me with a tenderness I have not felt in a long time. My body feels warm all over, and my fur coat slips off my shoulders and falls to the floor. I don't care. The dark-haired man picks me up and carries me into the adjacent bedroom.

"*Ma Chérie*, I have missed you, you know," he says with a silky French accent as he carefully places me on the bed. He takes his hand and uses his fingers to comb my dark hair, and push the loose strands behind my ears.

"I think the last time we saw each other for more than a *minute* was when we were in Paris, the second time together. *Rappeler*, remember? The first time was several years ago when we had finished off the arms dealers with your toxic *champignons*. The second time more recently at the ministry. *Oui?*" he says with that killer laugh.

"You are here, JP, and how did you get into my room?" I ask with ever so slight irritation, propping my head on my hand, elbow bent on the pillow.

"Come on, Lily, I am a superspy, *mais oui*," he says again with that laugh, placing the emphasis on the second syllable of my name. "You don't think we are going to let you and your curator friend handle this entire affair without my help. Have I not been with you at every critical moment in your service to us?"

True enough I think. He had been there, and always to make sure things were as they should be. He was there on my very first case, the one in Boston where he helped me poison an "intellectual runaway," a traitor. After all this time, I still feel that it was so unfortunate that the professor hadn't cooperated with the government. If he had, he might be alive today.

"Yes of course," I say out loud, and think, *at every critical moment*. There was no forgetting the convention center fiasco in Chicago where the world's chemists had gathered for an international meeting. Varying concentrations of cyanide had been added to foil-wrapped chocolate wafers by one deranged chemist seeking to destroy those attending the scientific convention. His plan was to have the vendors offer the candy at their booths along with the information on their products. I figured out his scheme, but only after I had tasted the bitter efforts of his personal revenge. Had the dark-haired man not been there, I would have died of cyanide poisoning.

The pressures from the New York case fill me like a balloon that is now ready to burst. Tension, pushing at the limits, is heightened with JP's surprise return. We hold each other's eyes with a simple look and my head drops on to the pillow. He leans over, kisses me on the lips, and my body arcs in response. God, he smells so good, like he's been sun dried after an ocean swim.

"Lily, Lily, I have missed you," he says softly. "Can we talk business a little later?" He touches my cheek, bends his head down to kiss my closed eyelids, and nuzzles my neck. I feel his warm breath on my skin, and the tiny hairs on my arm stand up as a shudder passes throughout my body. My passion unleashed, I loosen his tie, unbutton his shirt and pull the shirttails out from his trousers. The top button on his pants is unfastened and my hand slides beneath the waistband. Oh, he is aroused and it stirs me. My silky camisole top falls from my shoulders and the dark-haired man's lips brush my breasts. I slip beneath him and his tongue finds its way to that warm wet spot in the center of my core. My breathing deepens and I imagine he is looking at my face even though my eyes are closed. Then he joins me with the skill of a lover who knows how to please a woman, his woman. With my hands clinging around his powerful back, I open my eyes to meet his and we both know in that moment, we have the kind of union that only a supreme force could have created.

Here I am, making love with a man whose real name and beginnings I never learned. For me, he's always been just JP, the dark-haired man with intense blue-green eyes. He was a collaborator in the secret spy agency that has engaged my skills for all these years. The Agency took advantage of my anguish over a terrible loss, for their own agenda, and I have been unwittingly caught in an iron trap of despair chained to revenge ever since. But the dark-haired man changed our relationship, changed everything, when he sought me out in *La Cour Jardin* of the *Hôtel Plaza Athénée* in Paris. He found me ice skating in the little courtyard on New Year's Eve, and wrapped me in his arms as the snow began to fall. His warm embrace carried me back to his room, where we entered the New Year with shudders of ecstasy and an unbreakable bond of trust. He's the only man I have ever truly loved.

*   *   *

The following morning when I awake, I'm almost surprised to find a man's body next to mine. It's been a long time since I've shared my bed, and I'm reveling in the sheer delight of another human being's touch. His touch.

I roll over and look at the face of this man lying next to me. I'm happy. I stroke his hair and kiss his lips. There is no acid churning in my stomach, just excitement.

"Good morning *monsieur*," I say sweetly. "Shall I get us some coffee or perhaps even breakfast? I have a really intense day and I might add, so do you."

He opens his eyes, those gorgeous blue-green eyes and says, "Good morning my Lily," and pulls me into him. I taste his kiss, feel his strength, and hear him say, "*Oui*, breakfast would be nice, but I would rather have you." Then he touches my wrist and says, "I see you still wear the bracelet I gave you in Paris. We agreed you would never take it off."

I've never taken it off since the day he fastened it to my wrist. It's a simple platinum band intricately woven in a mesh web. Elegant without being too fancy for everyday wear, and a reminder of my dark-haired man.

I return the kiss, but as much as I want to be with him at that moment, I squelch my emotions and bring my critical mind into focus. I've spent years denying my emotions.

"Look, of course I should've known it was you calling the shots," I say, sitting up in bed and pulling the sheets up around me, "but when I didn't hear from you, well, I thought it might be someone else this time. Do you have any more information for me?"

"Lily, small IEDs still cannot be ruled out, but we are more concerned that this may be an attempt at mass poisoning. We've been suspicious all along, which is why we called you in from the start. The bankers may be at the heart of it. We are still working with fragments of information, but it is now becoming more clear."

Huh, I'm thinking. I knew it.

"Listen, I've been working on this other case and I really think the two may be related." I explode with great energy and begin to tell him about the younger people in the city who are coming down with sudden respiratory symptoms, and then dying of congested lungs filled with fluid.

"When I spoke with Becker yesterday, he told me that all the patients that the EMT Jim Cassidy had brought into the hospital had somehow been connected with Penn Station, or at least in the area around Penn Station and the Garden. At first none of us could see the link between the young pathologist Avy Bajian who died, until Jim went back to his apartment. Before going into cardiac arrest, Bajian said something about his wife and a date while he was in the ambulance. Jim called the wife later the same day and found out that they had tickets to go to a concert the night he died. You want to take a guess where?"

"Madison Square Garden," JP answers, getting out of bed, and stepping into a white terry cloth robe embossed with the hotel's name.

"Exactly!" I say, "And guess what he was doing the morning before he became ill?"

"Buying tic…"

"Yes, he was down at the Garden getting those tickets!" I say, interrupting JP before he can finish speaking. I can feel my excitement growing. He's now looking at me squarely, pulling me up from the bed. I don't resist.

"Lily, let us get out of the bed, wash up, and review the details of your findings. I could use a cup of *café* and something to eat so my mind will work better. Why don't you finish telling me your story in the shower," he says, putting his arm around my shoulder guiding me into the bathroom.

"Wait, is that my phone? Is it ringing?" I try and turn around to get it.

"I don't think so, Lily; later. The shower, *rapidement*."

Hot running water fills the room with steam. The shower door is obscured in fog, and splashes of the streaming water drown out the echoes of ardor, and all the external sounds like noise-cancelling headphones.

CHAPTER 9

THE WEST SIDE OF NEW YORK

On the other side of the city Eric Vandermeer made his way along the West Side of Manhattan using the time to think about the upcoming museum events. For him, New York City was the distillate of the East: a dark tincture filled with the essence of those who walked beneath stone monuments that brushed the sky. Walking the city streets with the pavement under his feet felt just as satisfying as the dirt on the paths in the forests he traveled when he was on a field expedition for museum research. There was a renewed freshness spurred by his discussions with his colleague Lily Robinson and he reviewed his predicament in his mind. He knew every inch of his museum, and what he thought were all the possible places one could hide or conceal an improvised bomb. Yet dogs, trained to detect a single molecule of explosive, had moved throughout the museum in waves during the week and found nothing.

He was terrified at the thought of a hidden bomb in a museum exhibit, remembering Lily's story of the Boston Marathon bombings. She had witnessed firsthand the unmistakable terror unleashed on innocent athletes and spectators as explosions produced death and limbs askew on the brick. Nurses and doctors were overwhelmed by the pools of blood as gurneys were wheeled into the emergency department and isolated legs were placed on stretchers next to the patients. Nurses slipped in the red on floors while yellow and black coded vests brought a never-ending onslaught of mangled humanity. Calls went out throughout the city for units of blood, and surgeons mustered their strength to hold a marathon of their own. They tried desperately to save lives, those with missing pieces, and those whose eyes had witnessed a lifetime of red stain flowing like a poison tide down Boylston Street. He found the vision haunting.

Eric also considered that maybe Lily had it right. He had to believe that any bomb carried through the doors of his domain would easily be detected unless of course it was hidden in a "Trojan horse." Or perhaps it wouldn't be a bomb at all, but something far easier to conceal, harder to reveal. The curator's anxiety mounted as he imagined the economic devastation if world bankers were to be the victims of a mass killing in an effort to disrupt the global economy, and bring chaos into the financial world. He also considered the consequences of the physical destruction to one of the world's most beloved and cherished museums. It would be terror at its highest level.

Once back in the museum, Eric Vandermeer again swept through the common areas with other agents at his side. There was no scent of a bomb.

"Sir," said one of the guards in an abrupt tone, "we've just covered the perimeter again and would like your permission to peruse the exhibit you will tour this evening. There are a lot of places to hide IEDs, and we just have to keep looking."

Eric nodded yes. There were obvious security agents as would be expected for a function such as this, but many of the government agents working with Lily and the curator were dressed either as museum guards or docents. Some were agents who had a high level of intelligence clearance and could recognize known terrorists by sight, and others were experts in bomb detection and disarmament. Yet they all blended in with the regular museum staff—acting as the just recently hired extras for the special event. The event assistant, a young woman named Alexis, had been quite helpful in organizing the dinner for the museum, and yet was unaware of the intrigue and threat behind the scenes. She had planned several fund-raising events for the museum in the past and was familiar with the protocol. Her reputation was one of efficiency and professionalism.

"Excuse me doctor," she said in a cordial tone, "we'll be setting up later this afternoon in the main hall. I'll see that the caterers are organized in the kitchen, and I think we have pretty much everything else under control. If I might add," she added a bit sternly, "please keep your security detail out of my way. We seem to have an awful lot of them today. I don't like to be interfered with when I'm creating a masterpiece. Oh, and I took the liberty of ordering flowers for each table. Lilies; I hope you like them," she said as she made her way out of the room.

Eric once again nodded yes, only partially listening to her words, and thought the event planner was not only efficient, but elegant, wearing a French designer scarf containing scenes of Napoleon on his horse. Alexis made a striking presentation. But his focus sharpened as he saw the silhouette of a woman in stilettos enter the room. There she was. Her unbuttoned suit jacket revealed her low-cut black tank top peering out from under her cashmere suit that Eric could not help but notice. She seemed to spill over the top with soft white flesh that had undoubtedly caught the curator's attention. He moved his eyes down to her shoes. *Leave it to Lily Robinson,* he thought. *We're in the middle of a crisis and she manages to wear her signature stiletto heels with the peep toes.* He never considered himself a man to know fashion, but since he had known Lily, he became attentive to the accessories of a woman's attire. He walked toward her, arms open wide for a hug, and she started asking about the changes in the museum security before he released her from his embrace.

Chapter 10

THE MUSEUM

I see Eric across the room. He's staring at me, undoubtedly noticing my shoes and my tank top. I wanted to turn up the fashion dial for the dinner tonight. It must be working.

"Good afternoon, Eric," I say with great enthusiasm, as he enfolds me in his arms. "I see we have metal detectors at every entry point now. That's a change. Are we going to search everyone's bag as well?"

"Well, that's the plan," he says, looking at his watch as if a little irritated. "We've been working all morning. I was waiting for you; thought you were coming in a little earlier."

"Sorry," I say, "Something came up and I got a little behind this morning." I'm smiling and thinking that's probably something James Bond would have said. Eric doesn't react. He seems stressed out and wants to take a walk through the exhibit, review some last-minute details. There's anxiety in his voice.

We walk through a dark corridor winding down a path filled with tropical foliage. Broad leaves of Dieffenbachia, or Dumb cane, green with variegated stripes like zebra skins tower overhead.

Eric lets out a slow breath and says, "You know Lily, this business has been exhausting. I didn't sleep well last night and I've been having some trouble concentrating lately. You see these dark circles around my eyes, don't you?" his fingers pointing at his face. He does look distressed and I take the opportunity to distract him and praise his work.

"These exhibits are clever, Eric. They get people interested in the natural world. I like the fact that several of the exhibits are interactive and draw the visitor in: you know, we get to sniff this, find that, solve this. The United States is lagging behind other countries when it comes to science skills.

Exhibits like these, ones that engage people and encourage them to become part of the show, could help rekindle America's quest for knowledge in the areas of math and science." We stop in front of a schematic of a house cut in a frontal plane depicting all the rooms on two floors with a basement below.

"Take this exhibit, for example. Here the participant can look at all the clues you've provided in order to figure out what happened. First, you find out that the person living in the house died during a cold winter snowstorm. You press the button, and you find a light blinking in the bedroom. That's where the body was found. You press the next button and a light blinks at a vent outside the house covered with snow. You get your last clue from the medical examiner. The body was a cherry red color when the pathologist began the autopsy. Then the person interacting with the exhibit gets to choose the cause of death: is it arsenic, carbon monoxide, antifreeze, or hypothermia? Well, that leads you to the last button, here." I point to the several metal buttons on the panel and then press the one indicating my answer for the cause of death.

"See, I'm right. It's carbon monoxide. The snow blocked the vent preventing the oil burner from getting enough oxygen. Insufficient oxygen resulted in incomplete combustion which produced carbon monoxide, that's CO rather than CO2 which is carbon dioxide."

I say this to Eric in such a way to emphasize the first syllable in both mon-oxide and di-oxide. I hope he's following me. I continue. "Carbon monoxide is particularly deadly, and since you can't smell it or see it, people don't know that it's present in a room, or even a house. The gas makes you tired, dizzy, headachy and eventually the victim becomes unconscious. That's why every household needs multiple CO detectors, not just smoke alarms. And that cherry red color, CO has such a high affinity for hemoglobin, the blood never gets fully desaturated."

After the monologue, I feel as if I'm gasping for air. I've lapsed into long-winded science speak, again. Eric gets it, and his face radiates satisfaction knowing that his exhibits are creative and clearly stimulating. Puzzles draw people in; the museum draws people in because figuring things out is what we like to do. It's what I like to do. Eric is looking into my eyes and realizes he knows very little about me other than my university job. I'm his puzzle. *Where is Lily's little silver button one can push to find out what makes her tick*, he thinks.

"Lily, you are an enigma," he blurts out.

He gets a big smile from me and I congratulate him on educating future generations of children and the adults as well. We walk out the back entrance of the exhibit and I can see the curator rub the right side of his head, as if he is bothered with thought.

By late afternoon, Eric and I had reviewed all our findings surrounding the dinner, but hadn't uncovered any additional information to change our original plans one way or the other. There was no word from JP either.

At one point, Eric lets me know that he likes my handbag he's seen me clutching tightly all day. Funny that he brings it up now. He guesses it must be very expensive for me to keep it so close. I laugh. The handbag is from a new Cuban designer, Delgado, I tell him. His shoes and handbags are flying off the shelves. They are quite coveted and now very hard to get. Prada has some real competition.

Yes, the handbag is expensive, but the priceless part is in its contents. Tucked deep inside the Delgado is a small ampoule of poison that John Chi had synthesized for me while I was in Hong Kong. As is my custom, the toxin is highly concentrated so that just a small drop produces lethal consequences. This reminds me that I need to get something from my oversized travel bag I'd left earlier in Eric's office while we were exploring the new exhibit.

It's probably near the closet in his office, so I leave him in the museum's special exhibit gift shop to check over the offerings. The place is stocked with books, poisonous spiders and scorpions frozen in plastic, geodes, rocks and minerals, and several pieces of clothing adorned with a skull and crossbones, a museum logo, or an exotic animal.

I exit the gift shop and wander past some of my favorite exhibits like the dioramas with preserved animals from the Northern Hemisphere. Large grizzly bears, brown bears and other native species make you feel so small when standing next to them. Unless you encounter these creatures in the wild, you lose sight of how big a grizzly bear can really be.

Turning left instead of right, I make one detour on the way to the curator's office. At the bottom of the back stairs is the kitchen. I need to see how the caterers are progressing with my menu. Located just to the inside of the door that leads from the caterers' vans into the kitchen area is a metal detector with some security guards in charge of screening backpacks, handbags and food bins. There's some commotion as one of the trained K-9s picks up a scent off a backpack, but it turns out to be just a book of matches when they look inside. Other backpacks and pocketbook searches have found nothing.

The kitchen is brilliant white, lined with subway tile from floor to ceiling.

Steam pours out from the tops of the pots, and oil sizzles in pans on the stove. The smell of garlic moves through the kitchen as the mussels are readied for the pot.

"Hey, Joey, get over here and peel these potatoes," the head chef says with his white hat slightly tilted to the right. "I need about twenty pounds, and you over there, yes you, donkey kong, get that parsley out of the bag and give it to Marty. Sometimes I think I'm working with a bunch of idiots."

I raise an eyebrow at the loudmouth chef, and he glares at me for being the intruder in his kitchen. So, I glare right back in return and walk over to the mussel pot. The aroma of garlic and shallots in the broth rise to the top and I inhale the bouquet like I would a flower. The flavor propels me and I feel as if I could eat a plateful of mussels on the spot. Not yielding to the urge, I focus on all elements of the dinner that must be perfect if poison is to be part of the menu.

Adjacent to the kitchen is a small bathroom. I pop inside for a quick lipstick check and notice a pretty blond leaning over the counter. As soon as she is aware of me, she closes her gold compact and pulls the top off the lipstick case. I do the same with my lipstick. We give each other a quick nod and as she turns to leave, I notice just a dot of white powder above her upper lip. I'm about to ask her who she is, but she slips out of the ladies' room like an eel sliding through a drainpipe.

I wonder who she is and what she's doing here. I'll check in with Eric when I see him since he worked with the museum staff to make all the service arrangements for the entire occasion.

Finally, I get up to Eric's office and this time, stop just outside admiring the large doors with glass squares on the top divided by worn mullions. It brings back memories of another academic center that had shaped my career and my life. I get lost in thought a lot, but have the discipline to quickly take me back into the moment. It's as if my fingers are always on the fine focus of life, like on a microscope, bringing me back so I can see things ever so clearly. I enter the office and walk over to the desk. I run my hand along the chipped wooden top and think about that other academic center when I was the research Fellow of a Nobel Laureate, my esteemed professor, who had shown me love and kindness. After his death, I had to transfer my research project to another laboratory and mentor, but I carried a part my professor's love deep inside me. It was my secret.

Ah, there's the travel bag just inside the closet door. This is the original bag

I carried with me on the train from Boston. I left it here yesterday when I went to Mercy to see Becker. I peer inside, my mind still trying to place the puzzle pieces. Let's see, there are several small notes from when I had talked with Becker on the phone, some chemical hand warmers so my fingers don't blanch in the cold, extra gloves for the same reason, and some literature that had been handed to me when I stepped off the escalators at Penn Station. These look familiar. Where have I seen them before? The dates on the flyer from the Garden are from concerts that have already occurred. I also have an unopened perfume card. These contents are all vaguely familiar to me and I know they are meaningful. If I can just put the pieces together. I'm trying to work out the details and the cell phone rings again.

"Lily," says a French accent on the phone, "I will be over to the museum a little later. My men cannot detect any explosive material, so *ma Chérie*, it is up to you. We are working on coming up with the name, but we know this is a Russian run operation."

When I hang up the phone, and look at the screen, I realize I have a voice message that must have been left when I was in the shower. I thought so, but I got distracted. I'm missing quite a few calls lately. I type in my password to retrieve the message. The voice mail is garbled; no doubt from a bad connection. It's Leigh.

"Dr. Robinson, this is John Ch… I was delay in ….. and just started …….. week. Very interesting cases. The vial contain…… I also found ….. in ….. This morning ……. to confirm using MALDI-TOF."

Now I feel my heart racing inside my chest. *What did he say? He found something in the vial he had to confirm.* I play the message again, but still can't make out all the words. I have to call him back. I don't care what time it is in Hong Kong. Damn, he's not picking up and his mailbox is full.

Damn it. I need to talk with John Chi now. Where the hell is he?

I race back to the main hall where I find the room now fully set for the dinner. Beautiful white linens cover the round dining tables while the crystal and silver gleam under the lights above. Napkins are folded like swans sitting atop snow-white plates ringed with gold. Star lights, like those seen in the planetarium, dot the ceiling adding to the dramatic effect. Each table has a striking flower centerpiece. I see it, but I react too slowly. Large pale lilies, white petals dotted with pink, and stamens yellow, thick with pollen, surrounded by ferns and baby's breath emerge from glass bowls in abundance, filling the air with perfume. In my haste, I've slid into the room and now

I'm choking for air. My throat begins to close. I stumble back through the entryway, making faint wheezing noises, when the head chef arrives to survey the setting. He catches me in his arms as I'm falling and carries me to a nearby bench. I will die without medical intervention.

"Hey, I need some help here. Somebody call 911," the chef calls out. "Miss, miss, what can I do for you?"

I'm trying to catch my breath. There's no air moving out of or into my lungs. My head starts to spin, as the carbon dioxide builds up. I make a last-ditch effort to point to my travel bag that I had just taken from Eric's office. The chef hands it to me with trepidation, and with the little strength I have, I open the zippered side compartment, and pull out my auto-injector. First, I remove the blue safety release, then jab the tip of the needle into my outer thigh. The device rolls from my hand and I close my eyes slipping into blackness as the surge of epinephrine courses through my body. Slowly the CO_2 is released from my chest and oxygen rides the tides of shallow breaths. Then my ears start to work.

"What's going on here?" shouts a security guard.

"I don't know," says the chef. "But she seems to be breathing. I think she lost consciousness for a second there. Look I've got to get back to my kitchen. I assume you'll see that she gets medical help." I hear the scurry of several footsteps, imagine shadowy figures looming above me, and then the garble of a two-way radio.

A few minutes later I hear Eric running into the hall with several more security men.

"Lily, Lily, are you all right?" his voice sounds panicked. "What happened, tell me what happened?" I can't speak because my throat is still swollen, as are my eyes.

"Listen, Lily, they've called 911. Why don't I put you in an ambulance and go with you to the hospital?" I shake my head vigorously indicating NO. I attempt to stand up, but Eric puts out his hand to stop me.

"Lily, I don't think this is a good idea."

My head is still down, and I try to collect my thoughts even though I can't find my voice. *What just happened? I went to the kitchen, looked over the meal, went back to Eric's office to retrieve my bag, then, then my phone rang. Yes, that was it, my phone rang. It was JP. He said something, but what?* There was another call too, but I just can't remember. My memory, as well as my breath, had been stolen.

Reluctantly, Eric hands me over to a security agent, so he can attend to the guests who are just beginning to appear. The guard will sit with me while we wait for medical assistance. He leads me off to a more secluded area, and I try and take some deeper breaths.

The guard keeps his radio on so we can hear what's happening. His contact lets him know that the guests are arriving at the entryway, each one going through the metal detector. They are searching all bags or pocketbooks. I can hear the radio voice make a comment about all the camel hair and fur coats being sequestered in a nearby closet for safekeeping. He lets us know that the bankers are mostly men and that they have brought their wives, eager to meet the museum curator. Of course, I'm thinking. Eric is known for his charming manner, handsome good looks, and colorful talks. He will be leading the tour through the exhibit tonight. He's part of the show.

I know the itinerary. We had it well-rehearsed. By now each guest has probably been given a handout on the presentation. They'll mingle at first in a lovely exhibit of rocks and minerals, amethyst gems and huge geodes with sparkling center crystals, as they drink cocktails and shake Eric's hand fueling his hope that he can influence them to become cash donors for his work.

Next the bankers and their wives will be escorted into the special exhibit hall for a narrated tour by the famed curator. Even if he's not up to his usual indulgent telling, he'll keep the visitors long enough for the agents to check out the main dining hall. He's probably wondering what it was that nearly killed me. After the requisite amount of time, he'll gently usher them back to assume their places at the banquet table. When everything seems to be in order, he'll have the waiters bring in the first course. A small soup will be served to start: chilled vichyssoise with chopped scallions floating on a white creamy surface. The security detail, dressed smartly as waiters, will serve the food with flair, as they maintain a watchful eye on every guest. Eric will continue to mingle with the crowd, working his way around the room, shaking more hands while looking nervously about. I can picture it all now.

*   *   *

While waiting to regain my voice, I try to piece together the most recent events, once again, in my mind. One of the agents is still by my side, his two-way radio in hand, anticipating further instruction from his boss. It starts to crackle and I hear the voice at the other end say that the ambulance is here. The EMT is walking through the metal detector while his medic bag is being thoroughly searched. Another guard will escort him and he should be with us in a few minutes.

*   *   *

"Hi there, I'm the EMT-paramedic; someone called 911 and described symptoms of what sounded like an anaphylactic attack, you know, a severe allergic reaction when your throat closes up."

I weakly raise my hand and squeak, "That would be me." Finally, I have enough breath to make words. The EMT puts an oxygen mask over my face and asks me to take some deep breaths.

"You know, you should really come back to the hospital to be checked out. I'm going to take you to Mercy."

"Oh, no, I don't want to go to the hospital," I tell him, still struggling with my breath and barely audible, "Did you say Mercy?" I say coughing, "I, I have a colleague who works there." He's trying to keep the mask over my nose and stop me from talking.

"Deep breaths please. Deep breaths. Are you a doctor?" he asks checking my pulse. It's now getting close to a normal rate and rhythm. I can feel it.

"What kind of doctor are you?" he asks.

"I'm a pathologist, um toxicologist," I wheeze.

"Hey, you wouldn't happen to know the Chief of Service over there, Francis Becker, would you?"

"What did you say your name was?" I rally with a surprising push of strength.

"Um, I didn't say, but it's Jim Cassidy."

"JIM!" He steps back from me with surprise at the sound of his name. Now it's all flooding back to me. *What did Becker say? Jim Cassidy and the ED doc had found similar items in the handbags of some of the victims. Yes, yes, and the vial of white powder. I had given the vial to Leigh. That was it, Leigh had called me back, left a message, said something about the vial.* I find my voice just in time.

"Jim, Francis Becker shared with me the details of the patients he autopsied, and some of the cases that you picked up and transported to the hospital. The common denominator was that they all had spent some time down around

Penn Station." My throat is still swollen so I can barely get full sentences out. I can see Jim now as the slits where my eyes begin to part.

Jim is a little surprised to be hearing this from a stranger, but then he remembers something Becker had said about a pathologist, toxicologist friend and he assumes that I'm this person.

"That's right," Jim said, listening intently. "That's the one thing they all had in common. But there is one more curious thing. Stu Greene, the ED doc who saw many of the cases, found some of the same things in the handbags of the women who got sick. Many of them were wearing a red nail polish when they came into the ED, and some even had a bottle of polish in their bag. I also recall seeing many of these same items Dr. Greene found when I was looking for some form of identification of my patients. You know, all of them had handouts from the Garden announcing the upcoming concerts, and they all had these perfume cards wrapped in cellophane. At least most of them were wrapped in cellophane. They looked like the kind of cards you scratch and sniff. You know what I mean?"

"Jim, please hand me my bag, yeah, that big black one over there on the floor," I squeak. "I'm not sure about the nail polish. Polish usually contains hydrocarbon-based solvents and I doubt nail polish laced with poison could be absorbed through the nails efficiently. And remember that both women and men have shown symptoms of poisoning."

"Yes of course," Jim says. I jump right back in.

"It's all about the presentation." I can see the puzzled look on his face. "Every patient that came to the ED presented with respiratory symptoms, so the toxin has to be inhaled. And to get deeply into the lungs the toxin would have to have been aerosolized particles of a very fine nature. You said something about scratch and sniff cards?" My mind is clearing.

I open my large travel bag and pull out the perfume card. It's still wrapped in cellophane. I see the flyers and cards I had looked at when I was up in Eric's office. I knew they were familiar.

"Jim, you've got to go down to the main exhibit hall and find Eric Vandermeer, the museum curator. I can't go there or I may have another anaphylactic attack. I'm afraid I shot all my epi so that's it for me."

He looks at me with a grin and says, "Hey no worries doc, I've got more epinephrine if we need it."

With Jim and the guard heading for Eric and the guests, I try calling John Chi again. It rings seven times and on the eighth ring, he picks up the phone.

"Hello, this is Dr. Leigh." He sounds a little groggy.

"John, John Chi! Thank God. It's Lily. I've been trying to reach you. Where the hell have you been?" By this time I'm screaming into the phone, my voice having recovered most of its potency. My question is met with silence.

"John, the vial of white powder, it contained the toxin?" I ask.

"No, Lily."

"What? What do you mean? You said you found toxin in the vial. I don't understand." I'm confused and frustrated. My head is still foggy from the shock and epi. Maybe I missed something.

"Lily, the vial of powder? That was just cocaine. That's not your problem. You have a much bigger problem. In the blood and urine, I found the toxin and its metabolite. I still need to confirm, but I'm pretty sure. Lily, I called you earlier today and left you a message. Did you get my message?"

I knew that if John Leigh was about to confirm his findings, that he was probably dead on right about the toxin. His estimated guesses were better than most scientists' confirmed findings. I'll trust his preliminary results. There's silence between us. If I could see his face at this moment what would I see? Trouble. I hear his deep breaths.

"John, I have to call you back. I have to identify the source. Please, please. Keep your cell phone with you. Do the confirmation testing and if you don't hear from me first, leave me a message. Have you got that?" And then the words just fall out of my mouth, "Oh and John, please stay away from the ponies. I need you."

Of course, I know about his gambling and wondered about his delay in getting results back to me. John Chi Leigh was so gifted in his younger days that he could identify any toxin, any poison no matter how obscure. But his career hit a dead end after personal misfortune, and he had to support himself by analyzing urine from racehorses, looking for illegal drugs in the stake winners. I knew that in recent years he had decided to offer his talent to the highest bidders for synthesizing exotic toxins or detecting the seemingly undetectable poison. I knew that his gambling habit had created a need that only his brilliant mind could fill. He had at his disposal one of the world's most sophisticated drug testing labs and he was always willing to work late and lock up the building after hours. And I knew he had been contracted to kill me years ago, but as I said, I was willing to take the risk working by his side just to be able to inhale genius.

I'm sure John Chi feels like I'm scolding him and didn't appreciate my last comment. But he let me down and he knows we're under pressure.

I break the silence. "John, given the nature of the victims' symptoms the toxin would have had to have been aerosolized to make it an effective terrorist weapon."

"Lily, remember Gyorgi Markov?" John says. "Gyorgi was the Bulgarian journalist stabbed in the leg with the tip of an umbrella while he waited at a bus station in London. A tiny pellet was only discovered by the pathologist on autopsy. Remember?"

"Of course I do, John. The pellet contained tiny holes, machined drilled, and the toxin was confined within. They assumed that a heat sensitive gelatin covered the holes and melted after it was injected into the body. Why are you bringing up this case now?" I ask him.

"Because this toxin kills at doses of 0.1 microgram per kilogram. Very toxic, Lily. You better hurry." I can hear the phone connection has gone silent.

Now I feel a little panic in my chest. I call Eric, and pray he has his cell phone turned on.

"Eric, is that you?" I ask when I hear the hello.

"Lily, what the hell is going on? Eric says. "I've got an EMT down here, says you're doing a lot better, but something about perfume cards. What the hell is going on and what happened to you anyway? This is getting scary, Lily. I thought we were looking for a bomber, possibly poison, but this is out of control my friend." I can hear the frustration and anxiety in his voice. This case is wearing him down. He works for the museum; he's not used to all this cloak and dagger stuff. So, I set him straight.

"Eric, I think there's toxin contained within the perfume cards. Once you open the cellophane, and scratch the pad, you release the toxin. I think that's what's happening. Tell the agents to look and see if there are any perfume cards, I don't know where they would be, but for God's sake, if you find one, do not open it. Do you understand?" Now he sets me straight.

"Jesus Christ Lily, it's too late for that. We handed out perfume cards with the literature on the exhibit when the guests arrived. They were provided by a sponsor who made a large contribution of cash to fund a special display at the museum. Oh God, I don't know if any have been opened. Let me see what I can do. Lily, I need your help down here. Oh, and what did you say the toxin was?"

"Ricin."

Chapter 11

THE MUSEUM

JP is on speed dial on my secure phone. I want it to be faster. Speed dial is never fast enough for me. He's always been my contact with the Agency and he'll know what to do next. I remember that he told me he would meet me at the museum. He was going to give me the intel on the banker I was to poison. I never got the information. Maybe JP's team can't make the ID yet. Anyway, I'm not sure I can even get down to the banquet to use the toxin. I can't risk another reaction. Wait a minute. Where is my Delgado bag? Damn! I'm missing my Delgado bag. When I had the anaphylactic attack, my travel bag was with me, and I thought I had my Delgado too. I must've left it at the entrance to the main hall where the dinner was set, or was it in Eric's office? Shit! My ampoule of poison!

My chest is still wheezing, but I'm moving as quickly as I can down the stairs toward the kitchen. I have to be careful opening the door to the main exhibit hall. I can't risk inhaling anymore contaminant. All I can see are agents, dressed as waiters, moving through the crowd, quietly collecting all the literature including the cards. One of the staff is explaining to the guests that there was some misinformation in the literature and they wanted everything back, including the advertisements. I still don't know which banker is the terrorist and if he realizes we are aware of the toxin embedded perfume cards, he may slip away before being exposed. I don't have the hard data to know for sure that it is the cards, but I'm pretty damn sure. The Agency will have to act fast. From what I can tell, all the cards that have been collected appear to be confined within the cellophane. The agents have carefully packed the ones they've gathered in a container that had been used in the kitchen for the potatoes. The container is now under the watchful eye of a young, but serious agent dressed in a tuxedo. I feel like

I'm in a circus. It's difficult to know if they've got them all. Another agent is currently looking for the original box containing the cards that had been shipped to the museum.

I'm on my way to Eric's office to look for my Delgado bag when I see Eric standing by the entrance to the exhibit hall.

"Lily, Lily, over here." I can see he's motioning me to come over to him, but I wave him toward me, instead. I'm trying to avoid the large exhibit hall.

"Eric, here," I call to him.

"Lily, thank God, are you alright?" he says. "What happened to you, in there?" He's pointing to the main hall.

"Eric," I answer, carefully choosing my words, "who selected the centerpieces for the tables?" I can see Eric tumbling the thought for a moment like he's polishing a stone.

"Lily, it's not unusual for me to host a dinner like this for big philanthropic donors. This one of course has been a nightmare. All the agents, the potential bombs threats, the dogs, it's no wonder my head aches." I can see him rubbing his temples again.

"They haven't found a thing. Not one thing, Lily. And you're worried about some stupid advertising cards and who chose the centerpieces. The museum takes care of all the catering and usually uses an event planner, you know someone who brings the whole affair together. We've used this company before, and I'm sure this particular gal has been here, too. Ahh, I think her name is Alexis; yes, that was it. Pretty blonde; elegant neck with a nice French silk scarf. She did mention something about the centerpieces. Said she would use lilies. Yeah, it was her."

Now I'm turning the thought around in my mind like I'm polishing a stone in a tumbler. This must have been the woman I saw in the ladies' room near the kitchen. I'm wondering whether this was just a coincidence or an intentional act. I'd be shocked if it were deliberate. Very few people know of my allergy to my namesake flower. I don't know what to say. More importantly I've got to ship these perfume cards to John Chi. We need an analysis to determine whether this is the source of the ricin, or should I keep looking? Yet, I feel I'm right about the cards. I can't believe it would be the nail polish. If that's the vehicle it would have such limited penetration. It doesn't make sense. Scratch and sniff is a brilliant plan. I wish I'd thought of it.

"Lily, Lily. Did you hear what I said? The event planner picked the flowers. You said something about ricin. The flowers have nothing to do with the ricin. Right?" Eric says interrupting my thought.

"Eric, listen," I say. "Why don't you go and see if you can track down the event planner. Alexis, I think you said her name was. I'm going to look for my contact and see if I can get these cards shipped out tonight for analysis. Oh, and did Jim Cassidy leave? You know the EMT?"

"Yeah, he left. He said you declined to be taken into the hospital and he got another call. I'll see if I can find her, although they should be past wrapping up the dinner by now. I'm a little confused, Lily, but I'll catch up with you later."

Eric does look a little shaken. Now I've got to get to Eric's office and look for my Delgado bag. I need that bag!

I'm breathing easier now, and when I finally get up to Eric's office I can see that the door is slightly ajar. My antennae are up and I carefully push it open, eyes wide.

"Lily!" I hear JP shout when I walk into the office. "*Ma Chérie*, are you all right? I was worried about you." He scoops me up and wraps his arms around me. I cling tightly to him like I don't want to let go. I don't.

"Thank God you're here," I say, letting out a breath. "We've got a real problem. I don't think we're going to have to concern ourselves with bombs; I think it is poison, and it may be poisoning on a mass scale. We need to focus on all those people in this city headed for any activities that would incur large crowds. Concerts, sports events, that sort of thing. JP, did you find out which banker is the terrorist infiltrate?"

"Lily, we don't have the name yet, but we are close. He's Russian for sure. You said mass poisoning? What poison are you talking about?"

"I think it may be ricin."

"Ricin? Nasty stuff, *Chérie*. Reminds me of the old KGB." Then he starts in like he's the chemist.

"If I remember my chemistry, *Chérie*, that's a glycoprotein lectin composed of an alpha and beta chain linked by a disulfide bond." It's clear he's been studying chemical warfare and this toxin is well known to the Agency. I interrupt him. I'm the toxicologist.

"Very good my love," I say, "and frankly I'm surprised," I add with a touch of sarcasm. "Ricin is derived from the castor bean plant or *Ricinus communis* which originated in Asia and Africa, but can now be found in many regions around the world. You know," I say, now lecturing, "the detection of ricin in fluids has been traditionally accomplished by immunologically-based methods which can measure concentrations at approximately 0.1 ng/mL. Other methods such as matrix-assisted laser desorption-ionization mass spectrometry or MALDI-MS, as we like to say, have also been used. We've got to send the perfume cards to Hong Kong, to Dr. Leigh's lab for analysis by MALDI-TOF, immediately."

"MALDI –TOF?" he questions.

"Yes. TOF is *time of flight*. This is a method of mass spectrometry whereby an ion's mass-to-charge ratio is calculated via a time measurement. Ions are accelerated by…"

"*Assez* Lily, this is no time for your analytical mind or a lecture. We are wasting time. I will alert the Agency to scan Penn Station and notify the New York authorities. We are also going to need permission from New Jersey for access to any sports stadiums. Gather the samples you have and I'll have them shipped to Leigh immediately. Please let him know they are coming and that we need answers right away. The city is busy with events, Broadway shows, concerts, ball games. We have to figure this out before there is widespread panic. Are you finished here with the curator? *Mais oui?*"

"Yes, but there may be something else." I have to tell him about the centerpieces. "JP, I think we need to look into the catering company who planned the dinner. Did you know the centerpieces for the tables tonight were lilies?"

"And so?"

"And so? I'm deathly allergic to lilies. I had an anaphylactic reaction. Oh, and my Delgado bag is missing." I scan the room hoping to see my bag hidden by a pile of books or under a chair. Nothing. I'm hoping Eric has it.

"I didn't realize you were deathly allergic. I knew you didn't favor them. I suppose it's a good thing I sent you roses, my Lily," he adds. Not funny to me. "*Et*, check with Eric regarding your bag. You must have dropped it when you had your allergic reaction, *Chérie*."

"Things are getting complicated," I tell him. "I'll see if I can find Eric and his event planner."

I track down Eric in the little accessory gift shop by the exhibit. He wasn't able to find the event planner, but he found my Delgado, thank God. The caterers are already finished in the kitchen. Eric's going to follow-up with the museum staff in the morning and find out more details about Alexis. Some undercover agents are staying on duty at the museum, but JP sent the remainder out into the city, primarily downtown near Penn Station. I also phone Leigh and tell him to expect more samples, and make him swear he'll get on the analysis as soon as they arrive. I try and explain to Eric some of what JP and I discussed, but not all. I know if we can't contain this, there will be a catastrophic ending. But the boundaries are so ephemeral, so ill-defined it's like reaching the edges of the universe. How do you know you are there when you don't even know where you are going?

*   *   *

Eric and I walk back to the exhibit so we can channel the stress and talk while strolling through the history and science of the origin of the earth. We need to clear our minds amidst nature's cleverness without worrying about bombs exploding and terrorists invading. But, my mind won't clear and keeps spinning. "I really think it's the perfume cards," I tell Eric, "and the ricin is laced within the scratch and sniff patch."

"Enough, Lily," Eric scolds. "Can't we just take one quiet moment in the museum, now that we're pretty sure it's not going to explode?"

Eric stops by a cluster of exotic blooms that are part of an exhibit on flowers of the world. They are gorgeous. Orchids cascading down the wall and green foliage fill the background. Eric leans down, cups a flower in his hand and inhales. My God, I'm holding my own breath, as I watch him bend toward the flower. It crosses my mind that many things throughout the city could be contaminated with ricin, and there just isn't any way to know at this point. I'm watching him, and I can see his eyes roll into the back of his head, so that only the whites are visible. He hits the floor with a thud. His body shakes violently and his lips fade from neutral pink to blue.

"Oh my God!" I cry out, dropping to the floor, trying to find a pulse. Strange, what runs through my brain at that moment. What is it they say in med school? *What's the first thing do you at a code blue? Take your own pulse first.* My pulse is racing. Eric's is there, but weak and irregular. At least he's got a pulse, so his heart's still beating, but his breathing is labored. *This can't be happening*, I'm thinking, *not again*. I pull out my phone and dial 911.

"Stay with me, stay with me, Eric!" I scream at the quivering body before me.

CHAPTER 12

NEW YORK CITY

We're in the ambulance now. Thank God. The paramedic's started an IV and put an oxygen mask over Eric's nose and mouth. He's unconscious, but at least he's breathing on his own. I have to admit that I'm terrified. Yes, cool collected me. What if there are other museum exhibits that are contaminated with ricin, or maybe even another toxin. Whatever got to Eric was fast acting and only a few poisons I know of could fit that description. My mind is running. I can see all the possible niches that could be filled with poison. It's like honey pouring into a mass of hexagonal wax cells. The sticky honeycomb trap has been set.

We've reached the emergency department, and the medical team is triaging Eric. He's on a gurney and they're moving him behind the curtain into an examination area.

The emergency medicine doc starts barking orders.

"Okay people, we have a man here in his forties. Looks like a grand mal seizure, at this point etiology unknown. Let's go people, get in another IV. I want super access, and some bloods here. Let's get a set of lytes, lactic acid, CBC, for starters. Then I want some imaging of that head."

I don't say a word. I'm just watching it all unfold and analyzing. They start the second IV and draw blood. The oxygen mask obscures Eric's nose and mouth making him unrecognizable. He still has not regained consciousness. They move him quickly to the CT scanner for imaging of his brain while I sit and wait with all the other collaterals in the collective waiting room. There they are: family members and friends clinging to each other while waiting for news on the outcome of the massive trauma that played out just moments before. I understand their pain.

When I think about Eric, I realize that his sudden illness did not present in the same way as the other cases we've seen. Could this be a completely different poison?

I'm impatient and finally, after close to an hour, the attending ED physician comes into the waiting room. I quickly stand up to shake his hand, and greet this older man with graying hair who's wearing a slightly soiled lab coat, and scuffed running shoes.

"Hi, doctor. I'm Lily Robinson. I brought in Dr. Vandermeer."

"Nice to meet you. Are you a friend, or, ahh, of Dr. Vandermeer?" He's trying to ascertain my relationship to his patient. And by the way he's looking at my clothes, must assume that we had been out on a date. It's the stilettos.

"Yes, I'm a friend, and a colleague," I tell him, and also let him know that I'm a physician. "Dr. Vandermeer was well until this seizure. He had been feeling a little tired and complained of difficulty sleeping. I do know he's been under a fair amount of stress lately."

"Doctor, why don't you come into the viewing room with me," he opens his arm indicating for me to follow him into a room with a large computer screen.

The ED attending enters Eric's name and medical record number at the prompt and brings up a CT image of the brain. Eric's brain. I can see the outline of the skull, the separation of the hemispheres, and a white area of high signal intensity between the inner edge of the skull and the brain. It looks like it's displacing the brain toward the center line. I know what this is. This is not the result of a toxin.

"You see this area here?" says the ED doc as he points to the lucent area on the digital image, "your friend has a subdural hematoma. If we don't operate on this now, he could die."

Like I said, I know this. But that blood collection over the brain is not the part the catches my eye as I move in closer to scrutinize the image. I feel myself biting my lower lip, and my analytical brain begins to swamp my neural network and shut down all possible circuits to my feelings. I have to stay focused. I'm wearing my doctor hat now.

"That injury was most likely caused when he fell and bumped his head on the metal framed flower box before he hit the floor. It wasn't the cause of the seizure, but the result of the fall," I explain. I know that the sudden tonic-clonic seizure that Eric experienced could be caused by many things, including poison, but I'm not sharing any more information with the ED doc. Then I point to that bright white spot on the image of the brain that has grabbed my attention and ask, "What's this small white area in the left parietal lobe? It looks almost cystic."

"Well that's the million-dollar question, isn't it?" he answers. "We don't know. He's gone up to surgery now, and when the neurosurgeon is in there fixing that subdural, he's going to try and take a biopsy of that lesion."

I head back out to the waiting room, find a chair and hit the seat hard as I sit down. My cell phone is in my travel bag and I dig down trying to pull it out from the bottom of the chaos. Right in the side pocket of the bag, I notice a cellophane wrapped perfume card. I must have missed this one when we were collecting cards to be sent to Leigh. I can't touch it now; it's contained. I've got two phone calls to make stat. First one is to Leigh.

"John, this is Lily. I know it's only been hours, but have you found out anything else about the toxin? Was it just ricin or ricin and something else?" I need to know.

John Chi has hesitation in his voice.

"Lily, I just see the fingerprint of ricin, no other peaks suggestive of any other compound." Just from his intonation, I suspect that he is keeping something from me, so I ask him again if he's sure. He says yes. I don't know if I believe him. I decide to tell him what's going on with Eric, but only briefly.

"Yes, John, it could be another poisoning related case, but the etiology is not so clear. Please let me know if you find anything, anything else." I swipe off my cell phone and sink into the worn waiting room chair. The acid begins to churn in my stomach.

Mustering some strength, I dial again. Second call. The phone is ringing. Finally, he picks up after several seconds that to me seem like minutes. "Hello, Francis? This is Lily Robinson, I'm sorry to call you late at home, but it's an emergency. A friend of mine was brought into your hospital tonight and is about to have a brain biopsy. Who does your neuro frozens?"

It takes a few moments for Becker to register the nature of the call. Then he speaks, "Well howdy there, Lily. I believe Dr. Delacroix is coverin' tonight, but I'd be happy to come on in and give ya a hand. Truth is I just poured myself a nice bourbon and branch. I find that little bit of whiskey at the end of the day goes a long way to easing pain. Ya' know what I mean? Hey, anyway, I was just gonna sit with a book and my ol' fluffy cat. But a neuro frozen? Sounds good."

Good news for me, so I let him know. "Francis that would be great; I'd feel a lot better if you're going to be looking at the tissue. I'm really sorry to disturb you at home, but I needed someone I could trust."

Becker lets me know that it shouldn't take him too long to get here, then hangs up the phone. I close my eyes and take another deep breath.

An hour later I'm in the cutting room in the Pathology Department at Mercy Hospital where all tissues and body parts end up once they're removed from a patient. Becker notices that I'm not exactly dressed to be grossing tissue. He doesn't inquire as to my whereabouts earlier in the evening that would have prompted my wearing such an outfit. Instead he just offers me a plastic apron and some shoe covers so I don't get myself dirty. Then he says,

"Those are pretty fancy heels, ma'am," as he hands me the shoe covers. "Don't know if these wraps are gonna make it over those stilettos." We start a dialogue.

"Francis, about the cases you asked me to provide consultation for in December."

"Yes, the ME and the CDC think it might have been a new strain of virus. I guess I jumped the gun on that one." I sense some embarrassment, so I quickly interject.

"No, Francis you were right. It was poison. It was ricin." There's silence.

Becker walks over to his double-headed microscope and sits down. He pulls out a glass slide from a gray slide folder and puts it under the 40x objective lens. He looks at me squarely in the eye and says, "You see this area in the lung over here, Lily?" I jump into the seat opposite him and look through the scope. The view is filled with blue and pink stained lung tissue with obvious pathology.

"This *is* the result of a toxin, not a virus," he says with slow deliberation. "I was jest waitin' for ya confirmation, and Marie is still chomping at the bit."

There's a knock at the window. "Doc, I have a frozen for you," says one of the assistants from the OR. "It's on the guy with the subdural."

Becker pops the tissue on the cryostat, shaves a nice thin section, places it on a glass slide, dips it in stain and then sits back down at the microscope. I've not stirred from my seat. Becker is like a surgeon when he performs a "frozen section." During a frozen section or intraoperative consultation, a small piece of tissue is sent from the operating room to the pathology area. This is an opportunity for the pathologist to quickly read the slide while the patient is still on the operating table and let the surgeon know what they're dealing with: inflammation, infection, tumor. If it's tumor, then the report will be either benign or malignant, and if malignant, the surgeon will want to know whether all the margins are clear.

Becker moves the objective lens into focus and I can see lymphocytes and plasma cells, with variable edema, gliosis, fibrosis, and necrosis. "Francis, this looks like an inflammatory reaction of some kind," I tell him.

Then he shifts the slide around on the microscope stage and scans other areas of the brain tissue. "Ya see this hyalinized area?" he says, seemingly surprised, "It looks like a larva was here and it's degeneratin'. Tell me, does your friend travel to Mexico, Central or South America?"

I really don't know Eric's travel history all that well, but I do know that he is a field biologist and has journeyed considerably in those geographic regions to study and collect certain species of invertebrates. "What are you thinking, Francis?" I venture.

"Well, I'll be. It looks like neurocysticercosis, Lily," says Becker with some revelation in his voice. "Hmm, neurocysticercosis is a leadin' cause of seizures in the developin' world. It's caused by ingestion of eggs from the pork tape worm *Taenia solium*. Usually occurs in unclean conditions. After the eggs are ingested, they turn into larval cysts and can move into the brain and elsewhere. It's not somethin' we usually see here in Manhattan, Lily, but I've seen plenty of cases while in Texas from folks up from Mexico. And assumin' they successfully evacuate the subdural hematoma, your friend will be treated with an antiparasitic medication and good ta' go."

I reach across the microscope table and take Becker's large hand in mine and gave it a squeeze. "Thanks, Francis. I'm so glad you're here," I tell him letting out a breath I didn't even realize was trapped within my chest. Becker reaches for the phone and calls the OR with the report of his findings. I haven't let go of his hand and he doesn't seem to mind.

CHAPTER 13

NEW YORK CITY

Near East End Avenue around 89th Street, a slender woman with long blonde hair walked behind Gracie Mansion along the East River. She had a light spring to her step and reveled in the unexpectedly warm and sunny days at the end of January. She loosened her silk scarf from around her collar and unbuttoned the top button of her long camel-colored cashmere coat. She revealed a scoop-necked chartreuse silk blouse, and around her neck she bore a gold pendant in the shape of a spider's web. She reached into her oversized leather bag to take out her sun glasses to block the brilliant glare off the water, and saw the ampoule within her bag. *It hadn't been as difficult as I expected,* thought Alexis. *It's really all about connections, who you know.* Getting the toxin had been a bonus, how they would incorporate the toxin into their plan would take genius.

She walked down along the river until she reached a suitable stopping place and pulled out her cell phone.

"Hello, Grigory?" she said with a trace of an accent, "*Da,* it's Alexis. Well they are onto the cards at this moment, but I have another treasure we can work with. *Da,* you heard. Uh, huh. I can meet you near the UN if you like. *Da, da,* okay then, I will see you in a few hours if you have other things to do in the meantime. I will go ahead. *Dosvidaniya.*"

She patted her purse and walked from the river west to East End Avenue. She flagged down a taxi and climbed in.

"42nd and First Avenue please, the United Nations building," she said in her best American accent. The taxi spun around and headed up 86th Street before heading downtown.

*　　*　　*

Down in lower Manhattan near Chelsea, there was a small printing shop on the fifth floor of a medium-sized brick building. The equipment was fairly basic: a digital press, folder, cutter, stitcher and palette jacks. Primarily the shop was used to generate advertisement cards that were slipped between the pages of magazines. These were the kind of cards that advertised magazine subscriptions, insurance companies, and colognes. However, this shop had one additional feature. It had the means to integrate a scent into a card, and more specifically, had the capability to print cards that had encapsulated scent or powder that could be released when the pad was scratched with a fingernail. The ability to encapsulate a powder in microscopic particles also meant that it could be incorporated in other products as well.

Grigory Markovic moved toward several of the workers on the assembly line. He was a rather short man, with a bald head and a stern face. When he opened his eyes wide, the deep lines above his brows gathered like undulating waves while his steel colored eyes penetrated their target and created fear in those that viewed them.

"Listen up people," he said with a pronounced Russian accent, "finish up and put all materials in boxes to be shipped to this address. We have created thousands of cards for distribution up and down the Northeast and that is just the start of our operation. I would like to send the critical people on ahead, and you, yes you," he swept his hand towards a handful of workers, "those we just hired for the packing, please stay behind because we have plumbers coming to work on the building's heating system and I need you to make sure everything has been cleaned up. There will be extra money in it for you."

Markovic was currently functioning well below his level of authority. He did not like interacting with the bottom rung of the operation. But his superiors insisted he personally go to the factory to handle the situation.

"Grigory, this is our opportunity to take a big bite out of America. Why bother hijacking planes and crashing through skyscrapers? There is no need for suicide bombers and global spectacle. It takes too much energy. It's all about everyday life in America, the comfortable life, the life that few in our world enjoy. In those seemly insignificant and most natural places—coffee shops, food marts, natural waters, magazines, program guides and flyers— poisons will be sequestered and released. We will create an uneasiness that will penetrate the American consciousness. They will be suspicious of each other, not sure if the coffee prepared by the person behind the counter is tainted or pure. Not sure if the food they eat, or the water they drink will bring sudden death. They are already worrying about computer hacks and unauthorized surveillance. A disrupted economy is much more unstable than a single terrorist act that only unites the country ready to rally the troops and fight the evildoers. And as an added distraction, we will also flood the country with illicit drugs. Already our plan on increasing the availability of heroin and cocaine has provided us with a nice profit, and the Americans with an epidemic of drug addicts. Let them burn for their hedonistic ways." His voice was raised at the end with a chilling delivery of self-righteousness.

Markovic saw the beauty in the plan's simplicity. There would be an underlying, ever present erosion here and there of daily American life, as distrust and poison filled the niches like water etching at rock over millions of years. Eventually there is the formation of a canyon, deep and wide enough to hold sacrificial victims thrown over its sharp, steep edge.

That night the printers were preparing their last batches of cards before they shipped everything to the designated address and moved their operation. It was a well-conceived plan promulgated by a mastermind terrorist.

*   *   *

The following morning, in the small brick building in lower Manhattan, the upper two floors of the printing shop were still. When the fire department was called in to investigate a faulty burner and potential fuel leak, four bodies were found on the fifth floor and two were found on the fourth floor. The medical examiner noted that there didn't appear to be any trauma, or any signs of a struggle in the now all but empty printing room. All the deceased were cherry red in color. He took a blood specimen from each victim and would be sure to run it on the blood gas analyzer when he got back to the lab.

CHAPTER 14

NEW YORK CITY

Still feeling exhausted, disoriented and uncertain of where I am, I fully open my eyes. I'm in a hotel room of course, but I had such a long and fitful night that I pull the covers back up over my head to shut out the world around me, just for a minute. The morning has just slipped away. Finally, I quietly tumble out of bed and locate my Delgado handbag. After I picked it up from Eric last night, I was completely derailed by his seizure and I failed to examine its contents. I'm drowsy and need that cup of coffee. Come on mind, clear quickly. My heart begins to thump as I reach down inside the bag to check for my ampoule of toxin. I can't quite put my hands on it.

Shit, shit, shit! Where the hell is it? Panic is setting in. My heart rate is going up. The contents of the bag are now dumped onto the table and I've looked in every conceivable place. The glass ampoule is gone. It had been in my handbag the night before and the only time my Delgado bag was not with me was when I was having the allergic reaction. When I lost consciousness, and for only a moment, I was unaware of my surroundings. Anything could have happened. It was Eric that finally returned the bag to me. That was before he crashed to the floor and bled into his brain. Now that I think about it, Eric was the only other person besides JP who knew I was carrying something deadly, something exquisitely toxic synthesized by John Leigh. And now, the ampoule of poison is missing.

It's my cell phone. I pick it up. "Hello, this is Dr. Robinson."

"Lily, Becker here."

"Francis?" I try and move the octave of my voice down just a notch, so I don't seem as agitated as I really am. "What's going on?" I ask as if the events from last night hadn't been enough.

"Well, some new developments at the hospital this mornin'. We had three DOA's late last night. One woman in her late thirties and the other in her early forties. Both women had attended a dinner with their husbands, bankers, at that science museum, ya know, over by the Park. The third one was in fact, one of those bankers. I think they said he was from Germany. Head of a big bank, in his fifties. The city's going a little crazy this morning. Also got a buzz from Marie. Says she gettin' quite a few calls on folks dying in respiratory distress around the city and wanted to know if I had any more info. Lily, Lily you still there? Ya kind of quiet, this mornin'. Everythin' Okay?"

We have failed. Clearly the cards are still in circulation. What is the Agency going to do? To announce this would cause widespread panic, and wouldn't likely be supported by those sponsoring this weekend's sports extravaganzas, and mega concerts. But to not warn the public, wouldn't that be unethical as well?

"I'm still here Francis."

"Well, there's one more strange thing, Lily. I got a call from Jack Parsons over at the city hospital. He's Chief over there. He told me they just brought a body in from downtown to his place since Marie is so backed up. Called me about the case 'cause he had no idea what to tell the ED doc when they spoke. Said the guy was having a cup of coffee when about five minutes later his lips began to tingle and go numb. Then the guy started vomiting and felt dizzy. His coworker said his friend claimed he was having a floatin' sensation. Next thing you know he was paralyzed. Just couldn't breathe. By the time the EMT's got there it was just too late. I thought maybe you'd know if that struck a familiar chord. Lily, are ya still with me on this one?"

I'm holding my head in my hands. Oh God, someone's got my ampoule of toxin. This is out of control.

"Francis, where did the man have the cup of coffee? Was he at the museum too?" I ask.

"Ah, no. He was down in front of the United Nations building."

I'm trying to focus my steely clinical mind and shut out every ounce of emotion. I need to get a handle on this.

"Francis, let me think about this for a minute. I'm going to take a shower, make a few calls and I'll get back to you. Then we can decide how to deal with Marie."

"Okay Lily. But does that crazy case ring a bell for ya?"

"Yes, Francis. Loud and clear." I swipe off the phone.

Here's where you can let it all go. I walk into the bathroom, turn on the shower and let the water run over me. Yet, the hard spray is not enough to wash away the sum of all my feelings. It's not enough to remove layers of sorrow and guilt that have followed me through most of my adult years. The tears from my eyes mix with those from the shower head. Through the rising steam and a haze of tears I see the glass door part and a naked man enters the shower. I know his familiar form and lean into him. Now I begin to weep.

"Shush, *Je sais, ma Chérie*. I know." He kisses me gently as the water splashes off the top of my head and hits him in the face. Then he picks me up locking his hands together under my bottom. He whispers, I'm as light as a feather, a *plume*, he says, and I wrap my legs around his waist, my back braced against the cool travertine tile. We both know our story and it would read like this:

He wanted her more than anything else, but understood that their relationship was dangerous and forbidden. He had broken the vow of becoming involved with a collaborator. Not just involved, but in love. She had been untouchable, unreachable, hardened from years of isolation, cloaked only in sadness and intellect. Yet he had been able to tap into her core, her heart, and understood he had found his earthly equal, his soul mate. She found in him intellectual curiosity, security, and strength and determination. Both had found uninhibited sex, a willingness to bar none, to bare all when such vulnerability might very well mean death.

I'm sobbing now. And we cling together, not wanting to let go, not wanting to leave the warm, wet womb before striking our courage to face the inevitable showdown.

Part 2

The Bloom of the Rose Tattoo (many years before)

CHAPTER 15

FRANCE

Adrienne Rosario Moreau was born in Reims, France, located some eighty miles east-northeast of Paris. Her family was engaged in making champagnes and she grew up playing in the vineyards of one of the *Grandes Marques* champagne houses. The winery was founded in the mid-18th century by her father's ancestors and had prospered over many decades. Her mother, also from a family who made wines, came from the Piedmont region of Italy. Mother had northern Italian looks with light hair, pale freckled skin, and blue-green eyes. But when Adrienne was born, her mother only saw a wisp of brunette hair on her tiny daughter and named her Adrienne Teresa. Like her mother, and her saint name, Adrienne Teresa enjoyed digging in the rich soil surrounding luscious vines, rich grapes, and copious flowers. The family grew roses in the gardens directly behind the house where the abundant sunshine, heavy clay soil and careful picking of dead leaves and flowers kept the roses in bloom for most of the spring, summer, and early fall. Adrienne spent so much time in the gardens that her mother assumed when her daughter grew up, she would run the vineyard. Although her mother wished for more children, no more came her way, so all her love was showered on Adrienne who grew up surrounded by parents who cared for her like a delicate flower.

When Adrienne was twelve, her father died of cancer and left her mother struggling to manage the vineyard. Her mother had no head for business and so her brother who was working in Colombia at the time, sent them money when he could and helped arrange for the continued operation of the business. In return for his generosity, he asked that his sister send to him her only daughter, so when Adrienne turned eighteen she left her homeland, the white grapes of Reims, and joined her uncle in Colombia. Understanding only that he was a businessman, she tended his gardens and helped her aunt with all the household chores. She had always planned to return one day to France and her mother, but only time was able to escape her uncle's compound.

"Dear uncle," said Adrienne, "I would like to help my mother run the vineyard back in Reims. Please let me return home," she would plead with him on a regular basis. Just after she turned twenty-one her uncle's wife died, and the entire running of the home resorted to Adrienne.

"Now that your aunt has died, I need you to take care of all the domestic chores as I have no daughters of my own." Thinking only of his own selfish needs, he kept her isolated from most of the outside world, trapping her within the walls of the plantation and cutting off her emotional desires.

Her uncle Alberto was not a kind man. Although he had sent money to his sister to help sustain the ancestral vineyards, he had ulterior motives. He knew that the vineyards would one day be left to Adrienne and he wanted to have control over her, so that he could also have control over his brother-in-law's estate in France. Although his overseas business was very profitable, he understood that having a legitimate business in France would offset his tainted business affairs in Colombia.

When he had come of age, her uncle Alberto had left his home near Turin, Italy to attend a university in the United States, where he found his calling in business and product manufacturing. He understood how to run a winery having grown up in Northern Italy watching his parents manage the vineyard. While at the university he met a young man from South America who convinced him opportunities were abundant in his country.

"Alberto, I think we should go into business together," said his South American friend. "I have an uncle who has a very lucrative enterprise and could use someone like you. Someone with good business sense."

Alberto had no other viable offer at the time and being a young man with an adventurous streak, he decided to go to South America with his new friend. At the time, he only knew that the business involved coffee beans and he hoped to work at a prosperous coffee plantation.

When he arrived in Colombia he was struck by the hot humid climate and jungle vegetation. Driving up to his friend's uncle's coffee plantation he could see the tall trees intruding into a bright blue sky. The grounds were spectacular. The rolling green hills were dotted with coffee bean trees laid out in neat little rows as far as he could see. On some of the hills, there were trees that towered above the coffee bean plants providing shade for the trees below. Alberto needed to catch his breath, just a touch. It wasn't just the sheer verdant beauty; it was that they were in the foothills of the mountains, some 3,800 feet above sea level. He embraced his good fortune.

"Ah my friend, this is a fantastic place. I'm sure I will be very happy here," he said to his Colombian colleague. "When do I meet your family? Where will we stay? Will I be doing the books or maybe helping with operations?"

He had many questions that he had never bothered to ask his friend while he was at the university in America. He really hadn't given it much thought. All he knew was that he didn't want to return to Italy to his family. He had had enough of his parents, and his sister.

Alberto didn't start by doing the books or any accounting, buying or selling. He didn't even start in the office. He started as a fruit picker. He harvested the fruit with the rest of the staff picking the cherries off the trees in large bags and taking them to the plant where they would wash the fruits, remove the flesh, and expose the small brown seeds inside. These would be dried and later brought to market.

After several years of working on the plantation and learning how the operation was conducted, he was brought into the business office where he learned how to organize the cash flow and make the production extremely profitable. He became so useful to his friend's uncle, that when Alberto asked to marry his daughter, the owner said yes.

His friend felt somewhat proud that he had brought such a clever fellow into the family fold and considered him as a brother. He decided to share with Alberto a side of the business that had been kept separate from his uncle as well as his university friend. They started out early one morning and walked several miles into the jungle, their backpacks weighing heavily on their shoulders. Alberto consumed copious amounts of water and could not stop wiping sweat from his brow.

Halting in the jungle, Alberto's friend turned to him and spread his arms open wide.

"Now, this is the part of the operation that makes the really big money," Alberto's friend declared. "Only a few of the most trusted know about this. It's run by my father's family. I work here as well as the coffee plantation and try to integrate some of the product here with some of the product from my uncle's operation where you are working."

When Alberto stopped and had a good look around, he could see now that the vegetation had changed. Shrubs with wrinkly, ribbed leaves with cascades of white flowers that turned to reddish purple cherries were now hundreds of shrubby plants with smooth elliptical shaped leaves. Not dissimilar to his coffee plants, but upon looking closely he could see the subtle differences in the leaf shape. Several men were harvesting the leaves and bringing them to areas where large barrels were located. This was a cocaine operation.

"Come on. Let me show you around. It's unbelievably cool. This plant is called *Erythoxylon coca* and grows in our unique climate, just like the coffee bean plants. Once the leaves are harvested we put them in these large metal barrels and pour gasoline into the barrel. This is the beginning of the extraction process. We let them soak in the gasoline to remove the cocaine alkaloid, then filter the solution into another barrel with acid, like this one over here," he said, pointing to large metal blue barrel.

"We can easily remove the gasoline in this acid layer, and then we add sodium bicarbonate to the remainder to make a cocaine base. Once we have this basic solution, we filter it through these white cloths," he said picking up a large cheesecloth and holding it in front of Alberto, "and then we take the filtered solution and dry it into a powder. Come on, look at this."

He brought him over to a series of large tables covered with pans of solution, slurry or powder, all stages of the drying process.

"Look, you see what that guy is doing? He takes the powder base and dumps it into another barrel sitting in a hot water bath and pours in ethyl acetate. We stopped using ether after a couple of explosions. That stuff's pretty nasty, not that this is much better. While in the *bano maria*, we add ethyl methyl ketone and hydrochloric acid all boiled up. That gives us a nice cocaine hydrochloride. Pretty much hands on chemistry, wouldn't you say?" he added with a slight chuckle.

Alberto recalled that while he had majored in business, his friend had been a chemistry major in college. He had no idea that this would be the business, or the future his friend had been working toward.

"The penultimate move is really a drying step and a way to get out all the solvents. First we express the liquid manually, then use a hydraulic press to squeeze out even more. Finally, we stick the pans in these microwaves, and now have fine powdered cocaine."

Alberto could see the series of microwaves in a sturdy shed area, with black wires emerging from the backs of the machines and forming a massive tangle as they all snaked their way to boards with electrical outlets. It was a mini power plant fueled by multiple gas-powered generators.

This was Alberto's descent into a world he never imagined. He threw himself into the task, and grew the business in such an aggressive manner, that money flowed like maple syrup from a tapped sugar tree. It was sweet. Like his friend and colleague, Alberto also kept the two businesses, the coffee plantation and the cocaine operation, from intersecting, at least at first glance. He stayed married to the uncle's daughter and although she couldn't bear him any children much less a son, he remained loyal to her until her difficult death during one final attempt to produce a child. In his mind, Alberto had no choice but to "borrow" his sister's only child in order to present a respectable household.

Alberto's business savvy was so impressive that when the owner of the plantation, his friend's uncle, became incapacitated due to complications from heart surgery, the control of the coffee operation fell to Alberto. By then he had become hardened by the drug trade, and understood that money, greed and power were the obsessions that really made the world turn. He wanted in.

CHAPTER 16

COLOMBIA

Alberto used the coffee plantation as a front for the cocaine distribution operation. Coffee beans were harvested and sold as the smaller business, but he was able to use its product as a means for shipping the cocaine to Mexico and into the United States. In Mexico he had established distributors who could easily move the drug across the American border and distribute throughout the United States. Cocaine was big business. It was the second most commonly trafficked illegal drug in the world and although it had been losing ground in recent years, it still brought in good money. He knew that at one point, almost 4% of all 12th graders in the U.S. had admitted to exposure to cocaine and 0.6 % of the total population admitted to using cocaine in the previous month.

Adrienne, his sister's only daughter, was confined to the coffee plantation and was not aware of the coexisting illegal operation. This was fine with her uncle who needed soft-spoken credibility around the estate when inspectors or nosey land owners were on site.

*   *   *

Adrienne was unhappy and restless on the coffee plantation. She longed for France and the vineyard and was tired of the jungle. She wished for a husband and children, a family of her own. Some nights she would wander the plantation and gaze at the night sky. This was the same moon she could see from her home in Reims but the night air was hot and fetid here, unlike the cool crisp nights back home in the valley. Many nights she could hear her uncle argue incessantly with his comrades over trivial things, particularly when they consumed liquor. They would go on and on with a crescendo of voices echoing ridiculous non-problems, and sometimes the arguments would become heated and threatening. This disturbed Adrienne and sometimes frightened her. But she learned that men just liked to argue to both hear themselves talk and to stake out their intellectual territory. It was in the DNA, puffy chest to puffy chest, in your face. That was the way they did business.

One night the men were drinking more than usual. This evening they had visitors carousing with regulars who Adrienne thought came from Russia. She quickly finished cleaning up the kitchen and scurried off to her room.

She dozed off, but was awakened a short time later by a loud bang and boisterous talk. She had left her window open to get a little fresh air, and when she looked up and out toward the night sky filled with her moon from Reims, she saw the figure of a man standing outside her window. He was staring at her and when she caught his eye, he put his finger to his lips to quiet her. He bent his head low and entered through the window. Adrienne wanted to scream but was too terrified to call out. The man approached her bed, and she pulled the sheets up over her head. He sat on the edge of the bed next to her and could feel her body quivering under the covers. He peeled them back slowly and could see her freightened face covered with streaming tears.

"Please, please, don't hurt me," she pleaded. "My uncle runs this plantation. I am his niece."

"Da," he replied, and put his hand over her mouth.

He pushed her nightgown up toward her head and exposed her young white breasts. She started to cry, as he squeezed them in reciprocity with one hand while his other hand kept her mouth shut, and almost cut off the air she desperately needed. She winced in pain. She now felt his hand move between her legs, and smelled his hot liquored breath as he began to breathe harder. Something large and painful filled her and she tried to cry out, but the weight of him on top of her was suffocating. She could barely breathe, much less move. With his final thrust, he collapsed fully on her and she laid there in pain, too scared and bewildered to move. She struggled for air, and then his body rolled off her. He sat up, pulled up his pants, and buckled his belt. He turned and looked at her, and for the first time. In the moonlight that filled her room, she could see his hard-cold steel grey eyes.

"Tell your uncle," he said with a slurred Russian voice, "that we expect cooperation, and nothing less."

He turned abruptly and exited through the window with hard precision, just the way he had entered her room, and her body.

Adrienne could not move. She was frozen in her bed. She began to weep and buried her head in her pillow.

"What do I do now?" she cried out loud. "I am a disgrace. I cannot tell my uncle. No one must ever know."

She rolled over in her bed and became aware of the sticky red fluid trickling down her thighs. She felt the pain, and forced herself from her bed and walked to the bathroom. She let the water run until it was good and hot, and when she saw steam fill the sink, soaked a washcloth and cleaned herself off. She held up the washcloth and saw the flecks of blood in the congealed fluid. She could smell him and feeling an immediate wave of nausea, she rushed to the toilet and wretched until the pain in her stomach negated the pain between her legs.

CHAPTER 17

THE PLANTATION, COLOMBIA

The next morning she prepared breakfast for her uncle as was expected. "Adrienne, you're very quiet this morning," said Alberto, barely looking up from his plate.

She nodded her head, but did not offer any explanation.

"Well then, I'll be spending the day in the back country. I'll see you later tonight."

Adrienne spent most of her day in her small room, giving in to bouts of crying and despair. There was no one to confide in, no one to console her. She longed for her mother.

While she lived in the larger main house, she was surrounded by smaller houses on the compound where the wives of some of the workers lived along with their husbands. Even though she was sure her uncle had money, he did not spend lavishly on her and she led a fairly plain existence. One concession was a maid that came in once a week to help Adrienne with the housework.

When her uncle returned home he noticed that Adrienne was still sullen and quiet. He retreated to his study and let her be. This behavior continued for another month or so with not so much as a whisper of the events that occurred on that dreadful night. But Adrienne realized she had to do something. She had missed her period and now was having bouts of nausea every morning for the last two weeks.

"Adrienne, I have had enough of you. You have been morose for weeks and now you are sick each morning. I'm going to bring the town doctor in to see you tomorrow."

At this point Adrienne decided to tell her uncle her story. Maybe he would be so angry he would ship her back to her mother. All she could do was hope.

"Uncle, do you remember the night several weeks ago when you had visitors, I think maybe they were from Russia."

He raised his head off his chest and looked directly at her.

"That night, the man with the steely gray eyes entered my bedroom, and, and," she gulped back the tears, "and raped me." She was sobbing, bracing for a blow across the face. He had never physically abused her, but she worried that this would push him to the edge.

Her uncle sat quietly and then his fingers began drumming on the table.

"You mean the short man, stocky build?"

"Yes, he told me to tell you that he expected cooperation and nothing less."

By now Adrienne was feeling nauseous and excused herself. She vomited into the toilet and tried not to aspirate into her lungs the acid pouring from her mouth. She gulped for air between sobs. Finally, when her stomach was empty, she rinsed her mouth with cold running water from the tap. She turned the knob to the off position and looked up into the mirror over the sink. Her eyes were red. The whites had tiny red veins exposed like raw nerves and the rims were also red from rubbing. There were dark circles under her eyes reflective of a lack of sleep and an abundance of worry. *Oh my God*, she thought. *There is a baby on the way. I'm an unmarried young woman living in the jungle with my uncle. No, no, I'm a pregnant, young unmarried woman living in the jungle, with… I'm a disgrace.*

She went back into the kitchen and saw that her uncle was still sitting at the table. She knew nothing other than the coffee business, but he knew what this was about. There was no mistake. Intimidation took many forms and initially he had been unwilling to cooperate with the Russians regarding his distribution operation. They wanted in and they wanted to move other drugs using his coffee business as a cover. He had been resistant. He had been trusted to keep this "family" business running. He had managed over the years to keep everything separate, but he knew the market was slowly shifting away from cocaine. It wasn't so much the heroin the Russians were pushing, it was the fentanyl, the synthetic opioids, and other counterfeit opioid pills that were now available on the black market. His friend, the chemist, knew this trade well. He was the one who had wanted to push the business in this direction, he wanted to work with the Russians, but Alberto had resisted.

There was no additional blow to her body. Instead her uncle put his hand on her shoulder. She placed her hand on top of his. He quickly pulled his hand away and left the room. Adrienne sobbed quietly and moved through her day as if the morning had never happened.

*   *   *

The months passed and Adrienne's belly began to grow, and it was clear to everyone who saw her that she was with child. Her uncle had arranged for a midwife to be present at the birth and seven and a half months later she gave birth to a little girl. Finally, Adrienne had someone with her whom she could love and cherish. She named her child Bella, Italian for beautiful to honor her mother and her heritage. She begged her uncle to let her fly home to France, to her mother to show her, her grandchild. Her uncle had already sent his men to France to help run the vineyard for his sister and without her knowledge, used the champagne operation as another cover for his drug trade. This was seen as a strategic distribution point for getting drugs into Europe, and one he would not relinquish. He debated in his mind whether to let Adrienne go and in the end decided he would keep her with him in Colombia.

The child grew up with only Adrienne's stories of her life in Reims, her wonderful grandparents she would never meet, the champagne vineyards with its legendary climbing grapes, and the endless rose gardens which Adrienne had tended with love.

Little Bella seemed a happy child and quite content to stay with her mother on the coffee plantation. Adrienne's uncle had arranged for Bella to have a personal tutor so she could be home schooled. Adrienne had been fluent in both French and Italian, the native languages of her parents, as well as in English which she had learned in school. While living in Colombia she had mastered Spanish like her uncle. He too spoke a variety of languages having gone to university in America and having lived in both Europe and South America. Little Bella was exposed to such a rich linguistic environment that at a very early age she clearly had an aptitude for languages and had been verbal before most babies speak their single words. This gift delighted her mother, and even Adrienne's hardened uncle Alberto took delight in speaking with the child. For the most part, life on the plantation carried on until one summer day when Bella was about three years old and the balance of favor changed.

CHAPTER 18

COLOMBIA

Something had happened deep in the jungle. One very hot summer day her uncle and some of his men returned to the Compound covered in blood and agitated by adrenaline. Adrienne could only look through the curtains. She could see their lips moving and arms flailing, but could not hear their words. These were not the regular coffee plantation workers who were yelling and waving automatic rifles in the air. These were men who accompanied her uncle from time to time. She thought they were probably the security team, the branch of men from the Compound that protected the coffee plantation from criminals, and kept everyone and anyone on the Compound in their place. These men seemed to increase in number after the incident with the Russians some years back and her uncle would not venture far from the Compound without one or two of these men in his company.

"Do you think the operation has been compromised?" asked one of these men of Alberto.

"I don't think so. It was only one person who wandered too close to the cocoa sheds, and it was only an outlying storage shed at that. However, the idiot who followed him back to his research camp should be shot," Alberto said angrily. "There was no need to kill all those people. It will only bring the authorities out here. We are going to have to slow down the cocaine operation for a while until this passes. Make sure everything is well hidden and that the focus is at the coffee plantation."

Just at that moment, one of the men who had been out in the jungle reached the outskirts of the group. He looked as though he were carrying a small bundle over his shoulder, but on further inspection, the bundle turned out to be a child. The child had a bandana covering its head and eyes, and was motionless.

"What have you got there?" one of the men yelled across the Compound. "Is it dead?" said another.

When the man reached the huddle, he laid the child on the ground in front of them.

"I think she passed out. I couldn't leave her there. Everyone else in the camp was dead, and, and I just couldn't kill a small child," he said, obviously revealing his weakness.

"Now what are we going to do? Everyone will be looking for her. There will be a huge search," cried one of the men.

"Quiet!" yelled Alberto. "Everyone keep quiet. Let me rethink this. We agree that this is the only survivor of the camp. Correct? Everyone else has been killed. Well, researchers get lost in the jungle all the time. It is a brutal, unforgiving place for those who are not familiar with its dangers. Yes, they will be missed after some time if they don't report home, but we can go back and cover up our mess. So, let the authorities look. What they will find is that the jungle swallowed them whole," he said with confidence.

At this time the little bundle began to stir. It was a soft moaning at first and then a little cry. Her tiny hands struggled to remove the bandana tied around her eyes. Adrienne, who had been watching out the window, saw the child move and something inside her propelled her into action. It was her motherly instinct. She quickly opened the door and ran toward the group of burly men. Alarmed at this sudden movement, the men turned in her direction and raised their guns. Alberto shot his hand up into the air.

"Halt!" he yelled. "Everyone stay where you are." By now the little bundle was crying softly, curled in a ball with her knees to her chest.

"Mommy, mommy," she cried in soft, almost inaudible tones.

"What happened to the child's mother?" asked Alberto.

"I killed her with the machete, when I pulled her out of the tent. I didn't know at the time there was a baby in there. Who brings a little child to the jungle? Who does that?" he said defensively.

Adrienne heard this last exchange and trembled. She was appalled and moved gently toward the little girl.

"Come here little one," she said quietly in Spanish opening up her arms. She wasn't sure where this child came from or who she was, or what language she spoke.

The little girl looked into Adrienne's kind face and said in very clear English, "I want my mommy. Where is my mommy?"

Adrienne bent down so she was eye level with the child. She looked into her jewel green eyes rimmed with tears, and stroked her dark silky hair.

"It's okay, little one," Adrienne said in English. "You can come with me."

Adrienne looked hard at her uncle Alberto. "I will take care of this," and carried the little girl off to the house.

Once inside Adrienne ran a washcloth under the cold tap and wrung out the excess water. She washed the dirt off the little girl's face and stroked her hair.

"You're safe now. You're with me." She looked at her carefully and thought she was probably the same age as Bella. Yet they looked so different. Bella had fair hair and steel gray eyes, while this child had dark hair and green eyes with a pale ivory complexion. Adrienne thought she was a very pretty little girl and was curious to know about her.

"Can you tell me your name, little one?"

The little girl was frightened and cried again for her mother.

"Tell me your name, please, it's okay."

"My name is Rose," the little girl said. "I'm Rose and I'm three years old. Where is mommy, where is Maggie?"

Adrienne pulled the child into her arms and hugged her. She began to cry thinking of her own mother whom she missed every day, and her own daughter who lived with her in virtual isolation.

All this noise woke Bella who called out for her mother. Carrying Rose in her arms, Adrienne went into the bedroom to see Bella.

"Bella, look we have a new member of our family. You have a new playmate. Her name is Rose."

Even at three Bella was uncertain how she felt about this situation. Suddenly she folded her arms, stomped one foot and made a face. Bella had been doted on, was the apple of her mother's eye, and the singular attraction for all her mother's attention, until Rose.

Rose on the other hand, kept crying and asking for her mother. She was tired and hungry, as well as frightened.

Adrienne brought the girls into the kitchen and sat them around the table. They could barely sit in the chairs since the girls were so small. Adrienne had a small children's table set up in the kitchen but it only had one chair at the moment. She would have to fix that. She went to the refrigerator and took out an apple, cut it into several small pieces and fed it to the girls. She filled two small plastic cups with orange juice. Both of the girls were quiet while they ate and drank. Adrienne was not certain what the plan was. In her own mind she wanted to keep little Rose. Rose would be a regular playmate for Bella and it would be fun to have another daughter. She could say that it was a distant cousin's child that had come to live with them. Or maybe people would think she just had another child.

She would probably have to keep her hidden for a while just in case the authorities came around asking questions. She wasn't exactly sure what had happened in the jungle, and truly didn't want to know. There was nothing better than plausible deniability.

About two days later, the local police came to the coffee plantation. Alberto met with them and offered to show them around the Compound. Adrienne could see them talking and walking while she looked out the window. She turned her attention to the girls and moved Rose into her bedroom with some toys to occupy her for a few moments. Then she took Bella by the hand and walked outside to greet the officer.

"Hello," she said sweetly, "I'm Adrienne, Alberto's niece and this is my little girl Bella. May I ask what is happening here?"

The officer looked at her and smiled. "We have a report that some researchers are missing in this area. We have a band of men out looking for them, but so far we haven't had much luck."

"Oh," said Adrienne with a tone of concern in her voice. "I do hope you find them soon. The jungle is an unforgiving place with many dangers. Where did they come from?"

"They were from the United States. Some university-sponsored research project. If they are to be found, we will find them. It won't be the first time students have been lost in the jungle."

"Who reported them missing? Did you find anyone from their party?" Adrienne asked as Bella clung to her lower leg.

"We were contacted by the University who let us know that their group had not checked in at the designated time, and they still haven't heard from them. I have no further information at this time. Ah," he said looking at his watch, "I have to get going now. Thank you both for your time."

He abruptly turned his back to her and walked away. Adrienne shot Alberto a knowing look. Maybe no one knew about the child after all. She would still keep everything quiet for several months before she let Rose have more exposure in the Compound. It was clear that the security detail knew of her, but they had every reason to keep things quiet. Adrienne didn't know all the facts, but she knew enough, and had seen the guns and blood on the men's shirts. She shuddered to think of this child's poor mother, was it Maggie, having been struck on the head with a machete. Little Rose must never know the truth. It was too traumatic. Adrienne would soothe her and comfort her until Rose had no past but the one Adrienne created for her.

Adrienne kept her eye on the newspapers every day hoping to read a story about the lost research party. The first week there was a small article, just a paragraph about some missing university researchers who had gotten lost in the jungle. Then months later there was a follow-up article saying that they have never been found. There were never any specifics of the research expedition in the article other than the number in the party. No mention of names or even a child. This gave Adrienne a sense of relief. She would now work to reshape Rose's memory and help her forget her early tragic life.

For the most part, the two girls got along. They had each other for sharing chores, keeping their mother company and trading secrets. When Adrienne looked at both of them, she couldn't help but think of their violent beginnings. Bella was the product of a brutal rape, and when she stared into Bella's face she could see the steely eyes of her father. As Bella got older, she looked less like her mother's side of the family. Adrienne didn't know much about the Russian. Her uncle never spoke of him again. Bella felt this unease in her mother when they looked at each other. She had asked many times who her father was, but Adrienne would only answer that she had a brief love interest as a young woman and the man had died in a tragic accident on the coffee plantation. Bella never accepted this explanation and often asked her great-uncle Alberto. He was less forthcoming than her mother.

Rose, on the other hand was viewed with more compassion by Adrienne. Since she had no idea who her parents were other than they were American, Adrienne made up an entire fantasy in her mind of where Rose came from and who she came from. In her mind she felt more protective of Rose knowing that she was an orphan.

The girls sensed these differences, although subtle, in their mother's reaction to them, and as they got older they began to pull apart. Bella spent more time studying her languages and Rose showed a surprising interest in the healing arts. Initially she demonstrated an aptitude for taking care of sick animals, spending much of her time with the plantation horses, riding them and grooming them. Later, she expressed an interest in medicine and science. Adrienne wondered if Rose would be interested in becoming a veterinarian, but knew that this would be impossible as long as they were trapped on the coffee plantation.

Adrienne always celebrated both girls' birthday on Bella's birthday since she didn't know when Rose's birthday was. For their 13th birthday, Adrienne asked her uncle if she could take them to the town.

"Uncle Alberto. I'd like to take the girls into town for their birthday this year. They are growing into young ladies and need more than what the plantation can give them. It's time. Things have been going smoothly here and I see no reason we can't go."

Alberto thought for a moment and finally said, "Adrienne, you have spent most of your adult life on the plantation. I think you could go to town as long as there are some of my men to go with you."

"Agreed!" said Adrienne excitedly. "Thank you, Uncle," and with that she wrapped her arms around his stout body and gave him a hug.

A few days later Adrienne, Rose and Bella got into the covered Jeep and one of the plantation security men drove the forty-two miles into town. The girls sat in the back seat while Adrienne sat in front with the driver.

"I can't believe we are actually going into the town," said Rose excitedly.

"I know. I can't believe it either. I'm so happy to get off the Compound, even if it's only for a day. Magazines and newspapers are not enough and we have such limited television. There's almost no reception where we are. My God, you think we were living in the Dark Ages of Europe!" exclaimed Bella. "I don't understand why we can't have more freedom."

This comment did not come lightly from Bella. Even though she was a budding teenager, she looked older and felt older in her mind. She always wondered why they were trapped in the Compound, and why they never had the freedom that other young people had. She had seriously considered running away, but it was only now she realized that the Compound was a very long way from the rest of civilization. The drive was long. It wasn't that she didn't love her mother, or even love her "sister" Rose for that matter. It was just, well it was just that she wanted to fly. She was that type of girl. What good was it reading about the world when you couldn't explore it? There was restlessness in her. Bella looked at Rose who was staring out the window of the Jeep and wondered who she really was. *Didn't she just show up one day?* Bella had heard the men talking on the plantation some time ago when they thought no one was around. It seems Rose was plucked right out of the jungle from some American research party. She and Rose had talked

107

about it. Even so, Rose seemed so much more content with the Compound. She liked reading science books and spending time in the garden with their "shared" mother.

The little town was a wake-up call for the girls. Even Adrienne was overly excited.

"Girls, look, over there," she said pointing to a beautiful white stucco building with a red Spanish tile roof. The door was one story tall and shaped in an arch with bricks forming a frame around the perimeter. Windows were cut into the stone either as rectangles, squares or arches. The cobblestone walk seemed to flow in either direction and told of the history of the many who had tread its surface the last few hundred years. There were modern shops interspersed with small restaurants. Some had roasting meat on spits in the open air and the smell drew the girls to the windows.

"Oh wow, look at that church tower," said Adrienne, pointing to a creamy tall building capped with an ornate red dome and a cross on top. The windows were outlined in white paint and very reminiscent of Spanish design from centuries past.

It was interesting, but the girls wanted to see the more modern shops, those with the latest clothes, those that had make-up and perfumes, hair products and other things that teenage girls were interested in. The town didn't have much in the way of modern shops, but there were some that clearly had a Western or more European influence. The girls walked past a tattoo parlor on the edge of the town and peered in the window. They saw designs with ornate flowers, animals, characters, and letters. They were curious having read about celebrities who had tattoos and they understood it was more of a Western cultural influence than anything else. They moved along and settled at having a coffee and pastry at a small outdoor café.

"I like it here," said Rose waving her hand out toward the town. "I wonder what the big cities are like. Mother, why can't we take a trip to Bogotá or even Cartagena?"

Bella waited for the reply. She wanted nothing else but to leave the plantation. *Why they couldn't send me to school somewhere in a big city*, she thought. Maybe she could work one day as a translator, or international banker, or something exciting. Life was boring on the plantation. It was all coffee beans and coffee bean workers. How would she ever meet a boy who wasn't a coffee been picker?

"Yes mother, I agree with Rose. Why can't we go to a big city next time?

We're young, we need to fly free," said Bella with some force.

Adrienne was now questioning her decision to bring them into the town. She understood their plight and had echoed those same sentiments many times long before the girls came into her heart. Her life would have been so different if she had stayed in Reims, been allowed to travel Europe and meet a proper husband. She didn't want to seem bitter, so she made the most of what she had. She had done her family duty by helping her uncle with his household. She had made a big sacrifice giving up her own dreams of having her own husband and family. Although Bella's start in life had been traumatic and violent, Adrienne loved her daughter and was grateful for her company. Bella had a slight edge to her personality, but she was clever and forthright. When Rose came into her life, it was like finding strawberries in cheesecake. Rose was a luscious, rewarding, bright child who was inner-directed and kind. She was very different from Bella, so Adrienne could enjoy each of them in their own way.

"Girls, I know how you feel," said Adrienne choking up unexpectedly. "I came to the plantation at a young age myself. I had dreams of my own that were never fulfilled. I've missed my own mother terribly all these years and wanted her to share in your lives, but it never happened and, and…" Adrienne couldn't finish her sentence.

And for the first time in many years she thought of taking the girls and running—running from her uncle, from the plantation, from the confinement, from her brutal rape. *Why not*, she thought, *why shouldn't I try? Why would I let my daughters live the same life that I have?*

Adrienne wiped the tears from her eyes. Both girls stared at their mother with surprise. Adrienne had always shown the most upbeat spirit of anyone and was a positive force in their lives. She helped mold them into the young women they were by instilling in them a sense of independence, intellectual curiosity and personal strength. She knew Bella shared half her gene pool and that was strong French and Italian stock. Her family were pioneers who had tamed the land and worked hard their entire lives. Rose, well, her family history was unknown to Adrienne, but she assumed she was the child of a researcher who had been on the field expedition. Her parents would have been adventurous, brilliant, and world travelers. That was perhaps the seed of Rose's interest in science and the natural world.

"Bella, Rose," said Adrienne, blotting her eyes, "let's make a pact; let this outing serve as an opportunity for more to come. We'll enjoy our day here, go back to your great-uncle's plantation and show him we can be trusted to have many outings. Then after a while, these adventures will be commonplace, and we can plan something in one of the big cities. Okay?"

The girls sat quiet for a moment. They had never seen their mother so emotional. They rallied around her, and enfolded her in their arms. Neither Bella nor Rose said a word.

They toured a few more shops and then Adrienne said, "Girls, is there something here you would like for your birthday? Something special?"

The girls thought for a moment and then Bella said, "Actually, I'd like a tattoo." She heard gasps. "No wait, let me explain. Just a tiny one and some place where no one will see it. It's fashionable these days, lots of people have them. I've seen it in magazines. Please, please mother. You can get one too."

Rose said, "It could be fun, like our little secret, Mother. Why not?"

"If my uncle ever found out, I don't know what he would do. No, I don't want one, not now anyway. But I recognize it's a sense of independence of youth. Just a tiny one, and in a place that no one can see. Do you understand?" she said sternly.

The girls ran back to the tattoo parlor. Adrienne trailed behind already regretting her decision to let them have a tattoo at thirteen. But she felt a rebellious streak in her own consciousness on this day, a sense that SHE wanted to break away and do something just a bit dangerous. It was that kind of a day.

She recognized that she could get into a great deal of trouble, but decided to let it all unfold as fate would have it.

Once in the shop, the tattoo artist wanted to confirm with Adrienne that she was truly giving her permission to let these two young girls have a tattoo. She assured him it was all right, if he could demonstrate that his equipment was clean and disinfected properly. He promised that it was.

"I have many tourists who come to little towns like ours in Colombia and love the plants, birds, animal life, and the jungle. They want to commemorate their experience with a tattoo. Here's a book with our most popular designs," he said showing the girls and Adrienne a collection of colorful drawings.

"I'm not sure," said Rose. "Bella, why don't you pick first."

Clearly Bella had given this some thought. She looked through the book and pointed to a picture of a jaguar.

"You want a jaguar?" said Adrienne. "That doesn't seem very feminine. What about a nice flower?" She turned to Rose, "Rose, you should get your namesake flower, a beautiful red rose."

Bella interrupted, "I don't want something pretty. I want something fierce." She pointed to a picture in the book of an outline of a small black and white image of a panther with claws extended and mouth slightly agape. It looked like it was stalking its prey.

"I'm not so sure about this," said her mother. It's not a good choice. How about something less fierce, maybe a bird or star? You told me it would be small. Even this black cat looks big."

Bella made a face. She wanted what she wanted, but it was clear her mother was not about to give in. "Let me think then," she said in a petulant voice. She folded her arms and stomped one foot while squeezing out her lips. "Let Rose get her, her, rose."

Rose seemed fine with that choice. She really didn't want the tattoo after all, but didn't want to seem as if she were above it all. So, she settled for a small red rose. It was like her mother said, her namesake flower.

"Lovely," said the artist as he showed her an open flower with bright red petals and two small green leaves. "We'll use this one. You know the rose is an ancient symbol for promise and hope. It symbolizes a new beginning."

Rose had the tattoo etched on her skin, just below her right hip. It would always be covered by her panties and no one would ever see it. Unless of course she wanted them to. Rose was surprised at how painful the procedure was, but she never said a word. Her mother wrung her hands in anxiety, regretting having made this decision.

Brooding Bella finally settled on a drawing she liked. It was a spider. It had two distinct body regions and eight long legs emerging from the abdomen. It certainly wasn't something her mother was going to like. But Bella liked it and she thought it was a compromise between a flower and a jaguar.

"You want this one?" said the tattoo artist with a questioning voice. "This one? Not the little dove on this page?"

Bella was not a dove, and she was not a symbol for promise and hope either.

"Yes, I want the spider. They are helpful creatures, right, Rose? You see them in the garden all the time. They trap all the unwanted flies and other bugs in their webs," Bella said.

"Yes," said the artist "you could think of them as a symbol for trickery or treachery."

Bella also had the tattoo planted just below her right hip. Now the girls, and their mother, shared a secret and created a bond from this outing.

The driver/security guard that had been sent with them to the town didn't consider this place much of a threat. It was a small, sleepy, touristy town with many old Spanish-style buildings, a church and some shops. He had let the girls roam with freedom while he sat in a café and had *aguapenela*, a sort of sugar cane and lemon drink, followed by several cups of espresso after his meal. He had indulged in a bowl of *ajiaco*, a nice thick chicken soup with potatoes, corn, avocado and sour cream and flavored with *guasca*. He was fairly bored by this time and after looking at his watch, went to find the girls to get them back to the plantation before the sun set.

The Jeep had been gassed up and everyone was on board and ready for the drive back. The girls were tired, and their heads leaned on one another while they dozed off in the back seat of the Jeep. About eleven miles from the center of town, the road was blocked with a cart filled with straw and other plants from the countryside. In front of the cart was a small green pickup truck. The driver exited the Jeep and walked up ahead to see why they had been stopped in the middle of the road. He was prepared to offer help to the farmer if needed. As he approached the truck in front of the cart, he was not able to see the driver sitting in the vehicle so he inched up to the front bumper. When he did, a man in dark coveralls approached him and shot him right through the forehead. As he fell, his head bumped the front of the truck, and he cascaded on to the ground. The girls were startled awake by the noise, and Adrienne who was not asleep was petrified at the sound of the gunshot. The man in the coveralls moved quickly to the jeep and opened the door.

"Get out. Get out," he yelled, his voice slightly muffled from his bandana. The girls huddled together and Adrienne stepped in front of them as a lioness protecting her cubs.

"What is going on? What is happening here?" Adrienne said shakily, biting her lip as a way to fight the tears. She wanted to appear strong and in control. She couldn't quite see the man's face because the bandana covered his nose and mouth, but she could see his eyes.

The man in the coveralls knocked her to the ground. By this time both girls were crying and screaming. He reached forward and placed his body between them. He looked at Rose and he looked at Bella. He grabbed Bella by the hair and began dragging her toward the truck. Rose tried to hang on to her, but he swatted her down and she landed on top of Adrienne.

Adrienne was not conscious, but Rose was. She knew she would not be able to fight this man alone, so she made a mental note of what he looked like, the shape of his body, the color of his hair and his eyes, and when he pulled down the bandana as he threw Bella into the truck, she made a mental note of the rest of his face. She would not forget it.

The truck sped away leaving a dead driver, an unconscious mother, and an adopted orphan abandoned in the road.

CHAPTER 19

COLUMBIA TO THE U.S.A.

Rose stayed with Adrienne until she regained consciousness. She had found some bottled water in the Jeep, and with some tissues had wiped the blood off her mother's face.

"Rose, are you alright?" Adrienne said with panic. "Where is Bella? Where is my little girl?" She looked around the jeep and saw nothing but the dead body of the driver in the road up ahead.

"Mother, he took Bella. He dragged her by her hair and threw her into the back of the truck. It was so horrible." She cried and put her head down into Adrienne's lap. Adrienne stroked her hair and hugged her.

"Listen, Rose, we have to get out of here. Are the keys still in the Jeep?"

They opened the driver's side door and saw keys were still in the ignition. "Get in Rose. Get in."

Adrienne slammed the door, turned the key and hit her foot to the gas pedal. She was used to driving around the plantation, but not small dirt jungle roads when the light was slipping away. Yet, she could do this. If she had had to pick a tattoo back at the shop, she would have picked the dragonfly. In Asian cultures it represented courage and strength and that's what Adrienne possessed now.

When they reached the plantation and drove in through the gate, Alberto was immediately alerted. He had expected them home a little earlier, and was about to send out some of his men to look for them.

Adrienne exploded from the Jeep, caught her breath and ran up to her uncle.

"He took her. He just took her," she shouted and broke down crying.

"What do you mean?" Alberto said, "Who took who?" As he looked toward the Jeep he could only see Rose. Bella was missing. There was no security driver either.

"Tell me everything," shouted Alberto. "Everything."

She told him all about the outing, everything but the part about the tattoo parlor. That was her secret with the girls. Then she told him what happened when they were stopped in the road. She could barely get the word "gunshot" off her tongue.

He moved Rose and Adrienne into the house.

"Stay here. Do you understand? I want you to stay in the house."

Alberto went outside and got into his truck and drove off toward the smaller houses that were contained within the Compound. Adrienne closed the curtain and went to find Rose who was on the bed in her room with the covers pulled over her head. Adrienne went to lie down next to her and gather her in her arms.

"Shush, shush, I'm going to get you out of this place. I will keep you safe. You have suffered enough in one short life." She stroked Rose's hair and snuggled close to her.

"Ouch," cried Rose.

"I'm sorry," said Adrienne, "what'd I do?"

"My hip is sore, that's all. From the tattoo," said Rose.

"Of course, I'll be careful," said Adrienne hugging her ever more tightly.

Neither one of them felt like eating even though their last meal had been hours before while they were touring the town. Instead they just lay there quietly in the bed together. The two of them fell asleep until the next morning when the sun crept in through the curtains and tapped them on their brow.

They both got up from the bed and headed into the kitchen, still dressed in their clothes from the day before. Alberto was sitting at the kitchen table drinking coffee. He looked up from his newspaper when he heard them walk in. His face looked tired, and he had stubble over his chin and below his nose. There were dark circles under his eyes.

"Adrienne, my men are out looking for Bella. You understand why I can't ask the police to help. I swear to you that when I catch that bastard, I will personally slit his throat." He turned to Rose.

"Rose, I am going to get you out of Colombia. I'll send you someplace safe."

"And Mother is coming with me. She can't stay here. She's coming with me," Rose pleaded.

"Perhaps later," he said with uncertainty. "Can either of you tell me what he looked like?"

Rose jumped right in. "He was a stocky man wearing dark coveralls, like they wear in a garage. He had short dirty blond hair, with a slightly receding hairline and dark gray eyes. He had big feet too and spoke with an accent. I could recognize him again if I saw him. I know I could."

Adrienne swallowed hard. She had seen his eyes too, and she had seen them once fourteen years before. It was the steely gray eyes. They had unending depth; they were bottomless and soulless.

Her uncle knew too just by reading Adrienne's face. No words were necessary. Her body said it all.

"Rose, go to your room. I want to talk with your mother," said Alberto standing up and towering over her. His voice sounded tired, but firm. Rose obeyed and went directly to the room she shared with Bella. She was worried about Bella, and now her uncle was planning on sending her away. It was the unraveling of her second family.

"Adrienne, you and Rose are in danger here. I'll make plans to send Rose to a boarding school in the United States. Maybe now is the time for you to go back to France."

"But why can't Rose and I stay together? Why must we be pulled apart?

"I just think it's safer if we hide Rose at a boarding school. We'll send her along first. I have to make arrangements to get her a passport. I'll send you back to Reims. It's been your wish for these last, what, almost twenty years. Your mother, my only sister, is frail and could use your help. I need to take on these Russian bastards, alone. They have plagued the coffee plantation long enough."

"It's more than coffee beans, isn't it uncle?"

"What do you mean?"

"You know exactly what I mean," Adrienne said with some force. "I really don't believe for one minute that this is all about the coffee plantation. I've lived here for seventeen years and I'm not blind. I think you have other businesses which are why those American researchers were murdered many years ago and the Russians want some of whatever else you have to offer."

"Adrienne, I will make all the arrangements tomorrow. Help Rose pack and make her understand that you, that we, love her."

*   *   *

It was several days before Alberto had all the preparations in order. There had been no news on Bella. He had men scouring the countryside and nearby towns looking for her and the Russian. She had simply vanished. Multiple times during the last ten years, it had been brought to his attention that the Russian had been monitoring the activity at the plantation, and his daughter. Alberto had not taken the threat seriously, until now. He obtained a passport for Rose from the Black Market and used Bella's birthdate and Adrienne's last name for her documents.

Alberto personally took Rose to the airport after she engaged in a very tearful good-bye with Adrienne and a promise that they would be together in the future. Rose boarded a plane for Boston and soon would be a new student at a prestigious boarding school in Wellesley, Massachusetts. She may have been a year too young to enter the ninth grade, since they didn't know her true birthdate, but with some "donation" money that Alberto contributed, and the fact that Rose was so far ahead in her studies in Colombia, she was allowed to grace the halls without issue.

The change in venue was very difficult for Rose. She went from living in virtual isolation except for her mother and sister and the plantation workers to living in a dormitory with many other girls. Psychologically she was in pain. She spent many nights crying in her bed until her suite mates reported her to the house mother who in turn sent her to the school psychologist.

Rose had few early memories of her life. Adrienne had seen to that. All she could tell the psychologist was that she missed her mother and her sister, and even her great-uncle. The psychologist recommended that she get involved in the horseback riding program that the school offered. This seemed agreeable to Rose who loved animals and had ridden regularly on the plantation. Back home, she had enjoyed riding a horse over the hills filled with coffee plants, through jungle brush and around the open grassy fields.

Rose understood that there was no other experience similar to riding a horse; not riding a bicycle or, in fact, sitting in or on anything mechanical. To ask another living creature to trust you, to graciously let you climb on their back and move with them was a privilege. A horse has a sense of the person in the saddle, and can feel both confidence, and fear, in a rider. For those who sit poised with assurance, a horse will respond like a purring kitten, embracing a gentle bend of a rein or tap of a heel. Rose was such a rider. She took to horses as though God had put her there. She felt one with them, particularly when she was riding cross country and only had her horse for company. In Colombia these had been great times to think, and now in Massachusetts these were times to contemplate her lonely life and her deep yearning to be united with her family.

Initially, she wrote to Adrienne almost every day when she first got to the academy, but then made it weekly since she had so much schoolwork. The telephone calls were short and intermittent. This made it that much harder for Rose to connect with anyone. The first year was the hardest. Rose didn't know how to handle the holidays, and was forced, in a sense, to spend some time with other girls' families who were willing to share their homes with her. The most perplexing holiday was Thanksgiving. This was totally foreign to Rose and one they had never celebrated when she lived in South America.

"Rose," said one of her schoolmates, "this is a real American holiday. We're celebrating the first Thanksgiving where, you know, the pilgrims who came over to this country from England gave thanks to the Native Americans who helped them survive a really harsh winter. It's sort of an everybody holiday. My dad, you know, who is a faculty member here always invites students who have no place to go on this holiday." She caught the saddened look in Rose's eye. "I'm sorry Rose; I didn't mean it like that. There are plenty of students who can't travel home for a long weekend because their homes are just too far away. Like your home."

Rose thought for a moment. *Like your home.* She remembered something that Bella had told her once. Bella said she overheard some of the men talking one day about how Rose came to the plantation. She just showed up one day from the jungle. So where did she come from and who were HER people? Were her parents American? She always considered Adrienne her mother basically because she was the only mother she remembered or knew. But who were her birth parents? Bella was always asking who her father was and both girls would lie in bed at night and talk about it.

"Do you think your mother really had an affair with one of the plantation workers when she was young?" asked Rose.

"I don't know," Bella answered. "That's what she says, but I doubt it. She says he was killed in an accident, I think with some machinery or something. I'd like to think she met a foreign diplomat and they had an amazing love connection, but then he had to leave the country on mysterious business. That would be so cool."

"Yeah, that would be cool," said Rose. "But what about me?"

"I think your parents may be from America, and I don't mean South

America," Bella giggled. "The men on the plantation said there was some kind of expedition in the jungle or something, and then I think there was a catastrophe or, or explosion, or something."

"Well, why didn't anyone ever try and find my parents or at least where my home was if that were really true? Why won't anyone talk about it? It doesn't really make any sense, Bella," Rose said with some irritation.

"I don't know. This place seems to be filled with mysterious beginnings, I guess. Maybe Adrienne and Alberto are spies, and they are really married to spies, and your parents were spies, and the whole thing got covered up."

Both girls laughed, threw pillows at one another and tried to fall asleep.

CHAPTER 20

BOSTON SUBURB

Rose had used her riding at the school as means of helping her cope with her separation from her family. The emotional and physical connection with her horse allowed her to redirect her loneliness into determination and drive. Focused on both her academic studies and her horseback riding, Rose achieved top grades in her courses, and became a competitive equestrian. In addition to receiving high honors for her school work, particularly in science, she also earned a coveted spot on the student riding team. The four girls on the team developed a camaraderie and closeness while they worked at combined training and then competed together in eventing. Eventing horse trials consisted of dressage, stadium or show jumping and cross country. Rose liked cross country riding best as this was what she was most suited to. For Rose, dressage was too constricting and too controlled, while stadium jumping was all about rubs and knock-downs. Rose didn't care much for whether her horse's hoof touched a rail or knocked it to the ground while she rode over the fences. What Rose cherished was the freedom she felt when she galloped over an open field or through the woods jumping whatever obstacles were in her path. Since her teammates were better at dressage and stadium jumping, Rose felt as though she was the team's anchor, ready to bring the medal home with her final cross country ride.

During the fall of her junior year in high school, Rose's teammates asked if she would like to ride with them along the high ridge trail. This trail was well known for its rocky terrain, challenging jumps, and twisty turns where maple and oak trees were the most dangerous obstacles. Rose had been on the trail many times and knew the path well. It was a nippy early November day with cool brisk winds. Gusts stirred up fallen orange and red leaves and carried them noisily into the air under the horses' hooves. The horses were stirred as well, jigging along the trail, and letting a little "buck" slip out every now and then. But the girls from the school competition team were strong riders and could sit any horse. This was cross country riding at its best. After an exhilarating first go, the girls decided to go around the course on the trail for a second time. The horses would have seen everything once and would be more settled for this round. After the third obstacle, the group, riding single file, entered the narrow path into the woods at a slow canter. Rose was following a chestnut mare, ridden by one of her teammates, winding in and out of the trees when a beautiful doe popped through the brush and landed in the middle of the trail. The chestnut mare reared unexpectedly causing the rider to lose her balance and she slid off her horse onto the ground. Rose tried to avoid trampling her teammate by pulling to the right, but inadvertently rapped her knee on the furrowed oak trunk and crashed her head into a low bough causing her helmet to fly off her head. With a large "crack" Rose was knocked off her horse and fell unconscious to the ground compounding the head injury.

"Oh my God," said one of the riders still sitting her horse as she pulled up sharply. "Are you all right?"

"I'm hurt. It's my arm, but Rose is not moving. I'm scared. We need help."

With two riders hurt and on the ground, one of the remaining two riders agreed to race back to the barn for help, while the other remained at the scene.

All-terrain vehicles made it out to the course and took the two injured girls to the school where ambulances were waiting with red lights pulsing. Both girls were transported to a local hospital, but it was determined that Rose's head injury was too severe to be cared for locally so she would need to go to one of the Boston hospitals for intensive treatment.

It took forty-five minutes to get to Boston, and Rose was still unconscious when she was wheeled into the emergency department.

"What have we got here?" the ED doc said when Rose's stretcher came in through the sliding glass doors.

"Hi, doc," said the EMT. "I've got a 16-year-old girl, cracked her head on a large tree branch and was knocked out when she hit the ground. Blood pressure is stable, but a little volatile. She may have a fractured kneecap too."

"Horseback riding accident? She's still got on her riding boots," said the ED doc, giving Rose's body a quick survey looking for damage as they rolled her down the hall. "Still has not regained consciousness. Hmm," he said moving her hair to one side. "Bad head wound."

Rose was moved into one of the exam rooms and examined thoroughly. Blood was drawn while both neurosurgery and orthopedics were called for consultation. Getting a jump up on the waiting list due to her critical condition, Rose relocated to the CT scanner. When the films were completed, the radiologist and the neurosurgeon reviewed the scans.

"Looks like a depressed skull fracture," said the radiologist pointing to an area of the skull where the bone protruded into the brain tissue. She placed both hands into the pockets of her lab coat and turned toward the neurosurgeon, her brow raised.

"Yeah, but you see this tear here? This vessel is going to have to be repaired. Blood is accumulating rapidly and it could cause some real damage. I need to get her to the OR stat," said the neurosurgeon. Already dressed in scrubs, the neurosurgeon alerted his team and reviewed his findings before making his final preparation for the OR.

*   *   *

In the adjacent examination room, a junior emergency medicine physician conferred with the consultant about his unconscious drug overdosed patient.

"We're sending him up to the medical intensive care unit. He's still unstable in spite of our treatment. I'm surprised there are such strong symptoms of cocaine poisoning." He turned toward the toxicologist for answers.

Lily Robinson, dressed in a black wool skirt and white cotton blouse, topped by her lab coat and finished with black stiletto heels, reviewed the toxicology findings. "I think what you need to consider here is a drug packer. That's why the symptoms are persisting."

"What do you mean?" he answered.

"Look, this guy just got off a plane from Colombia. He was brought in with signs of cocaine toxicity. He's tachycardic, he's got hypertension, his temp is through the roof, and he's been seizing. His urine tested positive for cocaine. You've given him fluids, tried cooling the body, and given him benzodiazepines. It's not working. He's probably got a belly full of cocaine filled condoms. Some of which have ruptured by now. Let's get a portable film in here."

Sure enough, when they looked at the digital x-ray, they could make out the outlines of sausage-like objects filling the intestines.

"He's a drug mule, a body packer. Some drug smugglers use human transport vessels to get their drugs to market. Better get him to surgery STAT," Lily said, "or we'll be seeing him on the autopsy table."

As Lily was leaving the ED she stopped to let the team of nurses and surgeons frantically push a gurney out from the exam room adjacent to the one she had been using. On the surface lay a lovely young girl with dark hair, clearly dressed for a date in the OR. Lily could see that she was unconscious, but something about her face was compelling. The girl's eyes were closed, but Lily had enough of a sense of her to feel the familiar. She let them rush by and hoped that the young girl made it through whatever surgery was ahead of her. Then she caught the eye of the neurosurgeon.

"Hey Bill, looks like a tough one," Lily said.

"The young ones always are."

"Good luck then."

*   *   *

Lily thought about the young girl's face as she headed back to her office. It had been foreign, yet familiar. She hoped that surgery would go smoothly for her and thought about checking up on her in the morning. But she would never get the chance. Her assistant had written her down on the calendar as off service, and off to another meeting. She was leaving tomorrow morning, and headed somewhere. Lily's assistant and her colleagues had come to expect her frequent disappearances due to unexpected consultations. She entered her office and packed her briefcase as she finalized her plans in her mind for her trip to New York. The hospital had been just one quick detour on her way to her assignment.

Chapter 21

IN TRANSIT

Lily Robinson sat in the first-class compartment on the train to New York City. Splashes of color flew by the window as the New England hardwoods transformed from green to gold, orange, red and magenta. The leaves were barely hanging on by their stems just waiting for the abscission layer to fully form in response to the sun's diminishing light, and for the final cut to send them in their multicolored splendor, to their final resting place. The train allowed the perspective of seeing the natural world during travel. Lily could see gleaming interludes of patchy marsh dotted with multicolored grass and stacks of tall thin dead trees across the terrain. Reflected above was an exquisite blue sky with floating filigree clouds.

Lily's target was a chain-smoker of European origin. He had a two-pack-a-day habit and had tried for years to give up the vice that filled his lungs, but this was a minor addiction compared to the heroin his body once craved and his mind consumed. Opiate addiction knows no bounds. The poor, the middle class, the educated, the talented could all be addicted to heroin. Heroin addicts attested to the fact that once this drug flows through your veins, there is no going back. The drug changes your brain; the addict enters a state of such serenity that reality is too harsh an alternative. There are many opportunities and ways for withdrawal, but none had been very effective for Lily's target; he had tried everything. Yet he would try once again.

As the train slowed through the crossing, the light blinked red to red, like two eyes winking in turn. Lily had managed to occupy the seat next to the chain-smoker. He sat next to the window facing forward with his briefcase at his feet. Lily occupied the aisle seat and had her briefcase, identical to his, at her left side.

Lily knew that her mark was a known assassin, an equal by job description, but one whose methods were considerably cruder than hers. His elimination would remove a potential threat to a newly emerging world leader. He had been hired by the radical alternative party to kill a budding statesman. Overt violence was acceptable since this was a message to others not to oppose the current regime. There had already been one successful attempt to remove another popular politician from reaching her goal of president of a foreign nation, and world democratic leaders did not wish to see this repeated. The assassin's current destination was a foreign consulate near Madison Avenue in busy midtown Manhattan.

"Hi," Lily said to the assassin. "Beautiful day for a train ride. Blue sky and lovely coastal views."

He eyed her suspiciously.

"Yes, I suppose so," he said with a slight accent.

"Where are you off to today? I've got to meet my boss downtown to go over a brief," said Lily.

"Oh, you must be a lawyer," he said. "Um, I work on Wall Street."

The lies were free-flowing, and as he held her green eyes with nods of understanding, her eyes reflected only the deception she saw in his gaze. When the conversation dwindled, he picked up his newspaper and Lily discreetly gathered his briefcase and her handbag and walked to the restroom as the train rocked gently. Once safely inside the compartment, she unlatched the case and carefully replaced several items she found within with those of her own creation. The train rocked and jolted her, but she regained her balance and continued the exchange.

When she returned to her seat she found the assassin still reading the *Wall Street Journal*, likely to give credence to his cover of a Wall Street financier. She placed his briefcase next to hers. Lily opened her handbag and removed a small container filled with chilled grapes.

"Would you like some of these?" Lily said, offering them to her traveling companion. They were large, red, crisp globes bursting with fluid and flavor.

"Thank you," he said, as he liberally grabbed a handful.

Lily looked past the window at men fishing off the piers into sunlit waters, where phragmites reached toward the sky with feathery tops. Lily thought about her early scientific years working in the laboratory of a renowned channel biophysicist and their treks to South America. After she had completed her graduate work, she secured a position as a fellow in the biophysicist's laboratory to study the physiology of many toxins. She had traveled many times while working in his lab to the Colombian rain forests with their lush green foliage teeming with life forms. They were such a contrast to the stark New England coast. The brush had been impenetrable and needed to be cut with a machete as they searched through the thick jungle for "yellow gold"—just the kind of golden treasure Lily would come to appreciate.

"Will you please excuse me," the assassin said to Lily as he moved past her seat and headed to the restroom with his case in hand.

The craving was strong. It was an illness and nothing less. His head ached and he was perspiring more than he should in the cool of the compartment. He knew that in his business, focus and precision were the hallmarks of success. Above all, he would need a clear head and steady hands for his next encounter. He would prove to all of them that he still had what it took. He opened his case and removed two foil pouches. He opened each pouch, removed the clear patches, and applied them to his skin. He reasoned that at this moment more than one might quell his craving. Then he placed a small orange hexagonal pill under his tongue and waited for it to dissolve.

When he returned to his seat, the vivacious woman with the bright green eyes and charming smile was gone. He was disappointed. Unseen, Lily had departed at the Stamford stop with many riders and would take her car service to New York City. She wasn't planning on traveling all the way to Manhattan by train. She saw her car service parked by the curb.

"I'm here, Carl," she said, waving her hand.

She swung her black and white cashmere wrap with the bold raspberry stripe around her shoulders as the car door opened. Her left shoe, black suede embossed with silver, caught in the door frame as she slipped into the car. She straightened her shoe and settled into the back seat for the rest of the trip.

When the train reached Penn Station the conductor entered the car and found the assassin hunched in his seat. The passenger appeared to have dozed off so the conductor gently touched his shoulder to rouse him so he would not miss his exit. But the assassin was not sleeping and in essence, he had already made his exit. It had been a quiet and relatively quick death.

The police were called, as were the EMTs, but it was too late. They interviewed the remaining passengers, but none could recall if the man had experienced convulsions or any other symptoms while sitting in his seat. No one had heard him if he cried out over the sound of the tilted train wheels on the tracks. The assassin had slowly slipped into paralysis; first his breathing impaired, then his heart. After he was removed from the train he was taken to the Office of the Chief Medical Examiner in New York City on First Avenue. It was this office that established the first toxicology laboratory in the United States in 1918.

The assassin was autopsied. Nothing specific was found other than nicotine patches on his body and old track marks on his arms from substance abuse. The medical examiner would find swelling of the axons at the node of Ranvier when he subsequently peered through his microscope at bits of brain tissue.

Lily Robinson recalled hearing much later on the nightly news that a middle-aged man had been found dead on the high-speed express train to New York City. At this time, the cause of death had not yet been determined and Lily smiled when she heard that the toxicology results were still pending.

*   *   *

When Lily reached her contact in New York City she gave him her report.

"How'd it go?"

"It's done," she said dispassionately. "They're not going to find anything, other than some nicotine patches. He was trying to give up smoking. It must have been enough of a struggle to keep away from heroin. He was taking Suboxone for that anyway. It's an opioid substitute. But I knew he was using the nicotine patch for the smoking habit so I just got the same drug delivery patches and embedded my homemade brew."

"A homemade brew for the patch? What toxin did you use?"

"Batrachotoxin.

"Nice. Where'd you learn about that stuff?"

"Colombia. The Emberá Chocó Indians practiced the custom of tipping darts with frog toxins for use with their blowguns in their hunt for large game. The frogs are collected and held in a basket until the Chocó are ready to use the poison. One frog is removed from the basket and the tip of the dart is rubbed multiple times along the back of the frog where the poison is secreted from glands within the skin. They let the poison dry on the dart before it is inserted into the blowgun."

"So do you have some poison frogs in your lab, Lily?" he said sarcastically.

"Let's just say that I have collected enough *Phyllobates terribilis* to have a little stockpile."

"Phyllo what?"

"*Phyllobates terribilis*. It's a small frog, brightly colored, umm, golden yellow. It's about twenty-fold more toxic than its relatives and if poison were to enter through a small wound during handling, the results could be fatal to man, or woman. Even you," she added. "These dendrobatid frogs are the origin of the batrachotoxins (BTXs)—batrachotoxin, homobatrachotoxin, and batrachotoxin-A. Believe me, their tox lab is not going to find it. In fact, they wouldn't even know to look for it."

CHAPTER 22

BOSTON SUBURB

It was almost a month before Rose came out of the coma. Adrienne was able to come over from France to be with her adopted daughter. She sat by her side and then one day Rose opened her eyes and could see the face of Adrienne, but not clearly.

"Mother," she said weakly. "Are you here with me? Where am I?"

Adrienne called the nurses who in turn called the doctor. Everyone was so excited to see that Rose had regained consciousness. The doctor gave her a physical exam to check her eye movements and see how much memory or function had been lost.

"Rose can you follow my finger? That's right," he said as he moved his finger right, then left, up then down. "Can you tell me your name?"

"It's Rose. Where am I? What happened?"

"Rose do you remember you were out on your horse, you and the girls were riding the high ridge trail," Adrienne said. "That silly chestnut mare spooked at a deer and that started the whole chain reaction. You hit your head and needed surgery. Your teammate broke her arm, but she's all right."

"Sort of," Rose said. "How long have I been here?" she said, looking around at all the monitors, IV lines and nurses.

"Quite a while, Rose," said the doctor. I'm going to have to take you to another floor for a few tests. But I'm amazed at how conversant you are after just having come out of the coma. You took a nasty fall and tore a blood vessel that supplies the brain. I had to go into your head, drain out the blood that had accumulated on your brain and repair the vessel. We also had to fix that depression in your skull. Your brain sustained a bad bruise and you may have some repercussions from that as well. It might last for several months. You know, we weren't quite sure when you would wake up. Clearly you're from sturdy stock." He shot a glance over to Adrienne.

*   *   *

It would take Rose several months to recover fully. Adrienne stayed with her and they were able to celebrate Christmas together. This was a bittersweet time for them.

"Mother, hurry, open the gift I got you," Rose said bursting with excitement. Adrienne slowly peeled the wrapping paper off the little box. She carefully removed the top of the box and inside was a beautiful snow globe. The scene was clearly New England, with a family standing in the snow, about to get into a horse drawn sleigh.

"Now that's not something we would have seen in Colombia, is it?" said Rose. "I want you to think of us when you see the globe. Like we're a real family and we live in New England."

Adrienne could see the anguish on Rose's face. They had never been a "real" family, had they, just one made up of several bits and pieces.

"Thank you, sweetie. I'll cherish it forever. Now I have a little something for you. Actually I have two things for you. One you can have now, and the other needs to go somewhere for safe keeping. Promise me you will not open this letter until, well, until I'm no longer around."

This made Rose cry. "Mother please don't talk like that." She put the letter aside.

Adrienne gave Rose a tiny velvet ring box. It wasn't wrapped, but it was in a small gift bag filled with rose-colored sheets of transparent paper. It was elegant.

Rose opened the box and inside she saw a beautiful gold ring with a red colored gemstone. It was exquisite.

"Mother, it's beautiful. What is it? What kind of stone is it?"

"Rose, it's a very rare red diamond. It's been in my family for a very long time. Passed down from mother to daughter over many, many years." Adrienne had hoped one day to give the ring to Bella.

"Look inside the gold band. Do you see the inscription? It's a tiny grape cluster engraved on the band with the word *amour* which means love in French. We have a family legend that my great, great, oh I don't really know how many greats, grandfather had a small diamond mine in Africa as a young man. He happened to find a cluster of rare red diamonds and was able to sell enough to make money to buy the land we now have in Reims. Rose, we're talking somewhere about the 1700s. The ring is a real gem and very old. A legend, in fact. I want you to have it, as my daughter. You must treasure it always."

Rose started to cry again. "I know you probably wanted to give it to Bella. I supposed there is no news, is there?"

There was no news on Bella. Adrienne said that her uncle had contacted her while she was living in France to say that Bella had completely disappeared and it was most likely that the Russian had taken her. He couldn't confirm that she was alive, but then he couldn't confirm that she was dead either. Even so, he still had his contacts searching for her.

At this news, both Rose and Adrienne hugged each other and cried some more. Adrienne missed her daughters, and Rose missed her sister and her mother.

At the end of January, Adrienne considered leaving Massachusetts. In her heart she wanted to stay with her daughter, but with her own mother's health getting worse, she felt that she needed to return to France. Adrienne considered that Rose would be going to college in a year anyway, and after that, hopefully stay in America. It's where she came from after all. One day Rose would open the letter from Adrienne. Adrienne hoped that with time and reflection Rose would understand, and perhaps she would forgive Adrienne.

"Rose, it's time. I have to go back to France," she told Rose one cold bleak afternoon. With tears in her eyes, she continued, "You have grown into such a beautiful young woman. I'm so proud of you. Listen, we need to start thinking about colleges. I wish for you to have a career, something I never had. I love you and I will see you soon." Adrienne kissed Rose again and gathered her in her arms so tightly that Rose just let her body go limp.

CHAPTER 23

BOSTON

Lily had forgotten about the visit. It was clearly marked on her calendar USG, but she had been working on a lecture and didn't hear the quiet knock on the door.

"Dr. Lily, um you have a visitor," said her assistant as she gently opened the door. She looked around the room and saw Lily sitting at her desk staring at her computer filled with the image of some molecular structure. The desk was covered with papers and several books stacked on one end.

"Oh, okay. Show him in," said Lily.

Lily had a small office with a double paned window that overlooked several mature trees stuck in concrete, and as well a great view of the cityscape. The office was painted in a soft green shade that provided harmony and balance for her stressful life. Pictures of poisonous plants, and various academic achievements dotted the walls.

After a short pause, a man with brown hair and hazel colored eyes entered the room, closing the door behind him. His casual appearance, complete with a few days of beard growth and a collared shirt with no tie, appeared to be the Agency's standard uniform.

"Oh, I wasn't expecting you." She looked at her calendar and then added, "Sorry, I see it here. What can I do for you?"

"Lily," said the agent, "I want to review the Mt. Vernon Affaire. Can we go over the details, please? Our Chief is all over it."

"And why is that?" she said.

"We have another election coming up and we may have a few loose ends to tie up, if you know what I mean," he answered. His eyes glanced at the extensive book collection behind Lily's desk and the small jars of plant parts sitting neatly on the shelves.

"Sure, what do you want to know?" said Lily Robinson. "It's all in the record. We've been over this before."

"I know, but I want to hear it directly from you. Tell me everything from the beginning."

"Okay," she said slowly, "I was staying at the Willow Hotel on Pennsylvania Avenue about two blocks east of the White House. I remember that the delegates from a Western African nation, I can't remember which one, were also staying there. I remember them because each one was moving about in a flowing orange Bubu and black cap and they reminded me of a rosary pea. The delegates and their security team occupied most of the 8th floor and blocked off many of the entrances and exits and made it difficult for me to get around."

Lily loved Washington, DC. It was the jewel of the nation, gleaming white buildings on such a grand scale. To her, the nation's capital evoked images of foreign intrigue and deception, and Lily imagined what it would have been like to work during the years of the Cold War.

"Did you meet with your regular contact or someone else?" the agent asked.

"No, not the regular suspects," she said with a laugh. "Someone else. The meeting took place in a small boardroom in the hotel. I remember there was an oval wooden table with mismatched chairs in the center of the room. One of the prints on the wall depicted a battle between two sailing ships. It's funny how you remember certain things, isn't it?" she said to the agent. "It was "The Capture of HM brig-sloop Reindeer by the American ship sloop Wasp on the 28th of June in 1814" by Derek G.M. Gardner, RLMA."

"I am impressed that you would remember that detail."

Lily remembered it because today's battles were rarely fought on the high seas; they were more likely to be fought in the boardroom. In conflict, something was always captured, whether it was strategies, confidences, property, or the control of another person's will. What had Lily surrendered to become an assassin? There was a time when Lily was just a doctor and educator who specialized in toxicology. On many occasions she had been asked about the best way, the least detectable way, to poison someone. Several years ago, she read the obituary of a medical examiner colleague. The newspaper told a story of a wife dying of natural causes and a husband who died suddenly from shock and sympathy at his loss. Lily of course knew better. The medical examiner had been an associate who had pressed Lily for details on natural toxins and the best recipes for murder. He had committed suicide, but only after killing his wife. At some point, governmental agencies too learned of Lily Robinson's art and pressed her into service.

"What happened on the day of the murder at Mount Vernon?" he asked her.

She hated that word—*murder*.

"Yes, as you said, the assassination was to take place on the Mount Vernon Estate in Virginia. I wore my black silk and chenille suit and black patent leather booties with four-inch heels. That suit had bow-like pockets and three central shiny black buttons," she added.

The agent made a face.

"It was raining," Lily continued, ignoring his scrunched up nose. "The car service dropped me off at the entrance to Mount Vernon. I had my umbrella with me and I remember the driveway was pebbled. The worst thing for high heels—pebbles, and of course brick, which covers Boston!"

Lily's heels had stuck in the pebbles and impeded her progress toward the house. When she finally got to the doorway, after slowly walking up the driveway, she moved through the house directly to the small reception of people on the piazza which overlooked a rolling lawn and the glorious Potomac River. It wasn't a particularly cold night, so Lily had stayed on the piazza to breathe in the fresh country air. After some time she reentered the house and mingled among the guests.

"Most of the guests were in the house at that point. I saw my target across the room; he was a tall man of medium build wearing a grey custom-made suit and a salmon and blue striped tie. He had short blonde hair and striking blue eyes."

"Lily you always remember the clothes and the eyes," laughed the agent.

"I know."

Lily Robinson worked her way across the room to introduce herself and remind him of their seating arrangements for dinner. She took her place next to the foreigner. Lily had been told of his deceptions, of buying and trading sensitive secrets of her government and perhaps even having ties with the Russians. It was thought that a simple, quiet elimination would be best.

"We started eating dinner. We had a salad of goat cheese, field greens, and champagne vinaigrette. I first engaged in conversation with the wife of a dignitary, in order to distract him. I moved my left hand under the table and kept my eyes on his face. I saw him hesitate, just for a second before he placed a forkful of salad into his mouth and for an instant, I thought I saw the diplomat's face register momentary irritation. Oh, the toxin was very fast acting. By the time the entrée was finished, the foreigner was not feeling well and complained of a severe stomach upset."

"Wait a minute," said the agent. "I missed the part where you gave him the poison. I assume you put it in his salad. Right?"

"I'll get there," said Lily, almost as if she were teasing him.

"As I said, soon after the entrée he felt sick. He called for his car and left the Mount Vernon Estate. I stayed until the end of the affair and returned to the Willow Hotel only to find that the entrance hall was blocked by the African security team. Apparently, the rain had found its way through an open window and flooded the end of the hall so I had to find another way around to room 303."

"I know he was found dead several days later, right?"

"Yes, it was reported from Embassy Row that the diplomat had died. Seemingly he had a preceding illness that lasted three days. They did take him to the ED the day after the dinner where he complained of severe gastrointestinal symptoms initially thought to be flu or food poisoning. They tried giving him fluids, but his symptoms worsened. He also had high fevers, bloody diarrhea, and by the time he got to intensive care, he was already on his way to massive organ failure."

"So it was the salad right?"

"No, it wasn't the salad. I thought about using an umbrella tip filled with ricin, but decided on the more potent toxin abrin which was hidden in the heel of one of my shoes. By releasing a lever in the shoe, I exposed a hidden injectable device. The small gauge of the needle allowed me to easily stab the tip into the leg of the diplomat, producing a sensation no more annoying than an insect bite," Lily said with some satisfaction.

"That's quite a story."

"Yes, well we keep adding stories, don't we? You folks know I have a real job, right? When do you think this is going to end? Is it ever going to end?" It was as if she were pleading with him. She was surprised that she was stirring a mild protest, but the never-say-anything culture that the Agency operated under annoyed her.

"It's not my call Lily. Thanks for your time. Oh, and Pixie Dust says 'hello'," he said as he left the room.

The door closed behind him. Lily sat pensively at her desk. *Exactly whose call was it then?* she thought, and pitched her pen across the room.

CHAPTER 24

BOSTON SUBURB

In the spring of her junior year, Rose started thinking about college and what she wanted to study. She had always liked science and thought she might major in science in college. So, she scoured the Internet looking at top colleges for biology. She had grown to love Boston and was hoping to stay within the city limits. Her great-uncle had agreed to pay the tuition. Adrienne had asked him to help her. After all, Rose was their family.

"Hey, Rose, are you going to career night on Thursday?" asked one of her friends. "They're having some people come from the local area to speak about what they do. It's a Q and A too. Should be fun."

"Hey thanks. I hadn't thought about going, but now that you mention it I think I will go. It's in the auditorium, right?"

"Yeah. Check out the flyer on the bulletin board. Let's see, here it is. Okay, we are a school for girls, so I guess it makes sense that all the invited speakers are women. Umm, we have a CEO from a pharmaceutical company, that's Ellen Petrakis, then we have a woman who runs a large early educational center for pre-kindergarteners, Barbara Smith, and then a doctor/toxicologist Lily Robinson from one of the Boston academic medical centers. Hey, isn't that the hospital that you had your brain surgery at?" she said pointing to the name on the paper before she finished reading the entire panel.

Rose looked at the flyer. "Yeah, that's the one. I wish the neurosurgeon was coming. He was awesome."

Rose got a copy of the flyer and Googled all the women who had been named on the program. She was most interested in the CEO from the pharmaceutical company and the doctor. They were women in science and she pretty much felt that was where she should be too. She would take her mother's advice and start to think about a career.

When Thursday came, Rose dressed in a pair of faded jeans and a multicolored tee. She was pretty much ensconced in American culture by now. When she thought back to the isolated lives that Bella and she were living in Colombia, she cringed. How was that possible? It was like they were living in another century. Massachusetts had been good for her mind, and her spirit. She only wished she could have shared all of this with Bella. Bella above all, wanted out from the coffee plantation. She was stifled there, choked and struggling to survive. Her abrupt abduction was something that haunted Rose. It troubled her dreams and left her in sweat-soaked sheets in the middle of the night. Some nights breathing too was difficult and most days she thought of Bella when she dressed. There it was just below her right hip. The rose tattoo. Bella had wanted the spider and that was not what their poor mother had bargained for. It had started as an extraordinary day, and turned into a day that Adrienne and Rose would never forget for the rest of their lives.

After she dressed and put on just a touch of lipstick, Rose slipped the ring Adrienne had given her at Christmas on to her right middle finger. It was too big to fit on her ring finger. She wore it there to make sure it was very secure and that there would be no chance it would fall off. She knew it was very valuable. It really was a symbol, not just of love, but of family strength. The Moreaus were strong and she was strong.

Rose reached the auditorium after the event had already started. She ended up sitting in the back of the room but could hear everyone quite clearly even though she couldn't see the speakers all that well.

The stage was set up with a long table. There were four chairs behind the counter for the four women speakers. Each one had a nameplate set in front of them identifying who they were. There were also glasses of water set on the table top. When Rose entered the auditorium the first speaker had already begun. She was an impressive woman with dark hair and a full figure. Barbara Smith had created a very successful preschool program in Massachusetts that was about to launch nationwide. She was there to speak to the girls about devoting their lives to the education of the nation's children.

"What we need, ladies, are dedicated, effective teachers. Education is the backbone of our culture. An educated population is what makes this country strong. And education needs to start at a very early age. Parents who read to their children when they are very young, turn those children into power readers and eventually adults with curiosity and commitment."

Rose thought she was impressive. The idea of becoming a teacher was appealing to her. Maybe a science teacher would be the right choice for a profession.

The next speaker was the CEO of the pharmaceutical company. Ellen Petrakis was a powerhouse. She was a sturdy woman with short blond hair carefully quaffed so no strand was out of place. She was inspirational and told the girls that their goal in life should be to shatter the glass ceiling. Women were capable, smart and should not accept the notion that they couldn't be executives or leaders of any company.

"Ladies," Ellen said, "you are the future. Science and technology are defining our country today and you will be a part of that. You have the minds to create new cures for cancer, drugs to eliminate heart disease, and therapies for a myriad of neurological diseases. Women are drivers; they have the vision and the strength to move organizations forward."

Rose sat in her seat thinking about a career in the pharmaceutical field. It sounded awfully exciting.

The third speaker was the doctor from the hospital where Rose had had her brain surgery. It was Dr. Lily Robinson. She had dark brown hair. Rose could not see her eyes from this far away, but she had Googled her pictures and knew she had green eyes, just like hers.

"I'm here to talk to you about pathology and about toxicology," Lily Robinson said. "Pathologists are physicians who diagnose diseases from blood and other body fluids, as well as from cells and tissues. The most extraordinary thing about pathology is that there is something in it for everyone. We examine tissue biopsies, perform autopsies, do molecular studies, run hematology laboratories, and investigate culture plates made from your sore throats and your urinary tract infections." The girls in the audience giggled. "We handle the blood banks, transfuse red cells, exchange parasite-infected red cells for healthy ones, and exchange bad plasma for good plasma during apheresis procedures. We are also forensic medical examiners and in the legal setting determine the manner of death and the cause of death. Was it a natural death, or was it a suicide, homicide or accidental death? Was it a bullet through the heart or was it an illicit drug such as cocaine that stopped the pump in mid beat? Or could it perhaps be some undetectable poison that blocks the sodium channels in the heart muscle so it can no longer take a beat. I'm a toxicologist. I have great admiration for all poisons and toxins. Poisons in nature are part of the natural defense of an organism, whether it is a plant or an animal. Presumably these toxins act as protection against predators in the case of an animal, or from an herbivore, in the case of a plant and in some cases "chemical defenses" might even be directed against microorganisms."

The audience was mesmerized. No one said a word. They sat enthralled and listened as Dr. Robinson told of her work in both the hospital and in the field. So many hands shot up for questions, that the last speaker, a judge from the local circuit court, was robbed of much of the time she had been allotted. The career night overshot the programmed two hours, but every girl left that auditorium with the inspiration instilled in them by four successful women. Each girl was motivated to go into science or education, law or medicine. It had been a winning evening by any measure. Rose was stirred too, but she was most inspired by the formidable toxicologist. The doctor would become the role model for Rose's future career choice.

Lily Robinson left the auditorium and caught up with Ellen Petrakis on her way out.

"Hi Ellen, I haven't seen you for a while. How are things going?"

"Great, Lily. We have a lot of new projects. You know, it would be super if you could come by the place. We'd love to have one of your talks on forensic toxicology. We're always interested in some new toxin since many ultimately lead to new drug development. Sometimes I have to remind the younger folks that we wouldn't have digitalis for heart medicine if it wasn't for someone recognizing its properties from the beautiful foxglove plant. For that matter, I guess we wouldn't have penicillin if our Scottish colleague Alexander Fleming hadn't discovered a promising mold," she said with a laugh.

"I'd love to," said Lily. "I'll ask my admin to set something up. The only thing I love more is one of these high school career nights. It's so much fun telling young people about the things we do. It's what makes you want to get up in the morning. Doesn't it, Ellen?"

"You bet. Good night, Lily." She got into her electric sport car and slammed the door shut.

Lily got into her red car filled full of gas and drove all the way back to her cottage. It wasn't as long a drive to the coast at night as it was during a Friday afternoon. It was a peaceful drive, complete with soft music and free flowing thought, and when she pulled up to the house, there was one welcoming light on in the window. She opened the door with her special key, the one with the red hearts on the bow. It was because she loved the cottage so that she had indulged in a designer key. She threw the keys on the table and went upstairs to take in the nighttime view. The lights from the other houses across the bay shone on the water and left reflections of green, white, yellow and red. It was quiet. She went out onto the deck and stared up at the sky. The sky was clear and she could see the stars overhead, with just a whisper of the Milky Way. There were so many stars that night. There was the Big Dipper and Orion's Belt; she saw some planets and her favorite star cluster, the Pleiades. The seven sisters were located in the constellation Taurus. Sisters who clung tightly together, united as a shining beacon to guide the fairer sex. Lily looked up at the stars thinking how they were billions of years old. They were here before her and would be here after her. She held on to the railing surrounding the deck. She knew she had another assignment coming up in the Middle East and it would be a difficult one. The timing was a little uncertain.

Lily had always requested some time between assignments so that she could mentally prepare, meaning ease her conscience. Her admin had already scheduled her to be out of the hospital for the next few weeks, away for another "consultation." Lily just had one stop to make before she reached her final destination. Everything had already been prepared. She couldn't help but think of the irony of the evening. It was this night that she had spoken to a group of high school students about her work. She had tried to inspire them about preserving life, the art of medicine, the natural world, pathology, and toxins. Yet she left out a large part of what she did; the part where she assassinates the undesirable, the dangerous, and the threatening. What would the girls have thought about that? Would they be so inspired if they knew that Lily used her knowledge of poisons to rid the world of those determined to be unfit to live by her government and its allies? It was a question she frequently asked herself in one form or another. *How long will I keep doing this? Am I really a patriot or just filling a void, quelling my anger over a past I cannot understand and explain?*

She went back downstairs to her bedroom and took off her skirt and pullover top. Lily kicked off her designer heels, and yet stacked them neatly in the closet. She slipped into a silk gown, and went into the bathroom to wash her face and brush her teeth. The hot water filled the sink and she took a white washcloth with a dragonfly embroidered on the margin, and washed the makeup off her face. As she dried her cheeks she looked closely into the mirror and stared at her own eyes. She saw a little puffiness under the lower lids and dabbed on a rich anti-aging cream to fill the erosions etched by the claw of time around the corners of her eyes and mouth. Lily Robinson climbed into bed and pulled the covers up around her.

I'm afraid to close my eyes. I'm afraid to dream. I can never get through my dreams without waking up in a panic, she thought. To soothe herself, she thought about him, the dark-haired man with the blue-green eyes who had saved her life. They had seen each other again after Chicago. There was something about him that she couldn't quite put her finger on. The fact was that she didn't know much about him at all. He never talked about anything personal when they were together, but rather just stuck to the assignment. But she knew there was some connection there. Lily could feel it. She was certain of this. She closed her eyes, and hoped for sleep to come swiftly. She hoped not to dream. She wanted to wake up in the morning as if the night never existed. She wanted to block every emotion, every possible feeling inside her, and go through each day as if it were the only day. There would be no past, no history. There would be no pain, no sorrow and no guilt. The night air was still apart from the sound of water gently rippling onto the shore. The mist quietly moved in over the sea, and the faint sound of the foghorn could be heard warning sailors and vessels, and Lily Robinson, of the rocky dangers ahead.

Chapter 25

THE MIDDLE EAST AND INDIA

The Middle East was a battleground of religious differences and cultural divergences. The dark-cloaked assassin closed his left eye and fixed his right onto the telescopic sight mounted on his Dragunov SVD. His target moved into view. The beta-blocker taken an hour ago had steadied his heart rate and allowed him to focus on the American General. As his left ventricle squeezed out its contents and his heart muscle rested and filled with blood, he gently pulled the trigger just between beats. The General was hit in his left shoulder. Incredibly, the sniper had missed the heart. This failure was sure to be severely punished and the assassin quickly planned his escape. Only now he wished he had not taken a drug that slowed his heart rate. He wanted to run but his heart could not keep up the pace.

He found an opportunity to flee to foreign soil with a band of farmers transporting the fruits of their labor down the same road the assassin was traveling. After a persuasive argument with his gun firmly in his hand, the farmers agreed to smuggle him across the border buried beneath mounds of green flowering herbs. On reaching the other side, he slipped out unnoticed from the truck bay into the night. He rubbed his tired eyes and tried successive blinks to clear his vision. Over the last year he had noticed that his vision had become progressively clouded—his eyes frequently blurry, colors seeming to fade into the background. He stared into the distant lights and saw they were surrounded by halos. Yet, he had been confident that his skill, honed through years of martial training, could overcome any visual deficits. He had thought he had had more time, but clearly he had miscalculated. The proof was in the General's left shoulder. He would have to execute his plan now and not later, and it would take him several days before he reached his destination.

While counter-intelligence officials were interested in the sniper who had nearly killed the General, their critical target was the assassin's inspiration, one whose anti-western dream led terrorists across the deserts to rise up against a free and democratic world. Though his vision of tyranny and oppression was clear, the terrorist leader's eyesight was as clouded as the assassin's. Unaware of each other's final destination, both villains were pursued through several Middle Eastern countries until they reached India. There the trail became entangled as overlapping paths were buried by the virtual footprints of the teeming masses bound in brightly colored patterns of silk. American and British officials were not the only ones out hunting. Military police and highly-placed terrorist agents from the assassin's own country were also on the Indian subcontinent. All the pieces but one were on the chessboard. Pawns, rooks, knights and bishops lined up ready to defend good or evil. Then Lily Robinson positioned herself in the middle of the game. She would have the next move.

Lily Robinson had been at her seaside cottage when she got "the ask" to travel to the Middle East. She had been immersed in the sunset hovering over the water. Rose-colored clouds filled the sky, and robin's egg blue painted the background. It was glorious. She closed her eyes to smell the colors and feel the air as her feet dug deep into the sand. Then she heard her name called. "Dr. Robinson." She was jostled back into the present. Her feet were no longer standing on the seaside sands of her home, but instead were sinking into the vast desert sands of a foreign world. This was her one stop before she made her way to India to resume her role in fighting evil. She looked up. The man across from her held in his hand a small vial with the toxin of her choice. The Middle East would yield an assassin in the shape of a question mark. Segmented death, no longer hidden deep in dark crevices, now artificially packaged, would provide the means for stinging the terrorists right in the heart of their operation.

Lily Robinson made her way to the American Hospital in Mumbai where she was incorporated into the strategic plan by sympathetic allies. The surgery would be in a week. She would be sent from the traditional hospital to an associated but smaller, inconspicuous facility where less complex surgeries were performed. These were mostly cosmetic and eye surgeries carried out in secrecy with subsequent recoveries out of the critical public view. She would play the role of a doctor, not one who followed the Hippocratic Oath, but rather one who followed a greater oath, one of universal freedom for all, and at any cost.

On the appointed day, the ten operating rooms were busy with many small cases. The skilled surgeon in Operating Room One exchanged glances with the anesthesiologist and made sure the anesthesia was adequate before lowering his knife. He carefully slit the cornea, suctioned out the murky contents of the lens and replaced it with the implant. Although protocol called for operating on a single eye at a time, the assassin had convinced the surgeon, using the persuasive measures he knew best, to perform surgery in both eyes during a single operation. In addition, he had given strict instructions to shave the bump on the nose to reduce its ethnic appearance. He hoped that with his altered facade and improved eyesight he might escape his certain death and blend into an alternate culture. The surgeon continued with a small incision across the columella. After the skin was peeled off the underlying boney structures, he gently reshaped the bone and cartilage so the bump in his nose had all but disappeared. The doctor was certain his patient would be satisfied.

When the surgeon finished operating in OR One, he removed his gloves and gown, rescrubbed and entered the next surgical suite. He took a deep breath to try to quiet his growing anxiety and mentally prepare himself for his next challenge. His previous patient had been merely physically intimidating while his present patient was far more sinister. The surgeon understood that he would be operating on someone of extreme political importance. There had been many bodyguards, explicit threats, and large cash donations to the hospital. The surgeon knew his failure would mean severe consequences either for him or for his family. He surveyed the operating room as he re-gloved and prepared to repeat the eye surgery he had just performed on the assassin. Was it merely coincidence there would be two patients from the Middle East with requests for surgery that were not the standard of care? *Who asks for both eyes done at the same time for cataract surgery?* There would be no discussion here so he kept his thoughts to himself. His hand shook as he took up the blade, but the green eyes above the mask of the assistant surgeon across the table reassured him. He began the surgery, one eye and then the next, and each time, Lily Robinson handed the intraocular lens implant to the senior surgeon.

The assassin woke up in the hotel-like recovery room with only voices to fix on for clues to his whereabouts. The gauze and swelling concealed the outside world and left him vulnerable. As he became more aware of his surroundings, he sensed that the room must be filled with perhaps one or more patients cloaked beneath layers of white cloth to protect identities, and soft tissue. In the bed next to him was an unfortunate whose recovery was not progressing as anticipated. Blinded, the assassin could not know that it was his fuel for inspiration, his terrorist leader, who struggled in distress. He could only hear the excited conversation of the nurses and feel the air move as they brushed past him.

"Doctor, he has become very hypertensive, his heart rate is now 120 and he's having difficulty breathing," said the nurse with trepidation.

"Get me an intubation kit now," shouted the surgeon after one quick look at his patient. The assassin recognized his surgeon's voice. He tried to fight his drug-induced hangover so he could better hear what was happening. The surgeon tilted the distressed patient's head back into the "sniffing" position, opened the patient's mouth and visualized the vocal cords. With the laryngoscope in place, he gently inserted the endotracheal tube past the vocal cords and into the trachea. He could now hook the patient up to the ventilator that would breathe for him. The assassin sensed the dread of what was to come, shuddered, and was thankful that he would not suffer the same fate.

After several hours in recovery, slipping in and out of consciousness where he imagined himself looking down the barrel of a rifle, eyes crystal clear, the assassin was released presumably into the care of a hospital transport volunteer. He was led to the car and eased into the back seat under the gentle hand of his guide. One and a half hours outside of the city, the car pulled over to the side of the road. The driver pulled out his PSM pistol, turned around in his seat and shot the assassin directly into the temple. The bullet entered the temporal lobe leaving a small entrance wound and extinguished both the rational and non-rational soul of the sniper. The driver opened the back door of the car, pulled out the body and brusquely dumped the remains into the roadside debris, a simple blend of flotsam and jetsam in an ocean devoid of humanity. He was satisfied that he had fulfilled his oath to rid his ranks of incompetence and would now return to the homeland that he and the murdered assassin shared. He could revel in the glory of having eliminated the one who failed at killing the American General.

Lily Robinson flew from Mumbai to London. She would catch the flight to Washington the following day, but first she was to be debriefed by British authorities. She slipped into her black silk suit and donned her black snake and suede platform shoes. She bent down to fasten the ankle straps and caught a glimpse of her reflection in the mirror. Her aqua breeze top, ruched in waves, crashed over the simple black skirt, the stark contrast reminiscent of a tumultuous life threatening to wash away a dark past. Was it too hard to imagine how her life had been before her child had been killed while Lily was studying abroad in Colombia? The body was never recovered. There was no sense of closure, no understanding of the circumstances, and no forgiveness. Lily Robinson had been an easy recruit by the government authorities who took advantage of a mother's sorrow and a determination for self-punishment. The sting went deep, right into the heart, and just between beats.

She closed her eyes, took a deep breath and immediately filled her mind with facts. With her brain gorged with data there was no room for any emotion. She was composed and went downstairs to meet with her contact.

"Lily," the British intelligence officer began, "we confirmed that the sniper who was found dead by the roadside was the one that had attempted to kill one of your Generals. That was a lucky miss. Turns out this would-be assassin was taken out by one of his own, a clear act of eliminating ineptitude. More importantly," he continued, "you got the big guy; one of the highest-ranking leaders in the terrorist war with a face in the "deck of cards." Nice job. I heard his death was pretty swift. Died in the recovery room of that hospital/hotel near the American Hospital in Mumbai. The hospital administrator said it was highly unusual to die from complications from relatively minor surgery like cataract surgery. How did you manage that one?"

"I really prepared this assassination well in advance," Lily said unemotionally. "Through the cooperation of several governments, not just yours and mine, I was able to secure a position as an assistant surgeon for the day surgery unit. The thing was, I assisted at several surgeries that day to reduce suspicion that would surround a single patient, particularly one that didn't survive. We all knew this guy had registered at the surgical facility under a false name and tried to make it out like he was a well-to-do businessman. Even the operating surgeon understood he was someone of extreme political importance. It's usual in cataract surgery to operate on one eye at a time. That's the standard of care. I mean if something goes wrong, at least you have one eye left. There was one case I know of where five of the patients who were injected with anesthetic by the same anesthesiologist went blind in that eye after cataract surgery. Can you imagine? It's why you do one eye at a time. Anyway, this terrorist was very persuasive if you know what I mean, and got the poor surgeon to do the double operation in one day. My only regret was that the surgeon, unaware of the arrangement and my identity, also became a victim in such an unconventional war. I do feel guilty about that."

"But how did you poison him? What toxin did use?" said the agent.

"Oh, my plan was simple. I delivered concentrated scorpion toxin via the lens implants. That potent stuff was derived from a yellow jewel hidden in the crevices of the Middle East: *Leiurus quinquestriatus*.

"Scorpion toxin?"

"Yes, scorpion toxin. You know I love the toxins that act at the sodium channel one way or another. It's such fundamental physiology and the key to how nerves work. Without going too heavily into the science, nerves must generate an action potential in order to work properly. Think of the action potential as the propagation of a wave along the nerve. Sodium moves in through the channels or openings in the cell membrane and when the electrical potential inside the cell gets low enough the sodium channels close and the potassium channels open. If these channels are blocked, or even kept open by toxins, nerves can't work like they are supposed to. If your sodium channels are blocked you get paralyzed. Respirations stop if the nerves that stimulate your diaphragm to move don't work. Pretty clever of Mother Nature, huh?" she said. She took a breath and continued.

"I picked one of the more deadly scorpion toxins. The genus *Leiurus* is distributed in northeastern Africa through the Middle East. *L. quinquestriatus* species are found primarily in Egypt, Israel, Jordan, Syria and Lebanon, which is why I had to make a detour before I came to India. Scorpions are nocturnal creatures hiding by day in crevices, or under stones or under tree bark. They're found in both tropical and temperate regions in deserts, forests, mountains and savannas. So the take-home message, my friend, is to make sure you shake out your boots before you put them on."

*   *   *

When Lily returned from India she had difficulty reentering her "normal" life. It was one thing to help rid the world of terrorists, but another to take innocent lives. She hated all collateral damage. She wished she could have warned the eye surgeon of the danger so he and his family could have been saved. These were the times that she struggled to understand what she had become—the destroying angel.

For years she repressed the memory of her daughter, her beautiful flower. She had been dazed and confused by it all. Every time she tried to recall the details, her mind became blurred with uncertainty and fear. All that she could remember was how the seed was planted.

The father of her daughter had been an older man she'd met in graduate school while she worked as his research fellow. He was a brilliant scientist, a Nobel Laureate, twenty years her senior, who had never married because of the intensity of his world-renowned work. During their brief affair, Lily became pregnant and in spite of being a single woman, chose to go ahead and have the baby.

"Lily, perhaps we should get married so the child will have a real father," said her professor with great sincerity when learning of her pregnancy. "All my life I've wanted a child of my own, but never found the time to marry."

While Lily cared for him deeply, she wasn't sure that she was in love and didn't want to engage in a deceitful arrangement. Rather than conform to the custom, she desired to remain single.

"I'm sorry, Charles," she said, taking both his hands in hers. "I, I don't think I could marry you." Although hurt by the rejection, he offered to help her care for the child and begged to remain part of her life.

Lily considered his generous offer, but shortly thereafter, while conducting field work in Africa, he was killed in an accident when a cart overturned in the road, pinning him underneath. He bled to death in the dirt ruts of a foreign country with no hospital, no modern medicine, and no one to save him. The impact of his death was overwhelming for Lily Robinson. She delivered her child several months later, alone with no husband, no baby's father to hold her hand or stand by her side. She bonded to the child as only someone who had great love to give, but few places to share it could. With no brothers or sisters, and a father who had passed away when she was a young child, followed by her mother's passing several years later, her baby was the one human being with whom she could have a profound connection, but that connection would ultimately be broken too. Stolen from her. Resolved to go it alone, she focused on her science and used her keen analytical mind as a defense mechanism to limit intimate human interaction. Until she met him.

It was hard to get the dark-haired man out of her head. They had been together on almost all her assignments and she knew that he would be there for future ones as well. She also knew that he felt an attraction toward her as well, but neither could acknowledge their feelings. It was forbidden to have any kind of a relationship between collaborators. The danger was always that the mission could be compromised. Above all, emotion could never be part of the equation. Only clinical judgment based on facts could dictate the outcome. If you loved someone, that could change the course of history.

Lily struggled to keep her emotions under control. What if the time came when she had to make a decision between love or duty? She had given up so much for her country. Was it too much to ask that they give just a little in return?

CHAPTER 26

BOSTON SUBURB

Rose made plans early in her senior year to visit several colleges. She had made up her mind to major in science and she wanted to find a college that would prepare her for medical school. There were so many fantastic options in Boston that she was sure she would find a university right in the city that would have everything she wanted.

Rose filled out many applications and focused intensely on her college essay.

My family lives in Colombia, South America. I spent my childhood growing up on a coffee plantation that was run by my great-uncle. We lived a rural existence with little of the modern conveniences that I grew to appreciate when I came to the United States for my high school years. My sister and I lived with my mother on the plantation and were home schooled. We learned multiple languages since my mother was originally from France, my grandparents were both French and Italian, and everyone on the plantation spoke Spanish or English.

I always had a love for gardening and the natural world that propelled my curiosity and fueled my interest in science. When I was a junior in high school I was in a terrible horseback riding accident that required surgery and rehabilitation to help retrain my brain. I was inspired by the skill and kindness of my surgeon who encouraged my family to wait out my coma and then helped me regain almost all my function. I say almost all, because there is probably some tiny piece missing somewhere that I just can't find.

In the spring of my junior year, my high school had a career night with the most inspiring women. One doctor in particular captured my fancy, and right then and there I wanted to go to medical school to become a physician. She talked about medicine and pathology in way that everyone in the audience was engaged and curious about our future possible opportunities. To inspire students, to heal the sick, to care for future generations is my goal in life.

151

Rose didn't write about the day she saw her sister brutally dragged out of the car after their driver had been shot to death. She didn't discuss seeing her mother struck down in the road and left bleeding. She didn't write in her essay that both she and her mother assumed that Bella was dead.

Rose twisted the red-jeweled ring on her finger. It sort of reminded her of a rose too. It was all she had of her "family." She missed her mother. Adrienne had promised that they would spend Christmas together and Rose asked if they could spend Christmas in France, but Adrienne was too worried that if Rose left the U.S. at this point she may have some difficulty returning. There was always a chance, Rose thought.

"Oh, to be accepted to a college in the U.S. would be so great," Rose said out loud to one of her suite-mates.

"Rose," exclaimed her friend, "would you please just get those applications in the mail. Of course you will be accepted to the college of your choice. Let's see, you have top grades, you're on the horseback riding team, you're a member of the language club and the science club, and, and your SAT scores are the best! In fact, you make me depressed." Her suite-mate plumped herself down on the bed.

The next day Rose got all the applications emailed and hoped that going to college would be the start of a new chapter in her life.

*   *   *

When December came, Adrienne let her know that Rose would not be able to come to France for the holiday. Rose was disappointed. She had wanted to spend Christmas in France with her mother and grandmother. Adrienne could hear the disappointment in her voice.

"Listen Rose, why don't we rent a little house on the coast or maybe even go to one of the little islands off Massachusetts for a seaside winter Christmas? We can spend some time in the big city shopping the large department stores first and then drive out to the coast for the holiday. Come on. It'll be fun. What do you think?"

What could Rose think? What could she say?

"Oh Mother that will be fine. I can look at some places on the Internet and see what looks good. I'll make a few calls." Rose was disappointed. She longed to be in the France she had only heard about, dreamt about.

*   *   *

By the time the Christmas holiday came around they had their waterside winter cottage secured on the coast. Rose had to admit it was almost like her snow globe. There was freshly fallen snow, sparkling Christmas lights everywhere, and all the stores appeared to be giftwrapped. She was just missing the little family on the horse-drawn sleigh.

Rose and Adrienne had already shopped pre-Christmas in the city and loved seeing all the decorations in the stores. Christmas trees, icicles, tinsel, and snowflakes were all strung across store ceilings. They both took advantage of the last-minute bargains before Christmas day. Adrienne bought several cashmere sweaters and pairs of sheepskin slippers to take back to France. Her own mother would appreciate the soft warmth and cozy feel of these articles during the chilly nights in Reims. Rose, on the other hand, bought some jeans, tee shirts and warm hooded fleece sweatshirts.

Adrienne and Rose enjoyed a quiet holiday at the cottage and treasured their time together. They had walked the beaches during the day collecting shells and shiny rocks and sat quietly by the fire at night talking of their days on the plantation and of Alberto.

"Mother," said Rose, "did you call your uncle to wish him a happy Christmas?" She was sincere.

"No, not yet." Adrienne had never forgiven her uncle for his treatment of her, but was grateful he had seen to Rose's wellbeing by sending her to the United States. At least Rose was safe now.

The day after Christmas Adrienne and Rose decided to stroll the charming New England town and visit the local shops. They came across a small flower shop with enticing displays in the window. When they entered the store, in addition to many metal buckets with live flowers, there were seemingly hundreds of dried flower bunches hanging from the wooden beams running across the ceiling, and wreaths with dried flowers, greenery and starfish secured to the walls. Rose found a group of small metal vases containing realistic looking silk lily-of-the-valley flowers, tiny white flowers like beads off a sleek green stalk. The white metal vases had French writing on the outside that was pink and cursive. It said "*La Boutique de Fleurs, 12 Rue de Madeleine.*"

"Mother," Rose said excitedly, "I love these, can we please get some?" She stuck her hand deep inside the vase to rearrange the bouquet.

"Why not? Pick out a few arrangements that you like and we'll take them back to your dorm room," Adrienne replied.

Adrienne and Rose returned to their cottage and planned the remainder of their holiday week.

*   *   *

Lily Robinson had spent most of her Christmas holiday on the phone with the hospital. She was consulting on a patient in the medical intensive care unit who had overdosed on an unknown drug. She was waiting for the comprehensive toxicology report. Drug assay interpretation was complicated. The assays used in most hospital laboratories were limited in what they could detect. Some assays were designated as "class immunoassays," that is, they only detected certain drugs within a class of compounds that reacted with the immunologically reactive species used as the calibrator. If the urine had tested positive for opiates she wouldn't know which opiate it was. Was it a true opiate, a naturally occurring drug like morphine or codeine, or was it an opioid, a semi-synthetic drug like oxycodone? The answer couldn't be determined without more specific testing. To add to the confusion, synthetic drugs like fentanyl, and designer drugs crafted in China, wouldn't be detected by the assay at all. She'd seen many patients who presented like an opiate overdose with negative drug screens. She had sent out both the serum and the urine of her patient for a broad comprehensive screen using tandem mass spectrometry. This was a much more sensitive and specific method that could identify compounds that simple immunoassay screening could not. The only down side was this technology couldn't provide a very rapid turnaround time.

Lily took a trip into the small town as a diversion. She stopped at the grocery store to pick up some fruit and bread and then decided to stop at the flower shop to buy some flowers for her cottage. The store door opened and a little bell rang announcing a customer was on the premises. Lily saw the owner behind the counter.

"Hi Clara, Merry Christmas."

"Oh hi, Merry Christmas to you too."

"The store looks absolutely beautiful. Have you been busy?"

"Mostly before Christmas, but not too bad today. What can I help you with?"

"I thought I would just pick up some flowers to brighten the cottage. Anything new?"

"We have these really darling metal tins with lily-of-the-valley if you like that sought of thing. They're over there on the back bench by the dried hydrangeas."

"Clara, I love them," Lily exclaimed. "I'll take two tins."

Lily left the store and returned to her cottage. She put the flowers aside and checked her email for the toxicology results. Here they were. She glanced over the report and two positive drugs appeared in the list of the almost 150 that were assayed.

Hmm, fentanyl and its metabolite nor-fentanyl, she thought. *This drug is almost a hundred times more potent than morphine. No wonder he's not waking up. He probably has brain anoxia since he was down so long before they found him.*

She called the intensive care unit to update her report.

"Hello. This is Dr. Robinson. I have additional information on our patient who came in unresponsive with the drug overdose." She paused. "Yes, I'll speak with the attending." They discussed the case for several minutes and then Lily hung up the phone.

She had been so wrapped up in the overdose case that she had forgotten all about the flowers. The next morning she came across the metal vases on her kitchen counter.

"Oh you pretty little things. So sorry I ignored you."

She dumped the flowers out of the vase so she could rearrange them to her liking. To her surprise a beautiful ring rolled on the counter top. Lily picked it up and carefully turned it around in her fingers. She thought it looked very old. There was a gold band with an inscription inside that said *amour* and a grape cluster. The stone was a beautiful red brilliant gem, cut in the shape of a heart. This appeared to be someone's treasure.

Lily got into her car and drove back to town to the flower shop. The shop had a sign on the door with a clock face that read "will return in ten minutes." Clara must be taking a break.

Lily decided to stroll down the street to the café and have a cup of coffee while she waited for Clara to return to the shop. The café was a little crowded with post-holiday shoppers having a scone with their morning caffeine. Lily looked at all the patrons sitting at the counter or standing in line, when she noticed a young girl and her mother at the table in the distant corner of the café. What caught her eye was that the young girl was clearly upset. She was crying almost audibly and was inconsolable by her parent. *Poor thing,* Lily thought, *I wonder what that's about.*

Lily headed back to the flower shop. She could see Clara through the window.

The little bell chimed. "Hi, Clara."

"Hey, hi doctor, I'm surprised to see you again so soon."

"Well, you know those lily-of-the-valley flowers you sold me yesterday, the ones in the beautiful French tins. Well I found this in one of the tins."

She held out the ring to the store keep. The red brilliant gemstone caught the light and made it dazzle as if it had been the Christmas ornament atop a tree.

"Oh my God. That's the ring!" Clara exclaimed. "I can't believe you have it."

"What do you mean?"

"I sold some of those flowers in the vase a few days ago to a mother and daughter. The ring must have come off the daughter's finger when she was handling the flowers. They were in here earlier today in tears. Apparently it's a family heirloom. She did leave me a phone number so I'll call right away and let them know I have it. Thanks for coming by so quickly. They're from out of town and it would have made for a most unhappy ending to their otherwise cheery holiday."

"Glad I could help."

As Lily drove back to her cottage she couldn't help but wonder if the mother and daughter she had seen in the café were the same two people that the shopkeeper had talked about. There had been something familiar about the young girl, but Lily just couldn't quite put her finger on it.

*   *   *

Adrienne returned to France after the holidays and Rose returned to school to finish out her senior year. She waited eagerly in the spring for news on her acceptances to colleges and was delighted to see that she had a choice.

"OMG," squealed a suitemate. "I can't believe that you got into all these Ivy League schools. Which one Rose, which one are you going to choose?"

"I'm not sure." She shuffled through the letters and stopped at one in particular. "Maybe this is the one," she said, holding out a letter with an impressive crest on the top. "They'll give me a scholarship based on my scholastic achievement. I just have to keep that up through four years of college," she added. "Anyway, I think I might have a better chance at medical school if I go there."

Rose chose her university and would start there in the fall of that year. She would excel in all her studies and when she graduated college four years later, she would be faced once again with a shuffle of letters. This time she already knew which medical school would be her choice. She always knew where she wanted to go as she had her role model imprinted in her mind early in her junior year when she sat in the auditorium on career night in high school.

What a long way I've come from my life on the coffee plantation, she thought as she did her final packing to leave the boarding school for the last time. *Mother is so proud of me. I only wish I still had Bella in my life. She would have loved to share this with me.* She pulled on her jeans and took a long look at the rose tattoo just below her right hip.

CHAPTER 27

RUSSIA AND HONG KONG
One year prior to the current events

Long before the great city of New York was struggling with housing the growing dead from a seemingly unknown new epidemic, Russian radicals brewed their plan to create turmoil and destruction in the United States. They sought alliances with fundamentalist groups throughout the world who shared the same objective. They would stand united against the Americans. This common enemy would bind them.

In one small Russian village, Yuri, a man with a long beard, sandy hair, and much training in surreptitious chemistry could be seen at times carrying a large stone pot that contained a mixture of codeine, iodine, gasoline, paint thinner, hydrochloric acid, lighter fluid, and red phosphorus. This was his usual creation in order to make enough money to support his household. He had fallen on hard times in recent years and did the best he could for his family. He used this chemical combination to generate a fast-acting high, especially when heroin was scarce. However, the users of this product developed severe tissue damage around the injection site, causing gangrene and vein inflammation which resulted sporadically in amputation. In most cases the skin was left scaly and black from the corrosive effects, and the afflicted bore patches of crocodile skin signifying their entry into a world of drug abuse.

On a summer day, while Yuri was in the stone shed behind his house mixing his illicit substance, Russian agents had tracked him down, and he found them standing right outside his shed. At the time of this first encounter, he didn't know who they were or what they wanted, and feared arrest because of his forbidden drug making, but when the large man with steel grey eyes grabbed Yuri by the shirt, the plans were made clear.

"Yuri Ulrick, STOP, you little bastard. We know who you are," the man said with sarcasm in his voice. He frightened Yuri as he toyed with his emotions.

"Smart professor, or maybe even stupid professor," he said, laughing as he turned to his accomplice who was also laughing while he held a gun pointed directly at Yuri.

"You idiot, got the boot by big shot university because you were synthesizing designer drugs, and what's worse, you were dumb enough to get caught. You ran and tried to hide, but there is no hiding from us. Oh, look Maxim, he is still unbelievably stupid," the man said as he grabbed Yuri's stone pot.

"Still making and selling drugs to our children, huh?" he said as he started to spill the contents of the pot on the floor. His hand dipped into his pants pocket and he pulled out a cigarette lighter.

"What do you think Maxim? Should I light this shit on fire and we could watch him burn or should we just shoot him and make it quick?" Maxim raised the gun and took dead aim.

Yuri felt the sweat bead up on the back of his neck and thought he might soil his pants. He worried that this man would kill his wife and three children who were in the house preparing the evening meal. He didn't say a word.

The stout man laughed and put the cigarette lighter back into his pocket. He pulled Yuri in toward him and held him there.

"Yuri Ulrick, you will be allowed to continue your pitiful little life in exchange for a service to your country." He lifted his size thirteen boot and kicked the stone pot and its contents to the floor, clearing the table. He pushed Yuri down into a chair, opened a small leather pouch and dumped the contents onto the table. Several spiny fruits spilled onto the table top. He pried one sea urchin like fruit open and small dots of blood emerged from his thumb and right forefinger as the spines dug deep into his skin. Out popped a mottled seed resembling an engorged tick.

"This," he said pointing to the forbidden fruit, "is your future out of this hell hole."

There would be several more meetings to finalize the arrangements. The steely-eyed Russian was frequently accompanied by an attractive young blond woman who always wore a gold pendant of a spider's web. She took care of all the details and made all the travel arrangements for Yuri. There was an edge to her that Yuri found disturbing, but the chemist didn't really care. He knew what he had to do and had his direction even if his internal compass was without moral conviction. He merely relished the fact that he would have a chance once again to use the skills he had been trained for. He thought of himself as an exquisite scientist who had been unfairly dealt with. Here was his chance to prove himself and in the service of his country. His sponsors would infuse his small, secretive laboratory with the necessary equipment and resources, and with a little help he would be on his way to creating a very elegant toxin.

*   *   *

Although Yuri had been a highly skilled chemist, weaponization of a toxin was a fine art, and clearly Yuri would need some assistance. Like mercenaries who fought wars for any country, there also existed chemists for hire, for the right price. Yuri had learned of just such a scientist through a contact from a drug and slave trafficking ring in Hong Kong, one who could be bought if the money was right. He made the connection, and with his crude concoction, journeyed to Hong Kong for the next stage.

Hong Kong was a most exotic place for Yuri. Although he had been a university professor, he was a man from very modest means and had never been far from the place of his birth. Flying into Chek Lap Kok, Yuri could see the harbor lights and anxiety rose within him. He flew in on a dragon with fire breathing out of both engines and when the aircraft landed, Yuri reached for his duffle bag in the overhead compartment and exited the plane in a rush on unsteady legs.

He took public transportation along Route 8 and made his way to the Whitlow Laboratory. There he met a Chinese chemist of notable repute and one whose reputation for genius was well deserved. They entered a magnificent laboratory with sophisticated equipment for analysis, including multiple tandem mass spectrometers, gas chromatographs, and automated chemistry analyzers capable of performing hundreds of immunoassay procedures. It was every chemist's dream and even though Yuri had been given ample money to purchase the basic equipment for his project, nothing could compare with the fruits of a billion-dollar horse racing business. They entered a small room in the back of the building that contained additional equipment necessary for drug synthesis, and several fume hoods. It was here they came to a stop and sat down to discuss the details of the deal.

"Thank you for taking time to see me," said Yuri in his most obliging tone.

"I have cash you requested, with more to follow from my backers, once the toxin is delivered. This vial contains the crude product I have prepared and now only awaits your touch to aerosolize it. Once this is accomplished, I can smuggle it back to where we have a factory to embed the toxin into whatever merchandise we want." He placed a large Thermos on the table in front of the Hong Kong chemist.

The small man with his short black hair and black-rimmed glasses brought the Thermos to the hood and placed it inside. He donned an industrial strength respirator, slid the glass door down and opened the bottle, peering at the amorphous white mixture.

"Will be fine," he said without even so much as taking an extra breath. He voice was muffled behind the mask. "I can have this for you in about a month."

That night while Yuri paced his hotel room, the Hong Kong chemist worked in the lab turning the crude mixture into a fine powder, fine enough to be inhaled into the deepest part of the lungs, small particles that could work their way into 200 micrometer alveolar cavities, cross into the blood stream, and wreak havoc with the machinery that makes each cell in the body work. He worked into the early morning. He was exhausted. He hoped he had gotten this right, given that he had learned from the best. Yet there was always the risk that one omission in the procedure could produce an unforeseen problem. The chemist cleaned up the workbench so no trace of his presence could be detected. He locked the lab and exited the building unobserved via the North door. Heading South by train to the Jordan Station area, he continued his journey by foot to his apartment building. He climbed several flights of stairs to get to his flat. The room was sparsely laid out with a small brown pull-out sofa, a kitchenette with a hot plate, and a washroom with a combination shower and toilet.

The chemist absorbed his modest surroundings through the pores in his skin until the small hairs on his arms stood upright. *Soon I'll be out of this place and into a flat fit for a chemist of my stature*, he thought. Driven by mounting debt, he had made the decision to trade loyalty for betrayal.

He would grab just a few hours of sleep before going back to the lab to begin his regular shift, and then stay behind after hours to continue his tedious but necessary work.

Yuri waited for several weeks while his contact made the toxin. He had wanted to work side by side with a fellow colleague, but this was not permitted. So he kept busy reading chemistry books interspersed with those on the history of Hong Kong. Civilization had flourished in Hong Kong perhaps as long as 30,000 years ago. Stone tools and other artifacts of human inhabitants were discovered by the Hong Kong Archeological Society in Wong Tei Tung, but that was ancient history. Many people from Hong Kong spoke English after the colonization by the British. Yuri focused on practicing English so he could be proficient when, and if, he reached America. It had always been his dream to move to the United States.

When the Chinese chemist completed the job he would meet with Yuri to arrange a transfer of material. That meeting would set in motion the events that would begin to unravel the tapestry of American life.

Part 3

The Promise of Poison (the present)

CHAPTER 28

NEW YORK CITY

I open my eyes now to that feeling of exhaustion. Life is hard but death is even harder, especially the deaths piling up in New York that city authorities can't explain. My tired mind contemplates our inevitable end, and a visit I had with one of my favorite mentors during the last days of his life. It was spring just before all this chaos began. He chose to leave this world from his home and not from a hospital. He wanted by his side family, and those who felt like family, so he could reminisce a little, complain a little, and feel comfortable while doing both. Hospitals are a cacophony of voices, alarms, beepers, bells, and bright lights. They are stimulating places where it's impossible to find peace. Shared rooms bring multiple visitors, endless talking, and nurses moving workstations in and out of the room while patient care attendants scurry to find bed pans and adjust pillows. That's not peace. Peace comes from sitting by the ocean with your toes in the sand, from watching egrets hunt green crabs in the marsh, or eagles perch on ice floes during winter. Peace is getting lost in the beauty of hundreds of acres in the mountains of the American West while elk roam, vultures soar, and aspens quake. Peace comes from shutting your bedroom door and sinking into the mattress with the covers pulled up around your head. That's what I'd like to do right now.

Peace is what my mentor had as he embraced his "family" during those final days. He smoked just one last cigar, had one more Scotch for the hell of it, and told secrets he had hidden for years under a disguise of normalcy. I missed this experience with my own family. I was not with my father, or my mother, when they left me alone as a very young girl to care for myself and make my way in the world. My father died when I was only five and my mother died when I was just beginning my teenage years. I envy my mentor's grace with which he chose to exit life. He did it his way. His ashes were freed in the wind on a bright sunny day after his death. They floated over the blue Atlantic and touched the frothy waves until they dissolved within liquid that once gave birth to all life on earth.

*   *   *

Focus, Lily. Stay in the present. There is still the problem of the perfume cards, as well as my missing ampoule of toxin. I'm fully aware that it could only have been my toxin, the one that I had John Chi prepare for me that caused the death of the man drinking coffee somewhere up around the United Nations building. That was the ampoule of toxin I was going to use at the banquet to poison the terrorist, but JP hadn't yet made the final identification. I know he's close. My real fear now is that the enemy has had a nice trial run with a drop or two of poison in coffee, but what will happen if they decide to dump the contents into one of the reservoirs that provide water to the city? I had asked John to synthesize saxitoxin, an ocean-loving toxin, you might say. This is an algal-derived neurotoxin contained in shellfish. It's not uncommon, and can present a health hazard to individuals who live or vacation within coastal areas around the world. Mussels were on the menu for the dinner at the museum and the perfect hiding spot for saxitoxin. It's certainly within the realm of possibilities that even fishermen harvesting these shellfish might not realize they are contaminated. Sometimes it's not so obvious. Many coastal areas that experience regular shellfish contamination due to paralytic shellfish poisoning, or PSP, might have too low a concentration of algal cells to produce visible contamination, and yet it is sufficient to intoxicate shellfish.

Saxitoxin is a fabulous poison, in my opinion. This toxin initially produces symptoms of an abnormal tingling sensation like pins and needles (paresthesias) in the arms and legs, and numbness around the mouth. Those were the symptoms Becker described to me over the phone when speaking about the man who died near the UN. I knew then it was my toxin that had killed him. You've heard of "red tides"? The most common of these seasonal exposures is PSP usually associated with outbreaks of "red tide." Blooming of specific algae that contain red-brown pigments may result in the reddish appearance of water and hence are sometimes called "red tides." I remember there was a classic case reported *in Mortality and Morbidity Weekly* several years ago:

In the month of June, six fishermen complained of illness after eating the blue mussels, *Mytilus edulis*, harvested from waters 115 miles from Nantucket, an island thirty miles off the coast of Massachusetts. Within one to two and a half hours after consumption, the men, ranging in ages from 24–47 years, presented with the following symptoms: five men had numbness of the mouth, four had vomiting, four had paresthesia of extremities, two had numbness and tingling of the tongue, two had numbness of the face, and one had numbness of the throat. One fisherman also had periorbital edema and twenty-four hours later, all of the fisherman had lower back pain which lasted, on average, approximately three days. Two of the men required hospitalization for several days. Symptoms were proportional to the number of mussels consumed, i.e. the more mussels consumed the more severe the presentation of the illness. The individual who consumed between eighteen and twenty-four mussels, in addition to having severe paresthesias, also had loss of consciousness and was hospitalized.

These fishermen had harvested mussels in an area of Georges Bank where it was previously known by the Massachusetts Department of Public Health to contain surf clams and sea scallops contaminated with saxitoxin, a major causative agent of PSP. A closure notice was sent to all Coast Guard stations and fishing vessels in the affected area. Despite this notification, the six fishermen reported in this incident had not received the information.

The fisherman boiled the harvested mussels for approximately ninety minutes prior to consumption. Laboratory assays later determined that the saxitoxin concentration in the recovered raw mussels was 24,400 µg /100g and in the cooked mussels was 4280 µg/100g (while the limit for safe consumption is a saxitoxin concentration of <80 µg/100g). Presumably some of the saxitoxin in the boiled mussels had leached into the boiling water.

This toxin is an old story. Historical allusions to red tides appeared perhaps as early as the time of Moses (1491 BC). In Exodus (7:20-21) the description reads "and all the water that was in the Nile was turned to blood. And the fish that were in the Nile died and the Nile became foul, so that the Egyptians could not drink water from the Nile." Acute poisoning from eating shellfish (probably contaminated with toxin-producing unicellular algae) was reported in 1689 and described by Captain George Vancouver in 1793 during his exploration of the coast of the North American Pacific Northwest. His experience led to the naming of Poison Cove to designate the fatal spot where the mussels were consumed.

I've always liked this toxin. So does John Chi.

*   *   *

JP tells me that the government agents have not been able to track down all the cards, and the last known whereabouts of the ampoule was at the UN building. We both know that the weekend, loaded with sporting events, opening shows on Broadway, and star-studded concerts is fast approaching. We face a choice: warn the public and risk widespread panic or try to solve the problem quietly. It's not my decision. Troubled, I turn toward the window overlooking the northeast corner of the balcony off the bedroom. The sky is magnificent. Billowy clouds hang low over the East River and I see ripples along the water's surface pushed by the wind. Open sky and big expanses allows my mind to clear, but also leaves cracks for fear to creep in.

"So, what's the plan?" I ask my dark-haired man, our relationship cemented from our history of missions glued together with caring and loyalty. "What do we do now?" His face gives him away. He's sitting at the corner table, his hand rubbing the stubble on his chin. He's thinking. I see the furrows in his forehead and the crow's feet around his eyes intensify as he formulates our next move.

"Lily, what is the information from your chemist?"

I reach for my cell phone and dial Hong Kong. "John, John, it's Lily. Anything new, have you found anything that can help us?" I fear I have desperation in my voice.

"Lily, I am working on something that may help you. But I don't have it yet. I am looking at the cards. The scratch strip contains weaponized grade ricin. There are only a few chemists in the world that can create such a toxin with that fine a particle. And, and only a few labs that have the capability. Lily, I also see a little peak on the ricin fingerprint that I need to identify. The fingerprint is not the same on every card. Not sure what it means. I need more time."

"John, we don't have more time," I tell him. "Thousands of lives are in jeopardy. There's no way in hell we can track down all those cards."

"Lily, I need more time." And then there was silence.

I turn to JP. "John may have something," I tell him.

"*Et, quoi?*"

"I don't know. We'll have to wait."

Then out of nowhere, he asks me to come downtown with him to look at some structure.

"Why are we going to this building?" I ask.

"*Chérie*, there were several bodies found there this morning. You may be interested."

"Bodies? Are the bodies still there? I would think the ME would be all over that one."

"*Oui*, but my men have found something interesting. Get your coat, Lily, and let's go."

JP grabs his coat, secures his gun in his holster, and hands me mine. I mean my coat. I know how to use a gun and have a gun that the Agency gave me, but I don't carry it. JP helps me slip into the sleeves, turns me around to face him, and buttons up the front of my coat. I move in closer for a hug, and feel his gun.

"Now let us go, *Chérie*."

Twenty minutes later we're standing in front of a brick building on the edge of the Garment District. JP lays it all out for me.

"Six men were found dead here this morning. They have been taken to the medical examiner's office for autopsy. The ME at the scene said the bodies were cherry red in color."

"Oh, carbon monoxide poisoning?" I ask. "Was there a faulty burner or something?"

"*Oui*, it was certainly made to look that way, but we think there is more to the story. The fourth and fifth floor had been cleaned thoroughly, ah, professionally, before we got there, but my men have found a few interesting clues. First, it seems this building used to contain an old printing facility. It was used to print advertising cards. These are the cards they slip in between the pages of magazines. It closed many years ago, and the building remained unoccupied until just recently. It appears to have been bought by an Eastern European or perhaps Russian man who we think may be a front for a larger organization. We're considering those details now, *Chérie*. This may be our connection to the Russian operation, but we are not certain. If your John Leigh can determine who created the ricin, we may be able to trace that back to the architect of the terror plot."

I'm thinking, why is it taking John such a long time to figure out the ricin signature? This shouldn't be so difficult a task for him. Yet, it was something John said to me over the phone that keeps coming back to me: "Only a few chemists in the world can create such a toxin with that fine a particle," and one of them would of course be John Chi Leigh. Am I so stupid as to not have considered this? Is it possible that John is delaying getting all the results to me because he's the creative genius behind the toxin? It's certainly one explanation, but I can't be sure. It's always a question of who you can or can't trust. And where does the truth lie, anyway? I've already been down the long gullet of our government, swallowed by their half-truths and convenient facts. John Chi is a government unto himself. His first obligation is to pay his debts so he can survive. He seems to be a little off lately, even preoccupied, and I'm fairly certain he's gambling again. The pressure for him to obtain large sums of money would overshadow any sense of loyalty he may have for me.

"Lily, let's go upstairs and have a look around. My men are still there."

JP tells me that the fire department has declared the building safe. There's no longer any carbon monoxide floating in the air. We take the elevator up to the fifth floor. The printing press is sitting in the middle of a large open space. The windows that frame the room are expansive and span from about midway on the wall up to the ceiling. The window glass is embedded in wire mesh for strength and security. The walls are old tile, off white with chips in places that furniture had probably knocked up against. I walk around the room, trying to imagine how the operation was laid out. Would they have had to work in specialized suits and masks to prevent breathing in the toxin during the manufacturing stage? Once the cards were sealed in the cellophane, they would be safe to move and package in bulk. JP knows where my mind is stuck.

"Lily, the bulk of the microencapsulation may have been done elsewhere."

"What do you mean?" I ask.

"In order to make the cards with the embedded toxin, they would have to first encapsulate the toxin in a solid shell. The hard-outer shell could be a variety of materials used to cover the core. They could have used a number of different processes, perhaps core-shell encapsulation or microgranulation, that is, matrix-encapsulation using a vibrating technology. Our chemists and engineers are examining all the possibilities. Clearly, this printing plant was used to manufacture the cards. There may have been some limited microencapsulation."

I'm back on John Chi. Could he truly be tangled in this web? I'm not sure if I should call him and confront him directly.

JP's phone rings.

"*Oui*, yes *je comprends*." He turns to me and says, "Lily, I must go. Please, keep on your friend, the Chinese chemist. We need answers and need them *tout de suite, Chérie*."

I know JP, I know.

CHAPTER 29

NEW YORK CITY

Across the street from the brick building, Alexis stood well hidden from view. Lily Robinson would certainly recognize her if she were to come out into the light. Lily had gotten a good look at her face when she bumped into her in the museum. Alexis couldn't see what was taking place on the fourth and fifth floor of the building but she could imagine. She was waiting for word from Grigory. Just when she was about to step out of the shadow to get better reception on her phone, she saw a dark-haired man exit the building, but noticed Lily Robinson was not with him. This might be her opportunity, but perhaps Grigory would see it differently. Who was the real Lily Robinson? It seemed to Alexis that a professor giving a talk about toxins at the museum would hardly be spending time with government agents to this extent. She pulled the gold chain around her neck from side to side while holding the spider's web between her thumb and forefinger.

*　　*　　*

Alexis had spent the last several years in the United States honing her skills and perfecting her American accent. She had been trained as an operative for Russia at the highest level. She facilitated drug trafficking from South America and the Middle East down through Mexico and up into the United States. Recently she had worked with Chinese chemists to bring in designer drugs that could go undetected in conventional drug screens. Growing poppies seemed like a lot of work by comparison. Workers had to toil the fields, harvest the crop, and extract precursors before the heroin, the diacetylmorphine, could be made. Instead the Chinese had large clandestine labs that could easily synthesize great quantities of designer drugs. Fentanyl, carfentanil, and acetyl-fentanyl were all simple substitutes for heroin, and these drugs were more potent, and more deadly, than heroin. These were drugs that could be compressed into a pill form, gathered in a plastic bag by the tens and sold for hundreds. It was good money.

From single pills manufactured for the unknowing person on the street to large aerosolized chemical batches destined for mass attacks, these drugs were acknowledged to be particularly deadly. The *Spetsnaz*, or Russian Special Forces, were well known by forensic chemists to have used carfentanil during the Moscow Theater siege. After Chechnyan terrorists took over 800 hostages as they watched *Nord-Ost* in the theater one night in October of 2000, the Special Forces pumped in what was presumably carfentanil and remifentanil to subdue all living things in an attempt to gain control. Over 120 hostages and perhaps as many as forty rebels died. Carfentanil, 10,000 times more potent than morphine and 100 times more potent than fentanyl, was a supreme incapacitating agent and was permitted for use only by licensed veterinarians to tranquilize big game such as elephants. It was never meant to poison the unsuspecting drug addicts in Ohio, Kentucky and Florida who thought they were buying only heroin and not a drug that could take down a 2,000-pound animal with just 4 milligrams.

Drugs and poisons had always been used to shape political outcomes throughout history, but the stakes were higher now. Interfering in American politics had been a high priority for the Russian government and the government of other anti-American nations. The prime objective had been to disrupt the American way of life. It was to cast doubt across cultures, feed the uncertainty that rests within each person, and create fear that could not be quieted by any free leader.

Alexis and Markovic had worked side by side for the last year bringing the plot to its boiling point. Steam emerged from the top of the plan announcing that contrary to some historians, revenge was not a dish best served cold, but rather one where burning desire trumped all.

They had labored with the disgraced Russian chemist to catalyze the initial steps in the plan. He was the one who knew how to extract ricin from the castor bean plant, *Ricinus communis*. Castor oil could be made from the seed and ingested trouble-free by humans as a laxative. The heating process during the extraction of the oil denatured and deactivated the protein ricin. But in capable hands, ricin, not castor oil could be coaxed from the tick-like bean and used in lethal ways. Incorporation of weapon grade ricin in various venues throughout the United States would create suspicion in every corner of the box and with the lid closed, there was no way out.

The Russian chemist had been wasting his time making Krokodil. Krokodil or desmorphine was a poor heroin substitute that left its users disfigured with skin resembling the crocodile and sloughing flesh that often progressed to gangrene, lost limbs and even death. This was a small-time enterprise.

The ricin plan was on a much grander scale. The manufacturing had been completed, cards and other impregnated material had been shipped throughout the United States, and the testing step in New York had gone much better than expected.

The dinner with the world bankers had been a primer for the world stage. Some bankers had died, causing minor perturbations to the economy because of future uncertainty. Yet the terrorists hoped for wider global destabilization. Once the reports flooded the airwaves, the stock market would fluctuate and bad news would diffuse like waves of trepidations. It was tantamount to throwing a stone into a pond. Hysteria was already beginning to spread across the city.

There were so many big happenings in the city that never sleeps. A dizzying choice of gatherings of Americans that could be attacked while they attended concerts in the park or in concert halls, while they laughed at theater productions or cheered big sports events in basketball, hockey or football. They had agreed that the Super Bowl could also be a potential target since it was slated to air during the weekend. The latter was considered an American icon, a spectacle of indulgence with beer, chicken wings, supersized drinks and television commercials exuding capitalism in its unholy excess. Markovic's superiors considered all the possibilities. The bankers' gala was just the start.

*   *   *

Alexis had discovered that a local doctor, Lily Robinson, would attend dinner with the bankers. Prior to the event she researched all she could on Lily, as well as the curator who Lily would accompany to the affair. As the event planner, Alexis had control of many aspects of the dinner party, although some were still clearly under the control of Lily Robinson and Eric Vandermeer. The life of Lily Robinson that was splashed on the Internet, found in journal

174

articles or books was her professional academic career. Her alternate life, and her origins, could not be traced. Her government had provided her with a deep cover, a synthesized background and only allowed the facts it wanted discovered, discoverable. However, Alexis was able to unearth one fact from a rather obscure interview given very early in Dr. Robinson's career. In a small gardening magazine, Dr. Robinson spoke of the flowers and herbs that she planted in her own garden and just in passing mentioned that lilies, her namesake flower, were not a favorite and gave her some trouble. Alexis had taken a chance that those pollen-filled blooms at the banquet in the museum might prove useful, and they had. One additional bonus was a tip unexpectedly heard from the Hong Kong chemist that Lily Robinson would probably be carrying a highly concentrated toxin in her handbag the night of dinner. Alexis didn't know that Lily Robinson was a skilled assassin who used poisoning as a means of elimination. She only thought that if she did have a toxin with her, it would somehow be part of the story for the museum exhibit. Perhaps a local demonstration using the poison to paralyze a small animal would be part of the entertainment for the agenda. There were times when Alexis' brain was on fire and her reasoning was overwhelmed by flames.

Alexis had been at Markovic's side for most of her young adult life. He had taken her in as his protégé when she was a budding teen. At the time, he wasn't sure what her potential would be, but Alexis had proven to be an asset to the organization. She was smart, and she was good with a gun when she needed to be. She had learned to speak multiple languages and had a great gift for mimicking accents to sound like a native speaker. All her gifts, however, were blunted by her weakness for cocaine.

"Alexis, are you ready?" Markovic asked in a demanding tone. "We need to start moving things across the river." It wasn't just perfume cards; it was anything that could have a toxin encapsulated into it. "Make sure the men have the programs ready for the American football game."

All the programs containing the information on the football players had a sticky strip that sealed them shut until the person handling the guide ran their finger between the front and back cover to pry open the booklet. When this occurred, lethal amounts of toxin would be aerosolized with deadly consequences. Hundreds of fine particles would be released in the air as the attendees at the football game opened their books in unison. Likewise, contaminated fingers could inoculate the eyes and mouth, as spectators used their hands to rub their faces in the dying light.

Everything was set for the Sunday.

Alexis returned to the room that had been rented by Markovic. She found her compact nestled among her packed clothes and carefully opened it. Inside was a white powder.

She prudently poured a little out on her makeup mirror and bent her head over the powder and snorted. She closed her eyes and felt the rush. Her heart started beating faster and her pulse raced. She felt alive.

There was a knock on the connecting door.

"Alexis, let me in," Markovic said in a strong tone.

"One moment," she replied anxiously.

Alexis quickly cleaned up the cocaine and put the compact away.

"Da, Grigory," she said as she opened the door. Markovic strutted in and sat down on the edge of the bed next to her.

"You've done well," he said, taking hold of the gold chain around her neck and pulling her toward him. Alexis could smell the vodka on his breath. As much as she wanted to move away from him, she knew there was no escape. She hadn't been able to escape him for eight years, so she did the only thing she knew how to do. She allowed her mind to depart her body at that very moment. There was cocaine circulating through her veins now and cocaine was flowing into her brain. *Let him do whatever he wants,* she thought. *My body is here, but my mind is not.*

He leaned over and kissed her on the forehead. Then he moved his mouth down to hers. Her body stiffened. Her consciousness had already left the hotel room. She could see her mother and her sister and the house she grew up in. She didn't dare look at her own form. Her shell remained on the bed and took the full assault as it had over the last many years. She had been conditioned by, what seemed to her, to be a lifetime of abuse and Markovic had expected her to show pleasure in hosting it.

When he finished with her, she lay there quietly.

"Alexis, I want the ampoule of toxin you took from the doctor. Where is it?" he said in a stern voice.

"Grigory, I thought I was to use the toxin. It, it was my find," she said almost pleadingly.

"I never said that. True your cleverness got you the unexpected, but I will decide on what to do with it. Besides, you think too small."

How she hated him. He would steal her moment. She hated him, but she was also connected to him. As much as she wanted to run, she wanted to stay. He had opened her eyes. He had violently ripped her from her colorless existence and had shown her a bright world full of excitement and danger. And for those reasons she also loved him. Her captor had been her savior.

Markovic's primary focus had been the ricin-embedded cards and football game programs. Alexis' stolen ampoule of potent toxin stimulated him to devise several alternate plans. Markovic didn't know much about Lily Robinson, or why she had the toxin in her possession. However, unlike her mentor, Alexis knew what Lily looked like and had surmised that she was not just any guest for the curator's museum event. She imagined that one drop of Lily's toxin would create the sideline of confusion that Markovic was looking for. That was the power of poison.

CHAPTER 30

NEW YORK

Pristine water flows from upstate New York lakes winding its way through mountains and valleys until at last, 125 miles later, it reaches checkpoints near the city of New York. Prior to flooding a series of aqueducts, billions of gallons are treated with chlorine and fluoride, bathed in ultraviolet light to kill microorganisms, but never filtered. When Alexis first called Markovic on her way to the UN days before, his mind was already polishing an idea to create a diversion. He put his parallel plan into motion at that moment. After he had finished his work at the printing shop, Markovic and his men pored over the information about the reservoir systems of New York. The Hillview reservoir in Yonkers was the closest to the city before the water entered a maze of tunnels for distribution.

"We have opportunity here to create one or two distractions from our primary plan," Markovic said to his men. "Maxim will go ahead to prepare the way." He pointed to a satellite view of the area on his laptop and continued talking to the rest of his men. "You will meet here in this parking lot off the thruway near the casino and raceway. Leave the car there and head toward the reservoir. You can easily see the layout of the buildings on the grounds," he said pointing to the edge of the reservoir, "and this little map shows the internal workings of the pump house." Markovic's associates had been able to pull detailed engineering maps only available to New York City DEP officials, and those who knew how to hack into the system. From the DEP drawings Markovic's men could identify how the water flowed from the reservoir into the pumping house in preparation for distribution to NYC Water Tunnels No.1, 2 and 3. They had obtained security badges for the facility and spliced their own identities into place so they had free access to the system. The groundwork had been done and they waited for further instructions from Markovic.

*   *   *

Both brilliant and menacing, Markovic had provided the steady hand that had propelled the ricin operation. His mindset had been sculpted early in his life by his brutal creator. Raised in an abusive household by an alcoholic father and a mother frightened into obedience, Markovic survived by sheer will. Retaliation had been his life's goal, and anger, or perhaps it was fear, drove him like a snarling wolf backed into a corner. Yet it was his intense focus, his gift for conducting operations like Swiss trains, and his heart devoid of conscience that made him desirable to certain factions within the Russian government. Given his former connections with the illegal drug trade, he had been carefully chosen for this assignment. While working in the cocaine jungles of Colombia he had cultivated a taste for hard drinking, bar room brawls and brutal negotiations. Raping Alberto's niece was the epitome of intimidation and a way to secure better leverage with the Colombians. They had cut a deal. A set amount of the Russians' drug product smuggled from the Middle East would be shipped to France with Alberto's coffee beans in exchange for a percentage of the cash, and the Russians would no longer be able to conduct any business at the plantation. Alberto had wanted distance between Markovic and his niece.

*   *   *

JP and I are meeting with the rest of the team at the safe house.

"*Attention*," JP says in French. "*Et*, team, we found the link and have made the identification."

Our small group lets out a "hoo hoo." Now we have our target. JP continues.

"Most of the hands-on operations are being conducted by a Russian operative whose organization is partially fueled by Middle Eastern terrorist connections and by drug cartels operating out of South America."

I stiffen whenever I hear the words "drug cartels" and "South America." Something inside me feels uneasy at these words.

"The Russian's name is Grigory Markovic." He hands out a color photograph of Markovic to all of us with the physical specifications of the terrorist noted on the lower half of the picture. I've now memorized the image of a short man, balding, who has very intense steely gray eyes. Rather unforgettable in a threatening way.

"He also has an accomplice with him named Alexis Popov."

"Alexis Popov," I say. "The event planner from the museum bankers' dinner was named Alexis." I ask to see her picture. I recognize the young blond woman as the one I had seen in the ladies' room when I was at the museum. I had just left the kitchen. She was putting on her lipstick and had a dot of white powder above her upper lip. I wouldn't be surprised if it was a touch of cocaine.

"Here is what we know," JP says. "Their plan is to distribute all the tainted advertising cards throughout the city and at all the intersecting transportation hubs getting to and from New York down the East Coast. There are also some big sports events this weekend, the Super Bowl for one, and several concerts at the Garden. We have alerted all the authorities from both the State of New York and the State of New Jersey. They are instructed to pick up any and all distributors of these materials and of course the materials themselves."

"JP," I interrupt. "How do we know that the toxin is confined to only the advertising cards? Suppose it's impregnated into other materials?" This was not that far-fetched. I had already considered this in the museum when Eric and I took that fateful walk down the garden path. If the desired effect was mass poisoning, then there might be an opportunity, under the right conditions, for simultaneous aerosolization. Poison would diffuse down the concentration gradient.

"Lily, this is the information we have to date. We will focus on the cards. *Et—*"

I interrupt JP again. "What about my ampoule of toxin?"

"*Oui ,*surely it is just a distraction, Lily. You must know that this was pure chance that your toxin was stolen."

That sentence sits in my cortex for about two seconds before I react. *Chance, maybe.* But only JP and I knew the toxin was hidden in my handbag. And John Chi of course.

"Well my distraction killed a few people down by the UN building. I think we should look at the reservoir systems for the city," I say.

"*Quoi?* What do you mean, Robinson?"

"JP, they have a toxin in their possession that could potentially contaminate our water supply. Remember this toxin is highly concentrated and is not

180

destroyed by heat. If they tamper with our water source, we won't be worrying just about the air we breathe, but also the water we drink. It's what I would do."

"You have considered this?"

"Yes. Mass poisoning can be difficult, but clearly has been accomplished. There were the Tokyo subway sarin attacks in 1995. Sarin, a deadly nerve gas, was left to volatilize on the trains and sickened maybe 200 people. Poisoned water consumed by a group of individuals at a common venue is another way—Kool-Aid at Jonestown," I say, referring to the 900 followers of Jim Jones and the People's Temple who died in Guyana in 1978 after drinking cyanide laced Kool-Aid. "I've already looked at the maps. The Hillview Reservoir in Yonkers is the closest and would be my choice."

JP is quiet for a moment, then turns to one of his men and says, "Agent Parker, contact the local authorities and get some men over to the reservoir and check it out. *Tout de suite.*"

I'm not so sure that the toxin would be lethal if the dilution factor were great enough. Yet, individuals drinking the water could become acutely ill and that might be enough to create panic. I'm thinking it's better they should check it out than not. What other places would the terrorists choose to use my toxin and the ricin? I'm still working on it. And who is actually in possession of the ampoule? Alexis stole it, but did she still have it, or has she given it to her accomplice, Markovic?

I'm not sure what to expect next. And this is why most agents have their gun at their side. But guns are easily discoverable and confiscated. I have another plan. I go to the kitchen and open the freezer compartment of the refrigerator. Inside is a small Styrofoam box I brought with me from the cottage. I place it on the kitchen table, open the box, and unwrap a one milliliter syringe that had been prefilled with the contents of a clear liquid contained in the rubber stopped medicine vial. The Queen of all Poisons. I take some duct tape and tape the syringe just inside my left bra cup so it remains invisible. Just in case.

"I'm going to take a walk," I announce to JP as he enters the kitchen. "I need to clear my mind."

"I am not so sure that is a good idea, Lily," he replies.

"No, I'll be okay, really."

It's getting on to dusk. The light disappears early in the winter and it gets cold fast. I wrap my fur coat around me, and pull down the crystal fox headband. I decide to take a walk over to Central Park toward the old reservoir near 85th Street. I know that this reservoir had been decommissioned when the third water tunnel was completed. Now the closest functioning reservoir to the city is up in Yonkers—Hillview. The picturesque landscape in front of me is now primarily a walking or jogging trail around the 1.58-mile perimeter. However, the Central Park Reservoir was originally used as a temporary water supply while the Croton Water system was shut down for repairs.

I walk briskly on the jogging path to generate heat for my body and clear my mind. There are still quite a few joggers out here in their lycra pants and tops covered with layers of fleece making the best of the disappearing sun rays. I'm on part of the path that's not as open as the rest of the track. There's a man in the distance sitting on a rocky outcrop, smoking a cigarette. His silhouette is familiar. My antennae shoot straight up. I stop walking, move to the side and watch.

I stand and watch for what feels like eternity. The stream of joggers slows down and the light fades. Soon the moon begins to rise. What is he doing? Cold air tunnels its way through the gap in my coat between buttons and then I feel the hair on my arms stand straight up. It's Markovic. I feel this in my gut. Millions of people in New York City and by chance we would be together at this moment at the Central Park Reservoir. How is that possible? I'm stunned, and a little frightened. JP was right; I should not be out here on my own, at night.

Surely Markovic must know that this reservoir is obsolete. He puts out his cigarette and starts back toward 85th Street from the South Gate House. I keep my distance. When he reaches the Metropolitan Museum of Art, he makes his way around to the side entrance where the delivery trucks unload food and drink. He stops and checks his watch. Two minutes later a large tanker truck pulls up to the entrance. I recognize the sleek aluminum cylindrical shape of the tank as that of a water carrier. So I look up toward the roof and see a storage tank. It's not uncommon for buildings in the city to have a water tower perched above the structure to provide a day's worth of the water needs for the inhabitants of the building. However, usually the water is pumped into the tower from pipes below the ground, and not delivered by a tanker. I'm fairly certain that as part of the debrief this morning, we were told that the museum had experienced an unexpected pump failure in the morning and water delivery had been necessary for the anticipated Sunday crowd of museum visitors. I'm beginning to see the picture.

I watch the driver of the tanker step down from the cab and I can see Markovic approach him. They have a short conversation. I'm too far away to hear anything, but it looks as if they've exchanged something. Money? Instructions? I'm not sure. The driver walks away from the truck and disappears around the side entrance of the building. Markovic moves toward the flank of the tanker and climbs up the ladder that leads to the top of the truck. I get it. I know what's about to happen. I've got to call for help. I reach into my bag for my phone and feel that familiar stir of air behind me. As I turn, someone grabs me around the waist and puts one hand over my mouth. I'm trying to fight him off. I'm scared, ensnared and can't move. His grip is so tight, it's difficult for me to breathe. The air that has picked up carbon dioxide from my blood stream and is ready to explode out of my body in exchange for fresh oxygen-rich air is now trapped in my lungs. I'm losing sight of Markovic. My surroundings start to spin around me and I feel the blackness coming on as I drop to the ground.

CHAPTER 31

YONKERS, NY

Markovic's men carried out his threat at Hillview. Maxim and his team arrived at the reservoir during the night as planned and followed the detailed instructions written on the map they had of the pumping station. Using the IDs they had created while in Manhattan, they were able to gain initial access to the facility. The ninety-acre reservoir serves as a holding tank for the billions of gallons of water it receives each day from the Catskill and Delaware Aqueducts. The two uptake chambers are located on the north side of the four-chambered building, so they headed to the south side toward the two downtake chambers where water would be released into three city water tunnels, numbered 1, 2 and 3. When Maxim had gained original entry onto the grounds, he had used his computer to silently disable the security system, so there was no alert when his team entered the pump house. Once inside, they quickly over-powered the security detail whose job it was to keep the water supply safe.

Now that all systems were under their control, security cameras were disconnected from the live feed and were fed static images as a replacement. Maxim sent one of his men to retrieve the van they had parked near the stadium parking lot at the raceway. When the van returned, Maxim's men brought in large pipes and machinery and spread out all their tools on the cement floor.

"Maxim," said one of the men, "where you want me to dump this?" Over his shoulder was a form wrapped in a blanket.

"Put that one in the closet with two guards. Now let's us get to work."

Working quickly in the basement of the pumping house, the Russians shut off specific valves, diverting water to flow through alternate pipes. Then began the tedious replacement of dismantling the existing plumbing. They removed two of the main pipes where the water flowed into the tunnels and replaced them with ones that looked identical, but were lined with a thick layer of soft lead. Lead that would easily leach out into the drinking water flowing through the tunnels and travel to every faucet in the city. The concentration of lead in the body above 5 micrograms per deciliter triggers a medical alert in children. The amount of lead released from these pipes could potentially raise the blood concentration in the unsuspecting inhabitants of New York City to much higher levels. Lead exposure has no obvious symptoms, but can affect almost every system in the body and children are the most vulnerable. Their brain is still growing and signs of lead poisoning can produce developmental delay, learning difficulties, abdominal pain and hearing loss—deficits that begin small, but end with big consequences. Their plan was perhaps subtle, but effective.

Markovic's team worked without rest. When the task was complete, all the men exited the building through the rear door, except Maxim who stayed behind to take care of the loose ends. The Russians understood that the New York authorities would know that the reservoir had been tampered with. Officials had been up there earlier in the day to check out the facility at the urging of the Agency, but had found nothing. Markovic's team had waited patiently to return and replace the pipes when the time was right. New York officials would be back. It was just a question of time. Bodies would be discovered and subsequently, the DEP would be consumed with testing water samples for the next six months to determine where the defect was. The terrorists' objective was merely to disrupt everyday life, create areas of diversion along the way, and most importantly, produce influence over the American political scene.

*   *   *

JP looked at his watch and was fully aware that Lily had been gone for some time. She was an independent woman, but when they were working on an assignment together, he was in charge, not her. He found her so bold at times that some might say her behavior was not just calculated, but risky. Then again, these were the kinks in her armor that he found so attractive. Early in their relationship he had admired her encyclopedic knowledge of poisons and toxins and exploited that expertise to obtain sensitive goals created by the Agency. No matter what was said publicly, he knew that every government throughout the world recognized that elimination of specific enemies of the State were necessary. It's just that no one wants to admit to it, particularly in the United States. Although French, JP had always been assigned to the U.S. Agency through a little-known loophole exploited by both governments. Lily Robinson had been his early assignment for the actual field work, although other operatives were her primary contact people. He had been at her side ever since.

He fell in love with her after the Cambridge poisoning at the academic's dinner, but kept his feelings to himself, until no longer able to contain the mounting emotion, confronted her in Paris after they had assassinated three arms dealers. He found her ice-skating in a little courtyard on New Year's Eve and told her how much he loved her. Their physical connection was so electric that when they separated, it was if he had a limb torn from his own body. They were wired together, sharing electrons back and forth at the speed of light. They defied physics. Reaching her emotionally had been his biggest challenge, but over the years he had been able to break through her protective shell to find warmth and feeling within. While in the public view, they masqueraded as colleagues. This business arrangement served to cloak their alternate relationship as lovers, and rendered each some protection.

The dark-haired man was worried about her. He had called her cell phone several times and there was no answer. Lily would respond, unless she couldn't. The safe-house was filled with many agents and equipment. JP looked through Lily's belongings and found her gun, the trigger lock still on, sitting in her bag. She would be vulnerable. Then he stepped out into the main staging area and spoke to one of the other agents.

"Parker, locate Robinson's phone. She's been gone much too long. We should be able to track it."

Agent Parker looked at the cell phone tracker map on the computer and found a signal pulsating near the Metropolitan Museum.

"Boss, we have a signal here," Parker said, pointing to the computer screen. I can take a few men and pick her up."

Agent Parker and a handful of associates packed into a black SUV and rode to 5th Avenue and 80th Street, parking around the side entrance used for deliveries at the museum. Everything appeared quiet and Lily Robinson was nowhere in sight. Using their tracking device, the men moved into the location where the cell phone signal was the strongest, ever vigilant of their surroundings. Still not seeing any people in the area, they parted the bushes, and started searching closer to the ground. Lily Robinson's cell phone lay bare in the mulch. Agent Parker picked up his own phone and dialed JP. He explained that he had found her phone, but not her. It looked as if there had been a scuffle in the area, and they found a large button on the ground which they kept as evidence. Parker also noted that there was a path that led to the Central Park reservoir and the men had combed that area as well. Robinson was nowhere to be found.

JP absorbed all this information and formulated a plan of his own. He left the main room of remaining agents and entered one of the back bedrooms of the house. His briefcase was there, and he opened the lid and pulled a small device from the back pocket. He switched it on and a pulsating white light appeared. He obtained the coordinates of the beam, and entered them into his portable GPS device.

"*Mais, oui*, but of course!" he uttered to himself and left the room.

"Get the van ready, and the dogs, and get me Parker," he shouted at his team.

*   *   *

When I open my eyes, there is only blackness. I can feel something warm and sticky oozing through my clothes. I don't think it's coming from me, since I don't feel pain in my body. Just aches. Something warm is under me, but it's hard to tell since my hands are bound by my sides. It's as if I'm wrapped in a blanket. The growing fear creeps into every pore in my body so I center my mind, tune that fine focus, and recreate the time line. The last thing I remember is being outside the Museum and watching the water delivery. I could see Markovic climbing up the ladder onto the top of the tanker. I was sure he had my toxin and was going to dump it into the open valve. He was going to poison the drinking water destined for the museum. I tried to call for help. I got out my phone, and then it was as if someone took my breath away. Blackness. Now where am I?

I try rolling from side to side to loosen the wrap. There is something, no someone, under me. My guess is that they're either dead or unconscious since there is no movement, and if they're dead, I'm not sure why I'm not as well. The darkness is frightening. When I stop to concentrate I can hear some faint drilling sounds, and what sounds like pumps circulating, but that's all. Where could they have possibly taken me? I doubt we are in the museum, although this could be a closet anywhere. The rolling back and forth has loosened my wrap and I can now move my arms more freely. I wriggle up toward the top of the blanket and am finally able to pull my torso and my arms out. There's no more light out here than from under the blanket, but I can take bigger breaths, and I can feel my way in and around the tiny room. There's no light switch on the walls that I can feel, so this must be a utility closet with the light switch outside the door. The door is locked.

Now, I need to determine who else is in here. There's one, no two, bodies trapped with me. My fingers feel for their necks in search of a pulse. No pulse. I touch their faces and let my fingers close their eyelids. I sweep both hands over their bodies squeezing their arms, legs and torso. The clothing feels like something a security guard would wear. Patches are sewn on the upper sleeve and above the breast pocket. The holster is empty and I feel around for a gun, but come up empty. When I touch the chest, my hand sticks to warm, thick liquid. Blood. This one has been shot. Probably the same is true for the other one. Tingles fan within my belly as fear takes hold. I'm next. Wish I had my gun with me. But then I realize two things. They would have surely taken my gun by now, and then, as I reach inside my bra cup, I feel the presence of the syringe taped to my skin. I've got it. It may be tantamount to bringing a knife to a gun fight, but hey, it's all I've got. So, two security guards have been shot and dumped in a closet. What were they guarding?

The drilling noise goes on for what seems like hours. I have no phone and no watch. All I can do is think. We're probably not in the museum because if the goal was to put poison in the water, the contents would already have been unloaded into the museum's holding tank by now. This place seems more like a pump house given the background noise. That's it! A pump house. Markovic must be up at Hillview. We're at the reservoir. But why not kill me straight off? Why just incapacitate me and keep me around with the dead bodies? What does he need from me?

I'm not sure if I should try and break out just yet. It may be better to wait. So, I do. Sometime later I hear footsteps approaching and I review my choices, fast. Do I stand so that when the door opens I will be behind it ready to attack? Or do I pretend to be wrapped back in the blanket and wait and see? I choose the door plan since whoever is approaching might just stand within the entry and fire his gun into the room. I hurry to place the blanket over one of the guards so at least it looks like a body is under there. I slide back behind the door, my heart racing once again. Quiet, quiet, this thumping is so loud. He's outside the door, I know this. The door opens and a tall man in a black cap, jeans and sweatshirt walks in. It's not Markovic! This man, whoever he is, has a Makarov PM in his hand ready to fire. He's Russian. When he edges forward, eyes sweeping the room, I approach him from behind holding a heavy mop bucket ready to knock him down, but he's too quick. He turns and knocks the bucket down with his pistol and pulls me forward. His hand covers my mouth and nose, and I find myself gasping for air once again. He drags me out of the closet and I can see that I am in a pump room. So, this must be the Hillview Reservoir. What are we doing here? I manage to wriggle out of his grip just enough to speak.

"Let me go," I shout. "What do you want from me, what are we doing here?

"Ah, you talk," he says in a heavy Russian accent. "I take you with me for little insurance. I found you spying on my boss. Why? Who are you?"

He starts pushing me forward into an elevator. I look around the room before I get in. It's clearly a water pump house with huge curved pipes, switch valves and large metal hydraulic wheels. What have they done?

"Who am I?" I say. "Who are you?" I feel like Alice in Wonderland having a conversation with the caterpillar. He holds up the pistol and asks me again who I am.

"I was walking near the museum and became curious about the tanker truck. That's all. What are we doing here?" There's no reply and the talk stops.

The elevator goes up to the ground floor where we walk around to the rear of the building and exit. I'm outside now and I've lost track of the time. The moon is still out, but I think dawn will be rising soon. We start to walk atop a long wall that runs the length of the reservoir and divides it into two separate basins. Does he want to dump me into the water? I doubt he is using this as a shortcut to get to the other side of the reservoir. Up ahead there looks like there's part of the chain linked fence that has been cut away, allowing for an opening down toward the water. That must be the stopping point. My heart is thumping again and I'm sure he can hear it. There's a steep drop from the top of the revetment to the water below. He pushes me toward the opening and is now standing directly in front of me. This is my last chance, he says, to tell him why I was following Markovic.

"We found you following Markovic. I don't know who you are, and now I don't care. You had chance to talk, but time has run out. They should have shot you with others," he says. This is a clear signal my time is up. Not that I have a bargaining chip, but since I'm about to die, I pretend I do.

"We're on to your faction. We know about the ricin. You can turn yourself in and be a witness against Markovic. I know people who can make a deal with you," I tell him.

"It's too late for Markovic," he says.

I'm desperate. "Where was the toxin made?" I ask.

"Hong Kong. And that's enough talking for you."

Then he makes his move. I look over my shoulder and see that there's no place to go, except down. He inches me up toward the edge and as I lose my balance my left hand grabs his right shoulder to steady myself, and with my right hand I take the syringe which I had previously removed from the bra cup, and jam the needle directly into his carotid artery pushing the plunger all the way to the hub of the needle.

"What, you bitch," he yells. I try and turn so I'm no longer facing the opening and at the same time give him a knee to the groin. The Russian falters and pulls me with him as he tumbles down the wall. He's gasping for air. I manage to hang on to a piece of chain link as he hits the water. He's going down under, but I'm not. As a breath escapes, I quickly take another one in.

*   *   *

JP's men flooded the Hillview reservoir in Yonkers. They systematically moved through the building and made their way down into the basement of the pump house. When they opened the door to the utility closet, they found the remains of two men who had once stood in the facility protecting the water supply. They had been shot, and there was blood on a blanket that had probably covered a third body. Robinson. But she was not in the building. The men remaining back in the black SUV obtained visual confirmation on the identities of the facility's security guards. Another small van approached and they could see it was the K-9 unit when it slid into the space next to the parked vehicle. Two handsome Belgium Malinois' jumped out of the van and twirled on their leads until they finally settled with their handlers. The agents gave the dogs a scarf that Lily Robinson had worn. Their keen noses inhaled the scent and were then set free to track her down if she were still on the grounds. The dogs made a beeline for the almost 3,000 foot long wall dividing the reservoir into the East and West basins. When they reached the break in the fence they stopped, and the dogs started barking fiercely. The agent shined a light down at the water and he could see a body floating.

"Robinson, are you all right? Hold on," Agent Parker shouted.

*   *   *

Here I am holding onto to the bit of broken fencing trying not to drop into the water below. My coat is caught. There are dogs barking ferociously with their muzzles pointed in my direction, an orb of light adjacent to the moon, and I hear Agent Parker shouting at me. Parker then turns to one of the other agents and asks him to call in backup with a rescue basket so they can safely extract any bodies from the basin.

"Is there anyone else down there with you?" Parker asks.

"Yes, although I think he's gone under. I no longer can see him. He's all yours. He should be dead."

Within a few minutes, which seems to me forever, a rescue basket is lowered down carrying two divers in dry suits outfitted in scuba gear. One helps me into the basket while the other one drops to the bottom of the wall and then dives into the water looking for my Russian assailant. When I get back on land, they place a blanket over my shoulders as I download info to Parker trying to remember as much as I can. The blanket gives me an uneasy feeling. I walk back to the parking area and decline the offer to be taken to an area hospital. The blood they found in the utility room was not mine I assure them. Then I see that the palm of my hand is bleeding where the fence has cut through.

They're driving me back to the safe house. When I get there and open the door, there's JP standing at the entry looking concerned, but reserved. "Robinson," he says with slight alarm as he pulls me into the back room.

"What do you think you are doing? You could have been killed. This is not how you operate. Your job is not to chase the bad guys in the middle of the night. Lily, you have a very narrow role in the organization. We choose targets and you pick the right poison, *mais oui*?" he says. He's angry. I hear it in his tone. We're alone. I don't answer. Then he pulls me into him and we cling together. I wince in pain from my bruises and abrasions.

"I cannot lose you my *Ma Chérie*," he says as he twists the platinum braided bracelet on my wrist.

Our lips meet in a soft communion and I feel my body dissolve into his. I want him now, but we have business.

"JP, it was Markovic. I'm sure he has the ampoule of toxin."

The dark-haired man looks into my eyes. "Lily, my men are still up at the Hillview Reservoir. You are right. Something happened there. We are considering all the information you gave Parker."

"And?" I ask.

"We do not yet know how the Russians tampered with the water supply, but we are assuming they did. It will take time to unravel."

Then I let him know about the museum. "JP, Markovic may have used my toxin or some other toxin to poison a tanker truck delivering water to the art museum. I know he did something and we're going to have to alert city authorities about the holding tanks, and the reservoirs. I'll contact some of the best chemists in the country to start looking for toxins in the New York City water supply. Just get me some samples, and make it *toute de suite*." I see those distinguished eyebrows rise framing his crow's feet as the dark-haired man hears me, but he already knows all of this.

"Now, I'm going to clean up these scrapes and get some sleep. I'm exhausted," I say, and slowly retreat from the safety of his arms. "It's been a very long day. I'll try Dr. Leigh tonight and tomorrow if I don't hear from him."

*   *   *

One of the agents takes me back to my hotel room and makes sure the room is clear when we enter. JP had to stay behind to continue the investigation or he would have come with me. I wanted him tonight, and I could tell he wanted me too. Danger produces a series of hormones that sets the body on edge that sharpens your senses, and makes you feel alive. They stir the cauldron of sexual desire that can only be satisfied when two heated bodies come together. But the dark-haired man is not here, so I hang up my coat and sit down on the bed and my head falls on the pillow, but just for a moment. I haven't yet changed my clothes or wiped the dirt and blood off my legs, and I feel myself already falling asleep. I start to dream, but then something startles me. It's the free-fall sensation that jolts your body awake, just as it's drifting into slumber. The hypnic jerk. It isn't a noise, or a sudden movement in the room, it's a remembrance of the last meeting I had with my therapist.

"Lily, let's try again," the therapist says. "If we can break through you might find some resolution, some peace."

I have been through this many times over many years. Alone and in my bed, and in his office, trying to work out my dream, the details of my horror. I remember. I relax into his plush office chair and focus on his voice. I visualize the beginning of dawn over the ocean on a brilliant summer morning. A dazzling red and orange sky fills the atmosphere and sets my mind on fire. I'm there.

*   *   *

A woman with dark hair and wings, like an angel, floats through the woods. She speaks out loud but there is no one there: *I always had a passion for collecting—never for murder. My autumn walk through the New England woods, mixed with pine and oak, led me to small armies of fungi. Each soldier, standing tall with white gills and stems, bearing smooth pure white helmets, was ready to stealthily deliver death on command. This is me, what I've become—the Destroying Angel.*

The scene changes rapidly. Now I can see myself in the woods with a young man who is familiar to me.

"Dr. Robinson? Dr. Robinson? Ah, do you think we have enough specimens?"

I see myself looking up and into the face of one of the graduate students. He stands in front of me, young, with blond hair and brown eyes wearing khaki pants and a thick pile fleece parka. I say to him, *"I'm sorry, Stuart, what did you say?"*

"I wanted to know if you thought we had collected enough specimens, you know, for your next trip."

I watch the dream unfold before me, as if I were watching a movie. I see myself speaking with my graduate student and watch as the dream image of me pulls up the collar of my jacket as the wind nips at my neck.

"Yes, Stuart I believe we have enough," I answer him. *"Stuart, why don't you go ahead and get the car warmed up; I'll be there in a minute; I just want to look around a bit more."* I watch Stuart leave and move out of the scene and then I see myself sort through a few more fungi, but this time, I pick the Death Cap, *Amanita phalloides*.

The scene changes again; I'm no longer in the New England woods, but now in the jungle. I see myself remove my wide brim hat from my head and

193

wipe the sweat from my brow with the sleeve of my shirt. The jungle is hot. For the last five days we've searched the Pacific versant for small gold jewels. Within the folds of green foliage one jewel sits quietly beckoning to me. I carefully retrieve my net and cast it forward to collect my prize. A beautiful, yellow, poison-dart frog. It's then that I hear the noise. It's distant but clear. It's a pop, no, it's a pop pop pop. Gunshots. There are screams. I'm not sure but I think it's coming from the direction of the camp. My heart is pounding. I try to repress the bitter taste in my mouth as my stomach churns in acid. I drop everything and run back to the camp as if aided by angel's wings.

The camp is not yet in full view. But, I'm almost there. I enter the clearing and see the first body with blood soaking his university tee shirt. Stuart. I don't stop because I can see the bullet wound in his chest and I know he's dead. There's more, much more, too terrible to face, too terrible for my mind to embrace. My body stiffens, and I try to cry out, but no sound comes out of my mouth. I try again. There's steam in the air, red covering the ground, and there's only silence. I cannot find my voice.

My God. There's my tent. It looks still. I don't perceive any signs of life. Maggie, oh Maggie. Her body lays crushed just outside the parted nylon curtain. I can't bring myself to look down at her, so I just catch a glimpse out of the corner of my eye. I part the unzipped screen of the tent with the pulses in my wrists almost visible. There is only the emptiness within. My daughter is gone. I fall to my knees and shake with such grief that I feel my body shatter into thousands of shards of glass. Surely it is just my broken heart. I have been robbed of the one joy I loved above all others. My wails echo through the jungle as I lay helpless among the mangled bodies, soaking the blood from the ground into my jeans and into my soul.

* * *

I hear the therapist's voice. "Go on, Lily, you must get to the end of your dream."

The sky is ablaze. Clouds hang in the air suspended like red rockets as I struggle to return to the scene.

"I can't, I can't finish the dream," I shout in anguish. "I just can't." Only it's not a dream.

"You can," he tells me. "What happens after you find your tent empty? What happens next, Lily?"

"I, I don't remember. I can't find her body; where's my baby's body? There are so many bodies. There's blood everywhere. I wander around the campsite. I must be in shock. I don't know, I think I started walking. Yes, I walk back into the jungle. I, I'm exhausted."

I'm sobbing now, sitting in that plush chair; my body tense with knees curled to my chest as I tell the dream. The sun is finally emerging. It peaks slowly at first, but then it bursts into the sky like a hot fiery ball and announces morning. I feel the fire; the emotional flames singe my face and burn in my mind.

"Lily, try and focus," he says. You walk into the jungle. What happens next?"

"I don't know. I, I think I find another camp. Yes, that's it. I find another camp. The people there are surprised to see someone so lost in the jungle. Alone. Alone and lost. I, I can't explain to them what has happened. I don't know what's happened. They see I'm covered with blood and look all over my body to find my wounds."

I look into the therapist's face. I know we have struggled for years to get to this place. We both know that the wounds were not to be found anywhere on my body. Instead, they were buried deep in my heart, and in my mind, well out of the reach of all, except perhaps a shaman.

*   *   *

What Lily didn't know at the time was that she had walked into a foreign government sponsored clandestine operation. They had infiltrated the Colombian jungle to gather information on several drug cartels that were operating under the cover of coffee plantations. In the next decade they would work their way through the organizations until they would crush them one by one. When Lily Robinson had inadvertently discovered them, she was clearly in shock and traumatized, and had lost touch with reality. They discovered what had happened at her camp a day or so later, but could not reveal their cover so kept Lily with them until she was well enough to travel. She had lost most of her memory regarding the massacre and only remembered collecting frogs for her research. She was told her small daughter had died in a horrible accident in the rain forest. They never used the word murder, and they never recovered any bodies. The government managed to suppress all news and information about the incident so they could continue their work in secrecy. Lily Robinson and her daughter had been collateral damage. They kept in touch with her through the years and later, when the time was just right, pressed her into service to help them achieve their own goals. She had been an easy target. Once again, the tip of the scorpion's stinger went deep, right into the heart, and just between beats.

CHAPTER 32

NEW YORK CITY

I had no luck reaching Dr. Leigh the night before. I tried calling him again in the morning, but still no answer. Today is Sunday. The government is confident that they have collected most of the advertisement cards, and has decided not to shut down any sports events, concerts or entrances to museums. Except for one. In an unprecedented move, the Metropolitan Art Museum is closed today while the Water Authority checks the failed water pump and chemists analyze the water from the tanker. An alert has been issued city wide to urge citizens to boil their water for ten minutes (I'm not sure what that will accomplish since that only helps with bacterial contamination and not toxins, but it wasn't my call), and to buy bottled water for additional security. Supermarket shelves are being stripped bare like the day before an announced blizzard.

I go back to the safe house to check in with the dark-haired man.

"JP, do you have any more information since last night?" I ask him.

"Markovic is missing and there is another body of interest we have just discovered. It's been mutilated so it will be a little while to see if it is a match to him. However, the body we pulled from the reservoir last night belongs to Maxim Petrikov. He was Markovic's right hand man, but perhaps the two of them disagreed on some aspect of the operation. Petrikov may have done our job for us. Moreover, I don't think either of them was fully aware of just who you are and the role you play. It seems like a coincidence that Petrikov picked you up while you were stalking his boss at the museum. Oh, and by the way, we are all amazed that you were not killed in the fall last night off the wall, *Chérie. C'est un miracle.*"

"A miracle, yes. I think my coat snagging on the broken fence is what saved me. The Russian broke my fall to some extent, although I have to admit I'm pretty sore this morning." I rub my hand where the gash is and then over my left arm to soothe the pain.

"Lily, what did you use to kill him? It was you, *mais oui?*

"Come on JP," I say with a smile, "You know that's a trade secret." All he can say is *hmmm.*

Then he asks if I've heard from Dr. Leigh. I tell him, not a word and then realize it's time to turn Leigh in.

"Listen, JP, there's a good chance that Leigh is part of this." I wait for his response. Leigh has always been my choice, my pick. The Agency has never been too keen on him. JP is looking at me with that wrinkled eyebrow and waiting for me to continue. He has incredible discipline. So I fill in the blanks.

"Only you and Leigh knew about the poison I was carrying in my handbag. No one else. And, and, most compelling, there is no one on this planet other than John Chi who has the skill set to make this grade of ricin. The toxin was created in Hong Kong. It has to be him."

The dark-haired man sits quietly. Then he says, "I'll call some contacts in Hong Kong."

"Okay. I'm going over to Mercy Hospital and check on a few things. I'll meet up with you later. By that time, we should have a full-fledged catastrophe on our hands if they don't collect all the ricin filled cards." I leave the safe house and take a cab to the hospital. I have two stops to make, both at Mercy.

*   *   *

"Knock, knock. Hey how are you feeling?" I ask Eric Vandermeer. He has a large bandage wrapped around his head and looks tired.

"Lily!" he greets me with enthusiasm. "So great to see you."

I lean over and give him a hug, then pull up a chair next to the bed and start a conversation.

"Eric, no bombs at the museum. The exhibit is safe. The only thing that's missing is its famous curator." I can see his face brighten.

"Yeah, right," he says. "It's a good thing you were there when I managed to knock myself out. I guess it takes a pathologist to know that I have worms in my brain," he adds with a laugh.

"Hey, as long as you're getting better." Then I start in with a lecture reminding him that he needs to cook his food thoroughly the next time he's down south of the border collecting whatever it is he collects. *Taenia* eggs have a way of finding a path to the gray matter in one's head. Then he interrupts me.

"Lily," he says. "I've been thinking about the event planner, Alexis. I checked in with the museum administration to get some background information on her. She started working with the museum about a year ago. She has always been extremely well organized and professional with all the events she has helped put together for us. There is nothing unusual there. However, there is one interesting piece of information. I asked the staff to look at all the events she worked on. Every one of them was accompanied by a large cash donation to our educational fund and had those advertising cards inserted into the literature that we handed out to the patrons. What do you think?"

What I think is that those were all dry runs for the real event and by doing so in advance, it wouldn't look unusual if the perfume cards were included on this occasion. I let Eric know that I think it's very useful information although the Agency already knows that Alexis Popov is part of this terrorist group. She is clearly an accomplice of Markovic.

I ask Eric how long he thinks they'll keep him in the hospital.

"Not sure," he says. "Maybe just another few days." Then he asks, "Lily, what about those perfume cards? Did they find them all?"

I hesitate to give him an answer. Eric knows quite a lot at this point, but not everything.

"Let me put it this way," I say. "You might want to spend a few extra days in the hospital. There's no rush to go home."

I give him a quick kiss on the cheek and head down to pathology. Second stop. Even though it's Sunday, I might be able to catch Francis Becker in his office. His door is open. My good luck.

"Hi there," I say, as I pop my head into his office.

"Well I'll be darned. Miss Lily," he says like he was in a television western from the 1970s. "I was wonderin' when I was gonna see you again. Listen, Lily, seriously, the whole city's gone a bit crazy. That's why I'm in the office today. The bodies, well frankly the bodies have been pilin' up. Marie is overwhelmed and there just aren't enough pathologists in the city to do all the autopsies. We already called in some colleagues from Long Island, and maybe you want to come in and do a few yourself. Marie is thinking that if all the patients present with similar signs and symptoms, then maybe we don't need to autopsy them all. Some of these are just going to be a view based on clinical symptoms."

A view means that if there is enough compelling evidence as to the cause of death, then an autopsy won't be performed. For example, if a known substance abuser is found with a needle in their arm and the toxicology report is positive for heroin, then the medical examiner may choose not to perform an autopsy. The medical examiner may choose to view the body only and make sure identification is correct.

"Lily," Francis asks, "did ya' talk to Marie about the ricin? Last time when you and I met, you told me you thought the toxin was ricin. Has that been confirmed?"

In fact, John Chi has never gotten back to me, so it's not been confirmed. We deliberated what to tell the Chief Medical Examiner when we met at the safe house this morning. However, it was assumed that most of the cards would be collected and we might be able to avoid any serious discussions. The Agency is negotiating with other governmental units on just how much to reveal to the public out of concern of producing widespread panic. Marie would have to know eventually.

"No Francis, I don't think we've specifically told Marie about the ricin, just that there seems to be some new agent causing an epidemic of respiratory collapse. We've also noted that it doesn't appear to be transmitted person to person, so there are no special precautions that need to be taken. To address the perfume card threat, government authorities have issued a public bulletin to the effect that any wrapped advertising cards should not be removed from the cellophane wrapper and should be taken to the nearest post office for proper disposal since they may contain small pieces of glass that were inadvertently introduced during the manufacturing process. Clearly bogus but less threatening than saying they contain poison."

The public can't know the truth. To realize that the terrorists have penetrated their safe way of life, wounded the mighty eagle's wings and introduced toxins into the city in an attempt at mass destruction would create a panic that could not be contained.

I reach out to touch my colleague's hand. Pathologists are the invisible thread in the weave of healthcare. They confirm the diagnosis, for better or worse. "You take care, Francis," I say. "I'll follow-up with you in a few days."

"Lily," he says, "this time, let's not wait so many years. Ya know, I'm gonna be watchin' the Super Bowl tonight having some chips, guacamole and a bourbon and branch. Ya'll welcome to join me."

"Thanks for the invite my friend," I reply. "Sounds tempting, but I have other plans for tonight." And then I exit the hospital to get ready for the next round.

*   *   *

Alexis didn't understand why Grigory had not returned from the previous night. He had left the room with the ampoule of toxin as dusk was approaching. She had waited for him until midnight, but when she heard nothing from him, she went to sleep. Early in the morning she checked in with operations only to learn that they too hadn't heard anything from Markovic or even Maxim. There were no television news reports about an accident or a body being found, so she wasn't sure what to make of it.

She took a cab down to the warehouse where all the programs for the Super Bowl had been transported. Markovic's men were loading them into the truck ready to deliver the programs to the stadium for sale and distribution. Everything was right on target. With or without Grigory she would continue with the work. Alexis knew what she had to do, and although Markovic wasn't with her, she knew she still needed him. He had looked after her when she was ripped away from her home at a young age.

Last night, after he had finished having sex with her, when she was her most vulnerable, he said to her something he had said many times before. "You are like your mother."

What did he mean by that? Maybe one day she would ask her mother, that is if she ever saw her mother again.

She moved around the warehouse in and out of shelves and stacks of cartons looking for Markovic. Boxes of programs and perfume cards were waiting patiently to be loaded onto trucks. One of Markovic's inner circle approached her when he saw her stopped by the office area.

"Alexis, after delivery of these materials, we are getting out of here," said one of Markovic's men. "Everything is still going as planned. Last night we created diversion with the city's water supply. Markovic's a genius. Get your things out of hotel and meet us at airport. We keeping to plan, no matter what."

"What do you mean, no matter what? Where is Grigory?" she replied. "We need to wait for Grigory."

"We believe Markovic and Maxim are dead. Killed last night by Americans," he said dispassionately. "Intelligence knew about them and

201

they know about us. It's only a matter of time."

Alexis reeled at this news. Grigory could not be dead. And Maxim? He is too clever to be caught. "What are you saying?" she asked again, visibly shaken.

"Alexis, you are soldier. We need to move on for cause. Once programs are delivered our work is done. The toxin should produce mass poisoning. Then we can sit back and watch stock markets crash, real estate plunge and chaos consume America. Then we move in for spoils. Now get your things and meet us at airport at 1800 hours. Don't just stand there. Go. Go!"

He had delivered the news as if he had said dinner was ready and on the table. It was brutal. Alexis stumbled and fought back the tears. No one would understand. Grigory was cruel, but he fed her; he was unfeeling but he clothed her; he was without a moral compass, but showed her a direction she never would have found without him.

Alexis went back to the hotel. She quickly gathered her things and let herself into the adjoining room to sift through Markovic's clothes. There was nothing memorable in his personal belongings. Nothing that said who he was. Just clothes.

She returned to her room and locked the adjoining door behind her. Perched on the bed, she ran her hand across the sheets, straightened them out and fell on top of the covers, tears streaming down her cheeks. Once again her whole life was turned upside down. She would have to readjust, find a new mentor in the organization, or, possibly lead it herself? Always the strong and rebellious teen growing up, she knew how to adapt, and how to survive. She assumed her strength came from her mother who could adjust in the face of ever-changing circumstances. What was it, her mother had once said to them? "I had dreams of my own that were never fulfilled." It was her way of letting her daughters know that she wasn't about to let it happen to them. Alexis had adapted to a harsh reality, and now she would need to push on, only this time without Grigory.

She slipped out of her dress and pulled a fresh pair of underwear out of her suitcase. She slipped out of her panties and looked at herself in the mirror. No scars reminiscent of physical beatings, just invisible emotional marks that had stood the test of time. She turned her back toward the mirror and her head over her shoulder. There it was. Just under her right hip. The body of a spider with eight legs outlined in black and its spinneret ready to weave her plan. The artist had been right. She was living a life of trickery and treachery.

CHAPTER 33

HONG KONG AND NEW JERSEY

Consumed by the ricin conundrum, John Chi Leigh could not leave his Hong Kong lab until he had the resolution. He reviewed his findings multiple times and always came up with the same answer. Lily had shipped him a series of cards that had been collected from all over the city. Some of the cards had a manufacturing date of November, while the rest were made in December. He could tell this by a small line in the bar code that gave the date the card was made. He also assumed that this would be close to the date that the toxin was embedded into the card, but had understood that the toxin itself had been made much earlier in the year. The perpetrators of the crime would have needed time to extract the ricin, convert the crude toxin into a weaponized form and then join the two processes, that is, embed the cards' scratch strip with toxin. It was a course of action that was easily a year in the making.

There were only a few laboratories in the world that were capable of accomplishing this high level of chemistry. One was, of course, his own lab. However, the mainland Chinese were also very capable of creating sophisticated drug labs. They were currently manufacturing illicit designer synthetic opioids and cannabinoids, and if the money was right, there was no reason they couldn't, wouldn't, make chemicals for warfare.

Synthetic cannabinoids or synthetic marijuana, commonly known as K2 or spice, was something that John Chi had been very familiar with. These man-made chemicals could be sprayed onto other plants and mimic some of the effects of delta-9 tetrahydrocannabinol, the psychoactive ingredient found in marijuana. As the U.S. government banned the new compounds, chemists would simply modify a hydrogen, or nitrogen or hydroxyl group here or there and create a totally new drug that presumably wasn't banned.

While some of these new compounds could produce an elevated mood and a relaxed feeling, more often they created paranoia and hallucinations. Violent behavior, suicidal thoughts and racing hearts or worse brought young people into the emergency departments around the country. It was hard to prevent the Chinese from getting these drugs into the United States. Leigh knew that the DEA was continuing talks with their counterparts in Beijing to crack down on these chemists who fine-tuned chemical formulas just to stay one step ahead of the law. Now opioids were the bigger business. Even John Chi had been approached to get into this game. His lab and his knowledge could be parlayed into billions of dollars. Synthetic fentanyl was in demand now and would be easy for him to make, just a simple cookbook formula. Yet of all the villains looking for chemists to hire for their own revenge schemes or money-making illicit drug enterprises, it was the terrorists who were the most frightening. Scrutinizing the world for new toxins and ways to weaponize them could command an unimaginable price. It was a tempting proposition.

The signature that John Chi saw within the chromatogram was distinct. He knew where the crude toxin had been made. By the look of the extraction process trail, the toxin had been created in Russia, but it was clear the refinement had taken place in China, more specifically in Hong Kong. He recognized the small residual molecules surrounding the larger peaks as an indication of a novel technique, his technique, for making such a fine particle. This was his laboratory's work. John Chi Leigh had been betrayed. This was never part of the agreement.

*　　*　　*

While Leigh worked out his puzzle in Hong Kong, program guides had been delivered to the football stadium ready to showcase the upcoming Super Bowl held in a teeming corner of the United States. Fans were already tailgating in the parking lot while others were streaming into the arena to find their seats. Ticket scalpers remained out front in hopes of finding someone willing to pay thousands of dollars for a chance to be part of history. Government agents and local police had practically surrounded the sports center. Most of the cards had been removed already, but there were still thousands of cards throughout the northeast corridor.

Vendors lined up the beers, the chicken wings, hot dogs and soda, and sold program guides by the thousands. Millions of television viewers turned on their high-definition sets and sat down in groups of families and friends to watch the spectacle. They had created their own dishes of chips and salsa, foot-long hoagies and endless supersized drinks. It was Super Bowl Sunday. The equivalent to the ancient Romans lining the steep seats in the Coliseum to watch the gladiators battle with each other, and with a wild menagerie of exotic creatures. It was time to let the games begin.

*　　*　　*

Dr. Francis Becker stayed later at the hospital than he had planned. There was something about these cases that bothered him. Lily had told him that all the victims had been exposed to the same toxin. But Stu Greene, the emergency department physician said some of the patients who presented with similar signs and symptoms survived with supportive treatment, and some died. Why didn't they all die? On his own autopsies, he noted variable amounts of pathology, some bodies showing more extensive lesions than others. He would have to check with Lily. He decided to let these questions go until the next day and head back to his New York home.

Francis Becker sat down in his comfortable chair back at the apartment, pulled up a table of goodies and cursed his leg filled with shrapnel and pain. His fluffy cat rubbed up against his ankle, but she was not as good a cure as the Bourbon and branch. He let out a small cough, wiped the sweat off his brow with his shirtsleeve and rubbed his tired eyes. The TV set flickered and the first anticipated commercial filled the screen. He had the perfect seat for the unfolding spectacle.

Eric Vandermeer had not been able to leave Mercy Hospital as Becker had. He was still a captive. The image of Alexis floated in his head and he wanted to return to the museum as soon as possible to learn more about her. He pressed the call button by his bed and asked one of the nurses to fix his pillows for him so he could get the angle straight for viewing the TV. He had trouble focusing because of the double vision, but he wasn't about to miss the Super Bowl. He would call Lily in the morning.

Jim Cassidy was riding the ambulance around the city. "Hey, can you turn on the radio," he said to his driver. "I'd like to see if we can get the football game on and catch the score. Oh, we've got another call. Twenty-five-year-old woman found down near the Park. Let's get over there now." The number of calls regarding acute respiratory distress and pulmonary edema seemed to Jim, to be slowing down. But the number of opioid overdoses was clearly on the rise. The narcotics just kept bombarding the city's vulnerable population without an end in sight.

*   *   *

The dark-haired man and I wait in a specially-equipped van near the parking lot by the gates of the football stadium. It's as good a place as any on this Sunday night. The cards have been found all over the city. Our vehicle is ready to move out to any location in an emergency, and it carries a supply of Hazmat suits and fine particle respirators. The biggest fear the producers of the Super Bowl faced had been the chance of a major snowfall. There had been much criticism for having the game in a cold weather city and not under the safety of a glass dome or someplace where the temperatures were mild and the cold air didn't take your breath away. If only I could reassure the world that cold temperatures and even snow would be preferable to ricin. I've still not heard from John Chi. The idea that he would have a hand in this makes me angry. I trusted him and believed that he trusted me.

*   *   *

John Chi went to the drug synthesis lab in the far end of the facility and looked at all the equipment. The lab hadn't been used for quite some time. Everything one would need to make weaponized ricin could be found here. Over in the corner hung a mask used for highly dangerous work. He could tell that it had been hanging on the peg for a while. There was a little dust on the band and the filter didn't appear to be brand new. It had been used before.

He donned protective clothing, then removed the filter and rinsed it, capturing the fluid. He added various solvents until he had collected enough of the liquid to concentrate the mixture. Then he waited.

When the extraction was completed, he injected the mixture into the mass spectrometer. He waited patiently for the signal to emerge. There it was. Ricin. The same peak he had identified in samples sent from New York appeared here. The original specimens also contained the metabolite ricine, and another unidentified peak which he could also see in this analysis. The number of peaks appeared to be variable across the samples. One thing was certain, the creation of the weaponized toxin had been done in this lab, in his lab. He was furious. He went down to the security section of the lab. It was closed this early in the morning, but he was the laboratory's director and had been employed there long enough to know how things worked. He found a way to get inside and turned on the computer. He typed in his passcode. Access to the security files was denied. He looked around the desk and under the keyboard.

Ming, he thought, *from the mainland. How many times have we been told to never leave our password under the keyboard?* He typed in Ming's password and was able to log into the security database. He methodically searched back over the last year looking for any clues that would suggest who had access to the lab after hours. There it was. He found it. It was a single month, almost a year ago. The lab had been visited after hours every night presumably to process a backlog of specimens that had been shipped from Australia. There were several horse-racing clubs that sent their specimens to his lab because of its high-quality work, but Leigh had signed off on those samples himself. There would have been no need to work on these specimens after hours.

The number on the ID badge that had accessed the lab late at night was 0404. He went to the employee directory to look up the number to find the name. There was a sound at the door. John Chi Leigh quickly shut down the computer and moved away from the desk. A janitor came into the room to empty the trashcans from the previous day while Leigh stood behind the blue security lab coats neatly hung on a clothes rack. When he was convinced the janitor had left the area, he returned to the computer to find the culprit. He ran down the numbers, 0401, 02, 03, 04. His finger stopped on the name adjacent to 0404. Disbelief filled his mind. He bristled and sunk deep into the chair. The office door opened.

"Dr. Leigh, what a surprise to find you in my office. Is there something I can do for you?" said Ming. He looked at his computer. The screen was black.

"So sorry, Ming. I, I was looking for…"

"What could you possibly be looking for in my office, Dr. Leigh? I am head of security."

"I was hoping you had a log of all the specimens that came in from other countries."

"I think you should be able to find that in the billing office. But then that's not why you are here, is it Dr. Leigh?"

The football game has begun in the Meadowlands in New Jersey. I haven't seen any perfume cards, so there's probably no need to worry here at the sports arena. Any cards that would have been handed out at the subway or trains would have been confiscated by the authorities. The security cameras throughout the arena have links to monitors in the van so we can keep an eye on the entrances, exits and concession stands. Hundreds of cameras also focus on different sections of the stadium seating allowing us to scroll through the screens and see how the fans are doing. So far, they're enjoying the game. The score is 8 to 0. I feel complacent for the moment, and then something catches my eye.

I'm looking at the camera from the main concession stand and I see a short stocky man wearing a surgical facemask. Not that unusual given this is flu season. Many people wear them in large crowds to prevent transmission of respiratory diseases and the public has been warned that this is a particularly virulent flu season. But on closer inspection, it looks more like an N95 respirator, a facemask that is capable of filtering particles perhaps 0.3 microns small. My heart starts accelerating, I reach out and grab JP's arm and call over Agent Parker.

"Look at the screen," I say excitedly. I think that's Markovic. That's the man I saw at the Museum. I know that's him. Both agents scrutinize the monitor.

"Robinson may be right," say's JP. "Parker, take some men down there and check it out."

I've already slipped out of the van and rush over to the concession stand. JP will disapprove so I don't ask him. My security pass lets me go anywhere I need to and the van is not that far from the main entrance. I'm not going there to apprehend Markovic; I just want to know what he's doing here wearing a respirator. He wouldn't be wearing the mask unless he's expecting something to happen, and if the perfume cards are no longer in play, then what could it be?

When I reach the concession area, I can see Markovic standing to the right of the snack bar. It appears as if he is more interested in the merchandise than anything else. He's watching what the fans are purchasing. What am I missing? I can see Parker and the other agents approaching and Markovic sees them too, so he starts his exit. I know I can't stop him, but I can get in his way to slow his escape.

Our bodies collide. "Stop," I shout. "Markovic, where's the toxin?"

He's startled, and then with complete composure, answers with those steel gray eyes staring at me above the mask, "Ahh, Dr. Robinson. Enjoy flipping through pages to satisfy your curiosity." Then he just bolts with Parker and the other agents close behind.

Flipping through pages? Flipping through pages of what? What could he mean by that?

* * *

Back in Hong Kong, Dr. Leigh felt trapped in the chair in Ming's office. How was he going to explain himself? He really had no good explanation as to why he was there other than to determine which chemist had had access to the lab after hours about a year ago. Suppose Ming was also involved in this conspiracy? Dr. Leigh knew that even though he was the scientific head of the laboratory there were restrictions as to where he could and could not be, and Ming had caught him flat out.

"Ming, I have found some irregularities in my synthesis lab," said Dr. Leigh. He waited to see how Ming would react.

"Are you concerned about a security matter? If not, then the chemists are your responsibility. Good day, Dr. Leigh."

John Chi left the security office and headed back to his own. He was relieved and felt it was unlikely that Ming was involved based on his response. Unless of course he was letting Leigh go to see what he would do next. Leigh was contemplative when he entered his office and sat down at his desk to review his options. His reputation and personal integrity were at stake.

The stream of laboratory workers checked in and began to assemble at their benches. They donned all their personal protective equipment, lab coat, gloves, and eyewear, and where necessary, masks. They gathered urine and blood specimens from the refrigerators and began their acid and base extractions. Each specimen had been assigned an accession number and results would be given to the client under those numbers. Leigh went out into the lab to check on the work. He stopped at the bench of a young chemist dressed in his starched white lab coat.

"Good morning Dr. Lin," said John Chi. "What are you working on today?"

George Sun Lin looked at Dr. Leigh and smiled. Leigh had been his model scientist since he had started his own training as a student chemist.

"Good morning, Dr. Leigh. I'm doing an extraction for some potential designer drugs."

"Of course, they would give you the most difficult work. You are one of our best scientists. Isn't that right Dr. Lin?"

George Sun Lin was flattered.

"Dr. Lin, George, when you get to a stopping point, please come to my office so I can discuss an exciting project with you."

Dr. Leigh was the most renowned chemist in Hong Kong if not the world. His reputation was unmatched and George Sun wanted to be held in the same esteem. He would quickly get his sample into the chromatograph and see Dr. Leigh while he waited for his results.

"Please, sit down Dr. Lin," said Dr. Leigh. He turned to the bench that ran along the back wall of his office and unplugged the electric teakettle which had clearly reached the boiling point. "I'll make us a nice cup of tea." Hong Kong still felt the influences of the British way of life.

George Lin watched while the tea kettle settled and Leigh added some dried tea leaves to the cups. He poured the boiling water into the teacups and waited while the steam teemed over the top. "Best to let it steep awhile. It's a special tea from my colleague in America and it needs to sit to bring out its full flavor." He let the cups cool in the office air.

George Sun was thrilled to be in John Chi's office and having tea with him. John Chi handed the cup to the young chemist after exchanging a few pleasantries.

"I've had my eye on you for some time," Leigh said. "You have been studying many of my methods and techniques, haven't you?"

"Why yes, Dr. Leigh. I've read all of your books and have tried to follow all of your procedures for extraction and synthesis of chemicals and drugs."

"You are probably the most gifted young chemist we have in this lab today," said Leigh. "You most undoubtedly will go far. Where are you living now, George?"

"I'm living in a little flat past Jordan station, but I'm planning on moving this spring." He took a sip of the tea. It was still a bit hot.

"Oh, why are you moving?" Leigh responded.

"I wanted to have a nicer place, a bigger flat fit for..." His voice trailed off. Perhaps he had revealed too much. He took another larger sip of tea since the liquid was now cooler.

"So ambitious for a young man. I suppose you have extra money from the working overtime late in the lab?"

George became uncomfortable. His lips were numb and he felt as if he were drooling, just a little.

"What do you mean, Dr. Leigh? Umm, I'm not feeling very well at the moment. Maybe we could speak later," he said with a slight slur.

Leigh sipped his tea and said, "Oh, perhaps a little more tea to settle your stomach."

The teacup dropped from George's hand and broke when it hit the floor.

Leigh looked at him and could see he was struggling with his breathing.

"Tell me George, did you disclose to them you were George Sun Lin or did you tell them you were John Chi Leigh?

"I don't know what you are talking about?" His voice was indistinct.

"You know exactly what I am talking about. The ricin, Dr. Lin. The ricin."

George Sun Lin's eyes widened and his mouth assumed the shape of the letter O. He felt frightened and considered asking for forgiveness. He had no comprehension of Dr. Leigh's intent.

"I, I told them I was you so I could get the job. We all look the same to the Westerners anyway. He didn't suspect anything. What is happening to me? What did you give me?" His voice slurred and his pulse slowed.

"Who was your connection, George? Who gave you this job?" By this time Leigh was on the floor holding him by the front of his lab coat. George Sun was barely breathing now.

"He was Russian, that's all I know. He had, he had a very crude toxin. But I fixed..." These words came out garbled and then he stopped talking. Dr. Lin had used Leigh's name and reputation. He had sifted through his notebooks and listened clandestinely on some of his phone calls. He wanted more than anything to be Dr. Leigh.

John Chi let go of George's lab coat and his head thumped on the floor. Leigh quietly sat there and finished his tea. He looked at the tea leaves at the bottom of his cup and those splattered on the floor next to George Sun.

"Ah," he said out loud as if he had an audience, "my tea leaves tell me I'm to have good fortune and many long years ahead. But Dr. Lin, no such luck for you."

*   *   *

The half-time show is almost over. There have been no overhead sirens and no calls for medics other than the usual: alcohol intoxication, occasional drug overdoses, and minor cuts and bruises. I return to the van for a scolding by JP for playing Russian roulette, and try to understand what Markovic meant when he said *flipping through pages to satisfy my curiosity*. Why flipping through pages? Parker and the other agents have not returned and Markovic is out there somewhere. We almost had him.

The second half of the game is beginning, and there's a stir in the stands. We can see through the monitors that several rows of spectators are coughing uncontrollably and two women have passed out. There's a radio call for help and now a call has come in specifically for our assistance. A Hazmat technician, a medic and I suit up and make our way to the disturbance. Television cameras are instructed to focus on the game and on parts of the stadium that are not affected. JP is monitoring our intervention from the van ready to call in more aid in a flash. When we reach the stands, the medic and technician take the women by stretcher from out between the rows. They will be transported to the hospital. Spectators are alarmed to see individuals wearing space suits in their midst. I hear gasps from the crowd, so I try to assure the remaining people who are now feeling dizzy that everything is under control. I'm looking around for those advertising cards and don't see any. There are only souvenir programs left on the seats. Handling one carefully, I notice that the programs have been initially sealed with glue. I flip through the pages to see if there are any advertising cards inserted between the leaves. And then it hits me. Markovic has embedded ricin in the glue that holds the programs' front and back cover together to keep the pages within secure until the spectator separates the two. As this idea begins to sink in, my heart starts racing once again with the terrifying realization that thousands of programs are all through the stadium and mass poisoning is upon us. Individuals seated in that section are quickly evacuated from their seats and brought inside the covered part of the stadium. How do we empty this entire arena calmly and ask everyone to leave their program guide at their seat? I've got to be sure. I collect a few programs, my wits, and focus my clinical mind. *Why the delay?* I wonder. *If the programs were to spew the toxin at the opening, why now and not earlier?* I spend some time with the remaining victims who did not lose consciousness and whose breathing seems relatively normal now, and then go back toward the van with some programs and many questions.

When I get to the van, JP is waiting for an update. I tell him it's worse than we thought. I tell him that I believe the program guides may also contain toxin. I show him one of the programs I've collected from the stands, now safely contained in an airtight bag. "JP, we're going to have to interrupt the game and make an announcement."

The dark-haired man is now conferring with officials from the sports arena. Apparently, they've discovered a gas leak in the section of the stadium where the fans had gotten sick and felt that this had been the reason for the coughing and dizziness. It is possible. But then Markovic's clue has me flipping through the pages.

It's the third quarter of the game and the only score is by the favored team. JP has left the van to meet with city authorities to review exit plans and instruct someone to oversee the collection of any remaining program guides just in case my hunch is right. I haven't seen any widespread commotion after the initial false alarm, but my gut tells me it's the program guides. Though there's been no mass reaction in the stadium that we can detect, it's the only thing that makes sense. I can't explain it. I'm so engrossed in the puzzle, I don't realize the fourth quarter has ended. The favored team has just been kicked out of the park by the underdogs at a rousing score of 43-8. Fans are going wild, and I can just about hear my cell phone ring. It's a Hong Kong exchange. Leigh!

"Leigh, where the hell have you been?" I yell into the phone. Then I let him have it. "I have been trying to get you for the last two days. You do realize that there are a slew of events happening all day and all night in the metropolitan area. In fact, the Super Bowl is playing and it's almost over, no it is over. We've collected thousands of cards from around the city. Leigh, I'm pretty sure that the football souvenir program guides are also laced with ricin. The sports arena is still standing, but we did have some sick fans. We have additional agents at the Garden and throughout the city since any event could be targeted." I managed to spew it all out at once before he could get a word in.

"Lily Robinson," Leigh says speaking to me slowly. "There is no longer any danger."

"What are you talking about?"

"It turns out one of my finest chemists worked with a Russian to make the toxin and get it into a weaponized grade. But they made one critical mistake in the extraction process and created an unstable form. The stability of the toxin, I estimate, may be two months once encapsulated, then it begins to break down into a non-toxic compound. I found the signature breakdown product on the cards, and even in some of the body fluids you sent me. I expect that the ricin was made quite a while ago, and had already started to degrade. If the powder had been incorporated into a glue form, rather than a core particle, it probably would break down that much quicker."

"Oh my God," I say, my heart pounding once again. "We may have lucked out, Leigh." And to think I doubted him. "Listen, I need to give the team the all clear. We can talk tomorrow. Thank you, John. Really, thank you."

"Lily, one more thing. Do you remember when you visited me the last time, we exchanged gifts?"

"Yes, John. What's this about?"

"I gave you an ampoule of saxitoxin and you gave me tea leaves from your magic garden. Yes, I think I might like to see that garden one day. You invited me once."

"You mean I gave you dried leaves and roots from Wolfsbane or monkshood, the devil's helmet. It contains my favorite poison, aconite." He knows this; why bring this up now? "And of course, you're always welcome to visit me, and my garden," I tell him.

"Well that Chinese chemist and I shared a cup of tea while we had our little chat this morning. He had your tea, I had my tea."

I get it now. "John, you poisoned him?"

"Yes, Lily Robinson, with the Queen of all Poisons."

CHAPTER 34

NEW YORK CITY AND BOSTON

I contact JP and his team to give them the good news that the toxin has been degrading into an inert compound. We're not completely out of danger and we'll need to have the program guides checked to see if the ricin is indeed incorporated into the glue. John Chi is a complicated man. I feel guilty that I doubted him, and he will most likely hold that against me. I'm sure he suspects that I had my suspicions. I hope we can move past this, but the reality is that I will always worry that some unforeseen circumstance will push him over the edge to choose the wrong side on the war of good versus evil. How strange that he chose that phone call to share with me his desire to visit me at the cottage. It must have been the tea. It's got me thinking about being up at the cottage. With all the excitement and stimulation of the last few weeks, the solitude and the comfort of the quiet by the sea would be a welcome embrace at this moment. I know it seems banal, but I miss hearing the long call of the gulls and the wind rushing through the marsh grasses. There's solace in the natural world.

JP and I are now back to the safe-house satisfied the Agency will handle the details for tonight. We made it work in spite of all the odds, and clearly, poor chemistry had played a role. One student's failure had been a remarkable success. JP's men never caught up with Markovic, and Parker returned for further instructions. They're now in contact with INTERPOL and are pursuing Markovic across all borders. He is out there and we will have to deal with him. I'm not certain what his relationship is with Alexis, but it's clear to me that she has had a hand in this. The Agency is going to be consumed with this investigation for months and collecting all possible sources of ricin will be paramount. This is not over, by any means. Here's the problem. We know about the perfume cards and now possibly the souvenir program guides. But

215

there may be other tainted products out there that we don't know about. This is why the perpetrators of this crime are called terrorists. I feel the terror, and sleeping in the coming weeks will be difficult. JP can see I'm stressed, but he has the bigger burden of follow-up and tying up loose ends. I have another life to go back to, but this is the life he lives every day. He is a remarkable man.

*   *   *

"Robinson," he says. "Let us see if we can get a chopper to take you back to Boston. I'll go with you."

"That would be great," I say. "I'm emotionally and physically drained." He reaches for my arm in a professional way to escort me, but in his eyes I see so much more.

Coming in over the city at night is beautiful with the Zakim Bridge lit up in purple and the Prudential Center and Hancock Building looking majestic when viewed flying up the Charles River. By the time we reach the city of Boston, the T has already stopped running. It's quiet. Boston is a city that sleeps all night. We get to the apartment, and I throw my bags on the bench and head straight toward the bedroom.

I sit down on the edge of the chair, unbutton my blouse, get up and step out of my pants. Then I feel his arms wrapping around me from behind, and his beard stubble prickly on the back of my neck.

"*Chérie*, you know I love you, *oui?*" says the dark-haired man with the intense blue-green eyes. He carries me to the bed and touches my lips with his forefinger. He sits up momentarily and removes his shirt and pants while I watch him. He's not a young man, but he has the body of a man who keeps fit. Those biceps surely lift weights and he's chiseled from his chest to his waist. I take the vision all in. We make the kind of love that comes from intensity of purpose, drowning out all the background clamor of life. Afterwards, I lay there quietly on top of him with my head resting between his shoulder blades.

"I love you," I say, in a whisper. "I love you and I don't even know your name. You know everything about me, and I don't even know your name."

"Ah, my *Ma Chérie*," he says. "I have kept it this way to protect you. But it's too late now. *Je m'appelle*, my name is Jean Paul."

Jean Paul. I like the sound of that. Jean Paul. Of course, he's JP after all.

"Tell me about yourself, about your family, where you come from," I ask.

"Ah, Lily, it's not all that exciting. My family is from the Champagne region of France. My ancestors owned a magnificent champagne house in Reims. It was started in the seventeen hundreds by the forbearer of my father's ancestors. I believe it still exists as it once did, but is probably modernized. I have not been there since I was a boy."

"Does your family still live there?" I ask, while I straddle him and rub his back and neck.

"Oh no, my father didn't work on the vineyard once he was a grown man. He left that to his brother. My father moved from Reims and became a diplomat for the French government. He was the one who got me interested in this line of work. I was raised in Chanlandry, east of Reims."

"That sounds nice. It would be wonderful to visit the champagne region. Maybe one day we could take a little trip there." I say this, but I know it will never happen.

"Do you keep in touch with your family?" I ask.

"Both my father and my uncle passed away. As far as I know, my uncle's wife still lives on the vineyard."

By this time I feel myself nodding off and I'm struggling to keep my eyes open. I try and sustain the conversation before I fall asleep by letting him know that I never really knew my own parents that well. I have only one keepsake to remember any family and it's a gold ring that wraps around your finger like a snake. My mother gave it to me and said that my grandmother got it in Hong Kong. Sadly, I never met my grandmother, although I heard she was a woman with grit. Thinking about my family and my losses makes me want to withdraw from the world, and so I roll over onto the bed, close my eyes and pull the covers up over my head. I hear Jean Paul's voice like the television you turn on when you want to drift off to sleep.

"How *ironique*," I barely hear him say, "that you mention a ring from your family that was given to you. I remember my father telling me a story when I was a young man that my grandmother had a ring that had been in the family for centuries. It was a rare red diamond cut in the shape of a heart. The gold band had the word *amour* inscribed on the inside with a cluster of grapes to indicate the love of the vineyard and the luck my ancestors had enjoyed. It was a Moreau family treasure. Lily, you're quiet, are you awake?"

I feel myself drift off into a deep sleep. Somewhere in the back of my mind or in my dream, I remember a ring in a vase with *La Boutique de Fleurs* inscribed on the tin. It was a red stone, brilliant cut, fixed on a gold band. It was a long time ago.

*   *   *

The next morning I awake with a startle.

"Oh my God, I'm going to be late," I say. I jump out of bed and into the shower not ever realizing that my lover Jean Paul had already departed before the sun touched our faces. I quickly throw myself together, grab my favorite stilettos for later and drive to the medical school stretching a few yellow lights into red. I park the car, run to my office, grab the thumb drive in the top of my desk, and make my way to the lecture hall.

Oh crap, I'm thinking. They put me in the lecture hall that I truly dislike. I can never connect with my students in here. This is the room that has steep sides, and rows of seats that go all the way from the tippy top to the pit at the bottom. There, in the distance, is the podium. The room is almost full, but as usual most of the students are in the middle and back rows. I've got to get these students to move forward.

"You know you can come down to the front. I need to be able to see you," I say to the crowd waving my arms and hands to entice them to move forward.

It never works but I do it all the time anyway. No one wants to sit in the front of a lecture hall anymore. When I was in medical school, sitting up at the front of the room meant that the tape recorder could get good sound reception to record the lectures. Later, the tape could easily be transcribed through the night by one of the students to share with all who had paid into the consortium for typed notes. Now, all the lectures are PowerPoint and video recordings available to every student and posted on the Internet. If medical students come to class at all, they come with their computers and smart phones, and it isn't clear who the bigger attraction is: the professor down in the abyss or the video streaming in their hands. I will try to compete this morning. I will try to compete with the outside world for the minds of my students, and for the freedom of this country that means so much to me. If only I could have shared this world with my precious flower.

*   *   *

There was one young woman sitting in the middle of the lecture hall who was focused on the lecturer. She rotated the brilliant red diamond around her finger. It was firmly set, secured by age, growth and young wisdom. She had waited a long time for this moment. She had come from the distant steamy jungles of Colombia. The memory of that day in the little sleepy town remained with her, as well as the artist's words: "You know the rose is an ancient symbol for promise and hope. It symbolizes a new beginning." And so it was.

Lily's Toxins

(The Real Stuff)

*(Adapted with permission from
Lily Robinson and the Art of Secret Poisoning, Nvision Publishing, 2011)*

Aconite/Aconitine: The Queen of Poisons

Aconite, Monkshood, or Wolfsbane (Aconitum species, e.g. *Aconitum napellus*) is a perennial plant originally native to Europe. It has deeply divided palmate leaves and flowers that are borne off a long stalk. Each flower contains five petaloid septals, one in the shape of a monkshood or helmet with blooms that vary in color from purple and blue, to combinations of color.

One of the most powerful plant-derived toxins, aconite can produce severe poisoning with as little as 0.2mg of aconitine, 5ml of the tincture, or 1 gram of the cured plant. The compounds (aconitine, mesaconitine and 3-acetylaconitine are the most toxic alkaloids) are primarily derived from the tubers or root stock of Aconitum species. The alkaloid content within the plant varies with the species, the geographic location and the time of harvest.

Symptoms of Poisoning:

Gastrointestinal manifestations of toxicity include the early onset of nausea, drooling (hypersalivation), and vomiting. Neurotoxic symptoms include abnormal sensations of tingling or burning known as paresthesias usually around the mouth (peri-oral), numbness, weakness of the muscles controlling speech so speech is impaired (dysarthria), weakness in the arms and legs which makes coordination of the muscles difficult and affects walking (ataxia), and fading consciousness leading to seizures and coma.

Aconite also affects the heart. The heart rate slows down producing what is known as characteristic bradydysrhythmias and then the blood pressure falls producing hypotension with life-threatening results. There conduction disturbances of the heart causes toxicity to advance rapidly, and life-threatening cardiotoxicity may be apparent within two hours of the ingestion. Death results from a fatal dysthymia (malignant dysrhythmia) or from direct myocardial depression and cardiovascular collapse.

For the Scientist in You:

Aconitine is considered an "activator" agent that opens sodium channels and it binds within the trans-membrane region known as "neurotoxin receptor site 2." This binding generates continual activation of the voltage-gated Na+ channel at the resting membrane potential, and simultaneous inhibition of channel inactivation. These activators affect both the autonomic nerves innervating the heart and the cardiac conduction tissues and both actions contribute to the clinical presentation.

Abrin and Ricin

Abrin

The rosary pea or jequirity pea (*Abrus precatorius*) is a plant common to many tropical locations and the source of the toxin abrin. While all parts of the plant are poisonous, it is the seeds (bright orange with a small black cap) that are primarily implicated in poisoning. The seeds or beads have traditionally been used for ornamental purposes (*Abrus* means "beautiful") as in prayer beads (*precare* means "to pray"), jewelry, maracas (Mexican shaker) or used as a folk medicine. Interestingly, because of their uniform size, the seeds have historically been used for weighing gold and jewels in Southeast Asia (1 carat =2 seeds).

Symptoms of Poisoning:

As a result of their availability in certain geographic areas, the seeds are utilized as a means of suicide in some countries. However, many poisonings with jequirity peas (and castor beans) are unintentional as a result of ingestion of beads from ornamental objects by children. Patients who ingest the crushed seed (whole seeds often pass through the GI tract intact) develop vomiting, diarrhea, and epigastric pain. As the abdominal pain progresses, patients exhibit bloody diarrhea and black tarry stools (melena). Central nervous system manifestations include altered sensorium, generalized tonic-clonic seizures, and diffuse cerebral edema with raised intracranial pressure. In later stages, patients present with toxic hepatitis, acute renal failure, and hemolysis; acute demyelinating encephalitis has also been reported.

Ricin

Ricin is derived from the castor bean (*Ricinus communis*) which originated in Asia and Africa but has now spread to many regions around the globe. These perennial shrubs have large, deep-green, divided leaves and produce spiny fruits that contain mottled seeds resembling an engorged tick. Whereas the outermost shell casing of the plant is used to make castor oil, it is the crushed inner seeds that contain the toxin ricin. Ricin has been considered historically for use in chemical warfare as it can be prepared as a rudimentary plant extract or in powdered, crystalline, or liquid forms.

For the Scientist in You:

Both abrin and ricin are glycoprotein lectins composed of an A and B-chain linked by a disulfide bond. Abrin is a toxalbumin (as is ricin) with an estimated fatal dose of 0.1 to 1 microgram/kg or one to two crushed seeds. The mechanism of action for the toxin is inhibition of protein synthesis. The toxin is composed of an A-chain with N-glycosidase activity that inhibits protein synthesis and a B-chain that binds cell-surface receptors and facilitates the A-chain's entry into cells. The A-chain irreversibly binds the 60S ribosomal subunit effectively blocking the binding of elongation factor 2 and the beginning of protein synthesis.

The Box Jellyfish

The box jellyfish or Sea Wasp (*Chironex fleckeri*) is considered to be perhaps the world's most venomous creature. The name is derived from Chiron (the centaur poisoned by the blood of the Hydra in Greek mythology; his name apparently comes from the Greek *cheiron*, "hand") and the Latin nex, "a murder" or "violent death"; so "the Assassin's Hand" is a well-deserved epithet. The jellyfish inhabits the waters of the southwestern Pacific and has been responsible for multiple deaths in the northern Australian waters.

There were sixty-four deaths from *C. fleckeri* reported from 1883 until 2007 when a 6-year-old boy in November of 2007 incurred a toxic envenomation. Children are at greater risk of death due to their smaller body mass. Although stings may occur anytime throughout the year, the official "stinger" season for the Northern Territory is October 1st until June 1st.

The bell or body of the organism is a translucent, box-shaped mass that can grow as large as a 2-gallon bucket (a diameter of up to 20 cm) with a weight up to 6 kg. The tentacles, which may be up to three meters in length, contain millions of nematocysts that act like "spring loaded syringes" and release venom when stimulated. The nematocysts fire venom into the skin within three milliseconds of being triggered distributing venom over a large surface area thus allowing for rapid absorption. The force of this strike is approximately 2–5 pounds per square inch, which is enough to penetrate the upper dermis of the skin and discharge venom into the microcirculation. Additionally, tentacles contain a sticky fluid that helps bind the tentacle to the victim.

Symptoms of Poisoning:

Box jellyfish envenomation syndromes include sudden cardiogenic death, and dermato-necrotic manifestations. Patients who are stung in the water have intense, burning pain and can die within minutes. A 10-cm length of tentacle is said to deliver a lethal dose, but this is variable. In patients who have box jellyfish envenomation, immediate emergency measures are required to treat hypotension, and arrhythmias, if present. For skin decontamination, applying vinegar (3%–10% acetic acid) will prevent the nematocysts from disarming during removal. *C. fleckeri* antivenom is available for treatment in ampoules containing 20,000 "neutralizing" units (Commonwealth Serum Laboratories, Australia) and is made using hyperimmunized sheep. The antivenom has been shown *in vitro*, to neutralize the lethal, hemolytic, and dermato-necrotic effects of both milked venom and whole tentacle extracts. However, efficacy in human envenomation has been debated.

For the Scientist in You:

Venom has been extracted by "milking" whereby live tentacles are approximated to a membrane and applied electrical stimulation causes the nematocysts to discharge causing the venom to be released on the opposite side of the membrane. The venom is then rinsed from the membrane and various toxins can be isolated for further study. However the characterization of *C. fleckeri* venom has been difficult because of its reported sensitivity to pH, temperature and chemical changes. More recent work by Winter and colleagues have demonstrated that nematocyst-derived venom without tentacular debris has provided suitable venom that retains its cardiotoxic effects. The venom is extracted by isolating nematocysts from tentacles, which then undergo lyophilization, with subsequent reconstitution. In the reconstituted mixture, the venom supernatant is separated from the nematocyst debris pellet and is relatively stable over a pH range of 5–9 and temperatures of 2, 20, or 30 degrees Centigrade. However, the toxins are inactivated by boiling which produces protein denaturation.

C. fleckeri venom is thought to produce abnormalities in ionic transport across membranes (for example in cardiac muscle) which result in altered membrane permeability. Sodium ions enter cells producing depolarization which enhances calcium ion influx (or decrease calcium ion extrusion). This increased cationic conduction across muscle and or nerve membranes may be nonspecific in that the toxin(s) acts more like an ionophore inserting into the membrane rather than utilizing existing cationic channels. Toxic skin reactions from the adhering tentacles include a characteristic crosshatched ladder pattern with subsequent wheals, vesicles, and later necrosis. In addition to direct tissue damage, the dermato-necrotic manifestations of envenomation are thought to entail the release of leukotrienes and other arachidonic acid derivatives.

Cyanide

In 1982 seven people died in the greater Chicago area after cyanide was substituted in acetaminophen capsules being sold in stores. Once the association was made between the product (Extra Strength Tylenol) and random deaths by potassium cyanide, panic ensued. Over 100,000 stories regarding the case ran in U.S. newspapers. While the perpetrator was never found (although there were suspicions of one individual), groundbreaking changes were made in the manufacturing industry that set today's standards for tamper resistant packaging.

What is interesting about this agent is the variety with which cyanide is present in the environment. It can be found as a solid, liquid, or gas, can be complexed with salts (most commonly sodium or potassium), with metals (such as gold, cobalt, mercury, or zinc), or with organic acids to produce nitriles such as acetonitrile. Cyanogenic glycosides are found naturally in many plant species. The *Prunus* species (peaches, plums, apricots) contain stones or pits, and apples have seeds that contain amygdalin, a cyanide precursor. Linamarin, another cyanogenic glycoside, is present in high concentrations in the cassava plant. Cyanide is also used in many industries, particularly metallurgy for mining and extracting gold, electroplating, pigment production, in agriculture, and in both clinical and research laboratories.

Symptoms of Poisoning

The threat of cyanide persists. Hydrogen cyanide (gas) and cyanogen chloride (gas or liquid) are known to be potential chemical terrorism agents, and the time from initial exposure to symptoms can be seconds to minutes, requiring immediate recognition of signs and symptoms. With moderate exposure, patients may experience giddiness, palpitations, dizziness, nausea, vomiting, headache, and breathing deeper and faster than normal (hyperventilation). With high exposure, symptoms are equally rapid and consist of loss of consciousness, seizure, coma, and cardiovascular collapse. Ingestion of cyanide can also produce rapid onset of symptoms and is life-threatening unless the antidote and supportive care are given emergently to the victims. Although the scent of bitter almonds is associated with cyanide poisoning (particularly in vomitus), the ability to detect the odor is genetically determined and absent in 20% to 40% of the population.

For the Scientist in You

As little as 200 mg of sodium or potassium cyanide may be fatal when ingested and hydrogen cyanide gas (HCN) is fatal at concentrations of 150–200 ppm. Both HCN and cyanide salts can be absorbed through the skin. Cyanide acts as a respiratory poison and affects all the tissues of the body but primarily those with high oxygen utilization and low tolerance for hypoxic stress (CNS and myocardium). The inactivation of cytochrome oxidase (a3) results in uncoupling mitochondrial oxidative phosphorylation with inhibition of cellular respiration. Patients exhibit severe lactic acidosis (concentrations of lactate 10 mmol/L) and the measured venous oxygen saturation may be increased since cellular oxygen consumption is blocked. As hypoxia ensues, the patient exhibits acute alteration of consciousness and gastrointestinal symptoms while cardiac manifestations include initial bradycardia and hypertension followed by reflexive tachycardia, then bradycardia and hypotension. In addition to the patient's initial presentation and a history of cyanide exposure, diagnosis can be made by measuring the cyanide concentration in the blood. However, as results from the laboratory will not be available immediately, treatment is based on the clinical/ history findings. Cyanide concentrations vary depending on whether the patient is a smoker or nonsmoker. Whole blood concentrations 0.5–1 mg/L may be toxic (cigarette smokers may have concentrations up to 0.1 mg/L) while concentrations of 0.26 mg/L are considered lethal. Cyanide, with a half-life between twenty minutes to an hour, is detoxified by the liver enzyme rhodanese (sulfurtransferase) to thiocyanate, which is excreted in the urine. Cyanide is measured by classical spectrophotometric methods (VIS) or by an automated headspace gas chromatographic method with nitrogen-phosphorous detector (HS-GC/NPD).

The Antidote

The Cyanide Antidote Kit contains amyl nitrite pearls, sodium nitrite, and sodium thiosulfate pearls. An amyl nitrite pearl is broken under the nose of the victim. Then 300 mg of sodium nitrite is given IV to produce methemoglobinemia (an alternate form of hemoglobin, a protein found in red blood cells). Methemoglobin has a higher binding affinity for cyanide allowing cellular respiration to continue. Sodium nitrite is followed by sodium thiosulfate, which converts cyanide to the nontoxic metabolite thiocyanate.

Hydroxocobalamin, vitamin B12a, is an alternative treatment for cyanide poisoning mainly used in Europe. Hydroxocobalamin contains the cobalt ion, which also has a higher affinity for cyanide and forms the nontoxic cyanocobalamin, which is excreted in the urine.

Batrachotoxin

Poisons in nature are part of the natural defense of an organism, whether it is a plant or an animal. Presumably these toxins act as protection against predators in the case of an animal, or from an herbivore, in the case of a plant. In some cases "chemical defenses" might even be directed against microorganisms. The discovery of these natural toxins by humans has led to their unique use by some cultures. Deep in the rain forests of western Colombia, the Embera´ Choco´ Indians practiced the custom of tipping darts with frog toxins for use with their blowguns in their hunt for large game. The frogs are collected and held in a basket until the Choco´ are ready for the frog's unique gift. One frog is removed from the basket and the tip of the dart is rubbed multiple times along the back of the frog where the poison is secreted from glands within the skin. The poison is allowed to dry on the dart before it is inserted into the blowgun. In brief, the blowgun, about 2.5–3 m in length, is made from a palm wood tree trunk (split and then quartered) utilizing two of the four sections of the split trunk. The quarters are hollowed out by hand, creating the center shaft (bore) of the blowgun. The two pieces are then glued together with tree resin, tied with plant fiber and then wrapped with bark bast. Darts, about 21–23 cm long, are made with the woody stem of the palm and are inscribed with spiral grooves to hold the poison.

The source of the poison used by the Choco´ is obtained from *Phyllobates terribilis*, a brightly colored frog, golden yellow in color and well hidden in the jungles of the Pacific versant of Colombia. This small frog, about 47mm in length, is about twenty fold more toxic than its relatives; if poison were to enter through a small wound during handling, the results could be fatal to man. These dendrobatid frogs are the origin of the batrachotoxins (BTXs) batrachotoxin, homobatrachotoxin, and batrachotoxin-A. The name batrachotoxin is derived from the Greek "*batrachos*," meaning frog.

Batrachotoxin is obtained not only from the skin of neotropical frogs, but also the feathers and skin of some passerine birds—and the Melyrid beetle. The history of the discovery of batrachotoxin is an interesting one, largely the work of John Daly and colleagues over several decades. Initially reported in isolated species of the frog genus *Phyllobates* (Latin for leaf climber in the family *Dendrobatidae*) in the 1960s, subsequent research in the 1990s showed that certain passerine birds from Papua New Guinea (genera *Pitohui* and *Ifrita*) contained feathers and skin from which batrachotoxin could also be isolated. To add to the mystery, poison-dart frogs raised in captivity on alkaloid free diets have no detectable BTXs in their skin. Thus, the putative source of BTXs is from the diet of these frogs or birds—insects. It is thought that the dendrobatid poison frogs do not produce the toxin *de novo*, but most likely sequester the alkaloid from their diet.

Symptoms of Poisoning

Cardiac manifestations of BTX intoxication include fatal arrhythmias which terminate in ventricular fibrillation and death.

For the Scientist in You

Batrachotoxin, a pyrrolecarboxylic ester, is a steroidal alkaloid (mw 538 Daltons) and blocks neuromuscular transmission irreversibly. It increases the permeability of excitable membranes to Na+ thus producing membrane depolarization, enhanced spontaneous transmitter release, and muscle contracture. It appears that voltage-gated sodium channels are the target of many natural neurotoxins that include batrachotoxin as well as tetrodotoxin (TTX), saxitoxin (STX), conus toxins, scorpion toxins and aconitine. There are neurotoxins that modify the Na+ channel (gating modifiers) such as BTX resulting in hyperexcitably, convulsions and death and those that block Na+ channels (Na+ channel blockers), such as TTX and STX producing paralysis, respiratory failure, and also death. BTX is classified as a lipid soluble neurotoxin that targets the type 2 receptor site (TTX and STX are hydrophilic and target the type 1 receptor site). What is most fascinating about poison-dart frogs is that they have BTX-resistant sodium channels. This allows the frogs to eat BTX-containing beetles without harm and to sequester the toxin within its own body without any ill effects! This is attributed to a genetic modification of the sodium channel macromolecule in *P. terribilis* rather than desensitization from repeated exposure to the BTX. Approximately 1000 g of BTXs can be found per frog skin in *P. terribilis*. In addition, BTX has an LD50 for mice of about 0.1 g per mouse. Moore and colleagues demonstrated morphological changes with injection of BTX in rat peroneal nerve including massive swelling of the axon at the nodes of Ranvier with retraction of paranodal myelin, as well as swelling of unmyelinated axons.

Amanitin (mushroom poisoning)

Mushroom poisoning is not uncommon. However, it is far more frequent in Western Europe (with 50–100 fatal cases per year), in Central Tuscany, Italy, and in Turkey than in the United States. But nonetheless, the Death Cap is ubiquitous and *A. phalloides* is accountable for the majority of fatalities caused by mushroom poisoning. *A. phalloides* usually grows in summer and in autumn, but since it can be harvested and stored, poisoning from amatoxins may occur at any time of the year.

Amatoxins are thermostable (cooking, drying, and freezing do not alter their toxicity). The fatal dose of amanitin is 0.1– 0.3 mg/kg. About 0.2– 0.4 mg of the amanitin can be obtained from 1 g of fresh *Amanita phalloides*.

Symptoms of Poisoning

The most important consideration in mushroom poisoning is patient history. The time the individual consumed the mushrooms, the time of onset of symptoms and how many mushrooms were eaten are all important in determining outcome. Without this information, the diagnosis and subsequent treatment are difficult. Only 20 to 50 grams of fresh mushrooms can produce critical liver and kidney damage and just three or four mushrooms are approximately 50 grams. Patients with amanita toxicity usually present within 6 to 12 hours after ingestion. Abdominal pain, nausea, vomiting and diarrhea (sometimes as frequently as six times per hour) are the predominant symptoms. Supportive care including fluid treatment is necessary, but without specific therapy death may occur in 50%–90% of patients. This is reduced to below 10% in patients receiving therapy. When medical treatment is not successful then liver transplantation is used as a definitive treatment. Liver transplantation has been used in both adult and in pediatric mushroom poisonings with success. However, if toxicity proceeds unchecked, patients progress to acute liver and renal failure, brain dysfunction, coma and finally death.

For the Scientist in You

A. phalloides produces 2 types of toxins: phallotoxins and amatoxin. The phallotoxins are not absorbed from the gut and are believed to be responsible for the nausea, vomiting and diarrhea. However the amatoxins, a group of bicyclic octapeptides, are rapidly absorbed by the intestines and bind to a 140-kDa subunit RNA polymerase-II in the hepatocytes. This binding interferes with messenger RNA synthesis. Cells of the gastrointestinal tract, liver and kidney have a high rate of protein synthesis and are especially susceptible to injury. Amanitin poisoning is distinguished by three clinical stages: an incubation stage, a gastrointestinal stage and a cytotoxic stage. During the latent or incubation stage (6–12 hours after ingestion with a range of 6–48 hours), the patient is generally asymptomatic. During the second stage, acute gastroenteritis occurs with abdominal pain, nausea, vomiting and diarrhea. Patients may develop severe dehydration, electrolyte disturbances, and increased liver function biomarkers [alanine aminotransferase (ALT), aspartate aminotransferase (AST), lactate dehydrogenase (LD); alkaline phosphatase] heralding the onset of hepatic necrosis. The production of coagulation factors and immunoglobulins decreases. This phase may last 2–3 days. Subsequently patients develop hepatorenal failure with jaundice, hypoglycemia, multiorgan failure, coma and finally death. Hepatic encephalopathy, a serum creatinine 1.4 mg/dL in patients with liver failure, a bilirubin 4.6 mg/dL and prolongation of the prothrombin time (twice the reference interval) are predictors of a fatal outcome.

Gastrointestinal decontamination including whole-bowel irrigation and activated charcoal are necessary in limiting toxin absorption. Antidotes to amanitin include silibinin (extract of milk thistle) and intravenous benzyl penicillin, thought to decrease the hepatocellular uptake of the toxin. These agents may fall into the category of inhibitory or competitive OATP1B3 substrates, which may inhibit uptake of the toxin. Administration of cimetidine, a cytochrome P-450 inhibitor which inhibits the uptake of amatoxins by the mixed function oxidase system, and N-acetylcysteine (NAC), a glutathione precursor that binds amatoxin-related free radicals, have also been used in the treatment of amanitin intoxication.

In one study, orthotropic liver transplantation was considered in patients with an interval between ingestion and diarrhea at less than eight hours. An international normalized ratio (INR) of 6 was considered reliable for deciding to perform emergency transplantation. Indications for emergency liver transplantation include a decrease in prothrombin index below 10% of normal (INR approximately 6) 4 days or more after ingestion. Histologic evaluation of the livers from patients with amanita toxicity reveals diffuse centrilobular to midzonal necrosis.

About 85% of the toxins are eliminated in the urine within six hours of intake and are detectable in urine for as long as 96 hours after ingestion; they are detectable in the plasma for approximately 36–48 hours. While detection of amanitins is important in the diagnosis, there is no correlation between plasma concentration and clinical outcome.

The Meixner test or newspaper test of Wieland requires blotting a sample of the mushroom to be tested on a piece of newspaper, adding concentrated hydrochloric acid and observing for the development of a blue color. The blue color is the result of a reaction of the substituted indole residue in the amanita toxins and the lignin in the paper. However, other ring-containing compounds such as psilocin (found in Psilocybe, Panaeolus and Conocybe mushrooms) and some 5-hydroxytryptamines also produce a positive result rendering the Meixner test nonspecific.

Crotalid Envenomation

Viperidae, subfamily *Crotalinae*, includes the *Crotalus* genus (rattlesnakes), *Agkistrodon* genus (copperheads and cottonmouths) and the *Bothrops* genus (*Fer-de-lance*). *Deinagkistrodon acutus*, formerly *Agkistrodon acutus*, is a venomous pit viper found in Southeast Asia and known by many names: the Chinese moccasin, the sharp-nosed viper, the snorkel viper and the "hundred-pace viper" ("hundred-pacer"). It is believed that after the victim is bitten, he or she will be able to walk only a hundred paces before perishing. In regions where the snakes may be more venomous, they are known as "fifty-pacers."

Pit vipers are venomous snakes with a heat-sensing pit anteroinferior to each eye, elliptical pupils (cat's eyes), and a single row of scales on their undersides—in contrast to nonvenomous snakes, which have no facial pits, round eye pupils, and two rows of scales on their undersides. All snakes are "cold-blooded" reptiles, that is, they maintain their body temperature approximate to that of the environment. Their forked tongues and highly developed nostrils contain receptors that can "taste" or detect odors in the air by focusing substances on the Jacobson's organ, a highly developed olfactory epithelium located in the palate. This helps to locate prey, which consists primarily of small animals and birds. Moccasins inject their venom through hollow, movable (retractable) fangs and, as with all venomous snakes, not all bites contain venom; these nonvenomous bites are known as "dry bites." To the consternation of some, venomoids are venomous snakes that have had a surgical procedure to render them incapable of administering venom with a bite (usually the removal of the venom gland). These surgically altered snakes are considered less dangerous when kept in captivity. Purists, however, feel that if one desires a less-dangerous snake, then the "keeper" should tend only nonvenomous species. *D. acutus* is found in southern China, Taiwan, and northern Vietnam and resides in mainly forested mountains, rocky hillsides, or under brush. This Chinese moccasin matures to 3 to 4 feet in length and is covered with brown or reddish brown triangles overlaying a grayish or reddish brown base color.

One review of snake bites found the highest rates of bites and mortality from snake bites in South Asia (Bangladesh, Bhutan, India, Nepal, Pakistan and Sri Lanka). India has the greatest number of snakebites per year (up to 50,000 fatalities per year) followed by Pakistan with over 8,000 fatalities per year. Snake bites are usually occupational hazards in these countries as numerous workers such as fishermen, farmers, plantation workers and herders come into contact with snakes. In addition, many of these workers live in outdoor habitats and are exposed to nocturnal snakes while sleeping.

Symptoms of Poisoning

The initial symptoms after a bite from a pit viper are usually pain and swelling around the bite, with physical signs of fang marks, bloody (hemorrhagic) vesicles, and tenderness at the bite site. Patients who present to the emergency department may have a history of nausea, vomiting or diarrhea, fainting, or near loss of consciousness. While most snake bites occur on the extremities, as a result of trying to handle a snake or walking in an infested area, there have been cases reported of penetrating eye injury caused by a venomous snakebite. In one such case, the victim was crawling along a hillside when he was bitten on his right eye. The patient presented with facial swelling, bruising around the eye, subconjunctival hemorrhage, corneal edema, and an abnormal protrusion of the eyeball. Although the patient received 2 vials of *D. acutus* antivenom, he continued to have progressive swelling of his airway and required intubation. Six hours after the snakebite, removal of the right eye was performed. The patient eventually recovered, but only after surgery, extensive supportive medical treatment, and systemic antibiotics.

Some snakes, such as those in the Elapid family (e.g., Australian death adders, African mambas, and Asian coral snakes) produce venoms containing neurotoxins that cause paralysis and death by respiratory failure. Other snakes in the Crotalid family, such as the hundred-pace viper, create venoms containing components that cause hemorrhage and tissue destruction. Rapidly progressive swelling in proximity to the wound usually constitutes a more severe envenomation.

The Antidote

Antivenom is used to neutralize toxins. Several countries produce specific antivenoms for individual snake species (see WHO Regional Office for South-East Asia). For example, China produces purified *Agkistrodon acutus* antivenin, which is the same as for *D. acutus*. However, one available antivenom product in the U.S. is Crotaline Fab antivenom (CroFab, Protherics, Nashville, TN). CroFab is a purified derivative from sheep hyperimmunized with the venom of 4 crotaline snakes, including an *Agkistrodon* species (cottonmouth snakes). However, with antivenom administration there is always the risk of an allergic reaction. While snakebites are less commonly fatal in the U.S. than the rest of the world, they are nevertheless of considerable medical importance and should be identified so that the appropriate medical care can be rendered expeditiously.

For the Scientist in You

These venoms produce not only extensive necrosis and hemorrhage that result in considerable tissue damage, but also coagulopathy and shock. In severe envenomations systemic shock is apparent with hypotension, altered mental status, respiratory difficulties, and marked coagulopathy. Laboratory studies should focus around the coagulopathies and thrombocytopenia associated with pit viper envenomations. Therefore, a complete blood count, platelet count, prothrombin time/international normalized ratio, activated partial thromboplastin time, and fibrinogen are usually included in the workup.

Snake venom proteins are the mechanism whereby animals kill or immobilize their prey. They are of considerable interest because they interact with diverse molecular targets, producing various pharmacological and physiological effects. Several snake venom proteins are used as biomedical research tools or in clinical applications. Captopril, an antihypertensive drug, was designed on the peptide inhibitor of angiotensin-converting enzyme derived from the venom of *Bothrops jararaca*. Venoms of true vipers (*Viperinae*) and of pit vipers (*Crotalinae*) contain hemotoxins, e.g., serine proteases. A therapeutic peptide isolated from *D. acutus* is coagulation factor X–binding protein reported to induce changes in plasma membrane permeability. Other substances such as thrombin-like enzymes are used for fibrinogen and fibrinogen-breakdown product assays.

The thrombin-like protease acutobin (40 kDa) is the major coagulating fibrinogenase of D. acutus venom, and contains a single chain of 236 residues including four potential N-glycosylation sites. Some venoms hydrolyze fibrinogen, releasing fibrinopeptide A, B, or both, while some may affect kininogen, plasminogen, and protein C. In addition to serine proteases, metalloproteinases and C-type lectins (CSL) are found in *A. acutus* venom. CSL are used to investigate platelet glycoprotein receptors. Qualitative determination of snake venom by sandwich ELISA is performed in Australia for species of snakes native to both Australia and New Guinea (Australian CSL Snake Venom Detection Kit, CSL, Melbourne, Australia).

Scorpion Toxins / Venoms

The scorpion *Leiurus quinquestriatus* is sometimes known as the death stalker. Scorpions fall in the class *Arachnida* into the order of *Scorpiones*. *L. quinquestriatus* is in the family *Buthidae*. There are approximately 1,400 species of scorpions but only a few are of medical importance. Clinically significant species hail from the genera: *Androctonus, Buthotus, Buthus, Centruroides, Leiurus, Parabuthus and Tityus*. New World scorpions such as *Centruroides* are found from the southern United States and Mexico. (*C. sculpturatus* is found in Arizona, eastern California, and western and northern Mexico) to northern South America and in the West Indies, while scorpions from the genus *Tityus* are found in South America. Old World scorpions are distributed throughout the Middle East, southern Spain, and the South of France (*Buthus*); North Africa, Middle East and Asia (*Androctonus*), the Indian subcontinent (*Buthotus*); and South Africa (*Parabuthus*). The genus *Leiurus* is distributed in northeastern Africa through the Middle East. *L. quinquestriatus* species are found primarily in Egypt, Israel, Jordan, Syria and Lebanon. Scorpions are nocturnal creatures, hiding by day in crevices, or under stones or tree bark. They are found in both tropical and temperate regions in deserts, forests, mountains and savannas.

The body of the scorpion is composed of a cephalothorax (prostoma) and an abdomen (mesosoma). Pincer-like claws are positioned in front of the cephalothorax and are used to catch prey while four pairs of walking legs come off the abdomen. The third component is the metosoma or scorpion tail, and at its end is the stinger (telson). The telson ends in the barb (aculeus) containing two poison glands. This apparatus is used to inject toxin into the prey. The scorpion diet consists primarily of insects and arachnids. Rather than hunt prey, scorpions wait for their prey, detecting them with sensory hairs located primarily on the pedipalpus (located on the cephalothorax).

Symptoms of Poisoning

Approximately 1.2 million scorpion stings occur worldwide each year. Envenomations can be classified as either Class I (local symptoms including pain and swelling at the site of the sting), Class II (systemic with symptoms of sedation, nausea, vomiting, and high blood pressure), or Class III (systemic with symptoms of cardiovascular, neurological and/or respiratory effects). Some epidemiological studies of Saudi Arabia have demonstrated that the majority of scorpion stings were recorded in the summer months, predominately in males, and between the ages of 15-30 years. Over 90% of patients received treatment and clinical severity was mainly Class I. Class II envenomation was seen in only 7.3% of admitted patients.

Treatment is usually supportive with particular attention to cardiac and electrolyte monitoring, intravenous fluids, sedatives and analgesics. Different scorpion antivenoms exist and are region (geographic species) specific.

For the Scientist in You

Envenomation with *L. quinquestriatus* (LQ) toxin produces both cardiovascular as well as neurotoxic effects. Animal models of envenomation show an initial increase in cardiac output and hypertension (the result of catecholamine discharge), followed by a second stage of decreased cardiac output (catecholamine depletion). This cycle produces cardiac arrhythmia and in combination with the increased oxygen demand can result in acute myocardial ischemia and infarction. Respiratory failure is a common complication with both cardiogenic and noncardiogenic components. Central nervous system symptoms include agitation, hyperthermia, hypertonus, seizures and coma, and are more often found in children. Scorpion toxins act on ion channels—primarily Na+ (and to a lesser degree on K+ and Ca2+)—prolonging the action potential and depolarization. Some investigators have explored the use of using polyvalent antivenoms with sodium and calcium channel blockers, as well as a multichannel blocker (amiodarone). Laboratory findings are usually not specific and include hyperglycemia, and leukocytosis; and cardiac ischemia produces a transient elevation of cardiac markers with associated ECG changes.

One randomized trial on *Mesobuthus tamulus* envenomation demonstrated a hastened recovery with the administration of both prazosin (an alpha 1 blocker) and scorpion antivenom, rather than with just prazosin alone. *M. tamulus*, the Indian red scorpion, produces significant cardiotoxicity, and although patients treated with both antivenom (monovalent anti-scorpion venom serum F(ab)2, Haffkine Biopharma, Mumbai) and prazosin had a shorter recovery as measured by several clinical parameters, there was no difference in deterioration to a more severe grade of poisoning.

BIBLIOGRAPHY

ACONITE

• Ameri A. The effects of Aconitum alkaloids on the central nervous system. Prog Neurobiol 1998;56:211–35.

• Ameri A. Structure-dependent differences in the effects of the Aconitum alkaloids lappaconitine, N-desacetyllappaconitine and lappaconidine in rat hippocampal slices. Brain Res 997;769:36–43.

• But PP, Tai YT, Young K. Three fatal cases of herbalaconite poisoning. Vet Hum Toxicol 1994;36:212–5.

• Catterall WA. Structure and function of voltage sensitive ion channels. Science (Wash DC)1988; 242:50 – 61.

• Fatovich DM. Aconite: a lethal Chinese herb. Ann Emerg Med 1992;21:309 –11.

• Kosower EM. A hypothesis for the mechanism of sodium channel opening by batrachotoxin and related toxins. FEBS Lett 1983;163:161– 4.

• Magnani BJ, Woolf AD. Cardiotoxic plants. In: Brent J, Wallace K, Burkhart K, eds. Critical care toxicology: diagnosis and management of the critically poisoned patient. Philadelphia: Elsevier Mosby; 2005. p 1325–33.

• Mizugaki M, Ito K, Ohyama Y, Konishi Y, Tanaka S, Kurasawa K. Quantitative analysis of Aconitum alkaloids in the urine and serum of a male attempting suicide by oral intake of aconite extract. J Anal Toxicol 1998;22:336–40.

• Sun AM, Li H, Huang ZH, But PP, Ding XQ. Analysis of the aconitine alkaloids in Chuanwu by electrospray ionization/tandem mass spectrometry. Chinese Chem Lett 2004;15:1071-4.

• Tai YT, But PP, Young K, Lau CP. Cardiotoxicity after accidental herb-induced aconite poisoning. Lancet 1992;340:1254–6.

ABRIN AND RICIN

• Audi J, Belson M, Patel M, Schier J, Osterloh J. Ricin poisoning: a comprehensive review. JAMA 2005; 294:2342–51.

• Crompton R, Gall D. Georgi Markov: death in a pellet. Med Leg J 1980;48:51– 62.

• Dickers K, Bradberry S, Rice P, Griffiths GD, Vale JA. Abrin poisoning. Toxicol Rev 2003;22:137– 42.

• Garber E, Walker J, O'Brien T. Detection of abrin in food using enzyme-linked immunosorbent
    assay and electrochemiluminescence technologies.J Food Prot 2008;71: 1868–74.

• Kinamore P, Jaeger R, de Castro F. Abrus and ricinus ingestion: management of three cases. Clin Toxicol 1980;17:401–5.

• Olsnes S. The history of ricin, abrin and related toxins. Toxicon 2004;44:361–70.

• Sahni V, Agarwal S, Singh N, Sidkar S. Acute demyelinating encephalitis after jequirity pea ingestion (Abrus precatorius). Clin Toxiocol 2007;45:77– 9.

• Subrahmanyan D, Mathew J, Raj M. An unusual manifestation of Abrus precatorius poisoning: a report of two cases. Clin Toxicol 2008;46:173–5.

BOX JELLYFISH

• Currie B. Marine antivenoms. J Toxicol Clin Toxicol 2003;41:301– 8.

• Department of Health and Community Services, Centre for Disease Control. Chironex fleckeri (Box Jellyfish).January 8.ttp://www.health.nt.gov.au/library/scripts/objectifyMedia.aspx?filepdf/26/02.pdf&siteID1&str_titleBox%20Jellyfish.pdf (Accessed March 30, 2009).

• Mbuthia J. Box jellyfish (Chironex fleckeri) envenomation. Clin Toxicol Rev Mass Poison Control System 1999;22(3).

• Pearn J. The sea, stingers, and surgeons: the surgeon's role in prevention, first aid, and management of marine envenomations. J Pediatr Surg 1995;30:105–10.

• Tibballs J. Australian venomous jellyfish, envenomation syndromes, toxins and therapy. Toxicon 2006;48:830 –59.

• Winter K, Isbister G, Seymour J, W Hodgson. An in vivo examination of the stability of venom from the Australian box jellyfish Chironex fleckeri. Toxicon 2007;49:804 –9.

CYANIDE

• Agency for Toxic Substances and Disease Registry. Cyanide toxicity. Am Fam hysician1993;48:107–14.

• Binder L, Frederickson L. Poisoning in laboratory personnel and health care professionals. Am J Emerg Med 1991;9:11–5.

• Blanc P. Cyanide. In: Faculty, staff, and associates of the California Poison Control System. Poisoning & drug overdose. 5th ed. Olson KR, ed.; Anderson IB, Benowitz NL, Blanc PD, Clark RF, Kearney TE, Osterioh JD, assoc. eds. New York: Lange Medical Books/McGraw-Hill; 2007. p 176–8.

• US Department of Defense Crisis Communication Strategies. Analysis: case study: the Johnson and Johnson Tylenol crisis. http://www.ou.edu/deptcomm/dodjcc/groups/02C2/Johnson%20&%20Johnson.htm

• Habel R, Roldan C. Toxicity, cyanide update, Aug 12, 2008.tp://www.emedicine.com/MED/topic487.htm

• Hall A, Dart R, Bogdan G. Sodium thiosulfate or hydroxocobalamin for the empiric treatment of cyanide poisoning? Ann Emerg Med 2007;49:806–13.

• Hall AH, Rumack BH. Cyanide. In: Haddad LM, Shannon MW, Winchester JF, eds. Clinical
management of poisoning and drug overdose. 3rd ed. New York: WB Saunders; 1998:899 –912.

• Gambaro V, Arnoldi S, Casagni E, Dell'acqua L, Pecoraro C, Froldi R. Blood cyanide determinationin two cases of fatal intoxication: comparison between headspace gas chromatography and a spectrophoto metric method. J Forensic Sci 2007;52: 1401–4.

• Leybell I, Baud F, Borron S. Toxicity, cyanide update May 18, 2006. http://www.emedicine.cm/EMERG/ topic118.htm.

• Pamidi PV, DeAbreu M, Kim D, Mansouri S. Hydroxocobalamin and cyanocobalamin interference on co-oximetry based hemoglobin measurements. Clinca Chimica Acta 2009;401:63–7.

• Yen D, Tsai J, Wang LM, Kao WF, Hu SC, Lee CH, Deng JF. The clinical experience of acute cyanide poisoning, Am J Emerg Med 1995;13:524–8.

BATRACHOTOXIN

• Albuquerque E, Daly J, Witkop B. Batrachotoxin: chemistry and pharmacology. Science 1971;172:995–1002.

• Daly J, Myers C, Warnick J, Albuquerque E. Levels of batrachotoxin and lack of sensitivity to its action in Poison-Dart frogs (Phyllobates). Science 1980;208: 1383–5.

• Daly J, Myers C. Tropical poison frogs [Letter]. Science 1993;262:1193.

• Daly J. The chemistry of poisons in amphibian skin. Proc Natl Acad Sci USA 1995;92:9 –13.

• Daly J, Spande T, Garraffo H. Alkaloids from amphibian skin: a tabulation of over eight-hundred compounds. J Nat Prod 2005;68:1556 –75.

• Dumbacher J, Spande T, Daly J. Batrachotoxin alkaloids from passerine birds: a second toxic bird genus (Ifrita kowaldi) from New Guinea. Proc Natl Acad Sci USA 2000;97:12970 –5.

• Dumbacher J, Wako A, Derrickson SR, Samuelson A, Spande TF, Daly JW. Melyrid beetles (Choresine): a putative source for the batrachotoxin alkaloids found in poison-dart frogs and toxic passerine birds. Proc Natl Acad Sci USA 2004;101:15857– 60.

• Moore GR, Boegman RJ, Robertson DM, Raine CS. Acute stages of batrachotoxin-induced neuropathy:a morphologic study of a sodium-channel toxin. J Neurocytol 1986;15:573– 83.

• Myers C, Daly J, Malkin B. A dangerously toxic new frog (Phyllobates) used by Embera´ Indians of Western Colombia, with discussion of blowgun fabrication and dart poisoning. Bull Am Mus Nat His1978;161:309–65.

• Myers C, Daly J. Dart-poison frogs. Sci Am 1983;248:120 –31.

• Summers K, Clough M. The evolution of coloration and toxicity in the poison frog family (Dendrobatidae). Proc Natl Acad Sci USA 2001;98:6227–32.

• Wang S, Wang G. Voltage-gated sodium channels as primary targets of diverse lipid-solubleneurotoxins. Cell Signal 2003;15:151–9.

AMANITIN

• Alves A, Gouveia Ferreira M, Paulo J, Franc¸a A, Carvalho A. Mushroom poisoning with Amanita phalloides: a report of four cases. Eur J Intern Med 2001;12:64–6.

• Beuhler M, Lee DC, Gerkin R. The Meixner test in the detection of alpha–amanitin and false-positive reactions caused by psilocin and 5-substituted tryptamines. Ann Emerg Med 2004;44:114 –20.

• Boyer JC, Hernandez F, Estorc J, De La Coussaye JE,Bali JP. Management of maternal Amanita phalloides poisoning during the first trimester of pregnancy: a case report and review of the literature. Clin Chem2001;47:971–4.

• Escudie´ L, Francoz C, Vinel JP, Moucari R, Cournot M, Paradis V, et al. Amanita phalloides poisoning: reassessment of prognostic factors and indications for emergency liver transplantation. J Hepatol 007;26:466 –73.

• Filigenzi MS, Poppenga RH, Tiwary AK, Puschner B. Determination of alpha-amanitin in serum and liver by multistage linear ion trap mass spectrometry. J Agric Food Chem 2007;55:2784 –90.

• Habal R. Toxicity, mushroom. Martinez JA, coauthor. http://emedicine. medscape.com/
article/167398-overview (Accessed December 2009). From Web site eMedicine.

• Hallen HE, Luo H, Scott-Craig JS, Walton JD. Gene family encoding the major toxins of lethal Amanita mushrooms. Proc Nat Acad Sci 07;104:19097–101.

• Himmelmann A, Mang G, Schnorf-Huber S. Lethal ingestion of stored Amanita phalloides mushrooms. Swiss Med Wkly 2001;131:616 –7.

• Karakayali H, Ekici Y, Ozcay F, Bilezikci B, Arslan G,Haberal M. Pediatric liver transplantation for acute liver failure. Transplant Proc 2007;39:1157– 60.

• Letschert K, Faulstich H, Keller D, Keppler D. Molecular characterization and inhibition of amanitin uptake into human hepatocytes. Toxicol Sci (Wash DC) 2006;91:140 –9.

• Robinson-Fuentes VA, Jaime-Sanchez JL, Garcia- Aguilar L, Gomez-Peralta M, Vazquez-Garciduen? as MS, Vazquez-Marrufo G. Determination of alphaand beta-amanitin in clinical urine samples by capillary zone electrophoresis. J Pharm Biomed Anal 2008;47:913–7.

• Soysal D, Cevik C, Saklamaz A, Yetimalar Y, Unsal B. Coagulation disorders secondary to acute liverfailure in Amanita phalloides poisoning: a casereport. Turk J Gastroenterol 2006;17:198 –202.

• Yildiz BD, Abbasoglu O, Saglam A, So¨ kmensu¨ er C. Urgent liver transplantation for Amanita phalloides poisoning. Pediatr Transplant 2008;12:105– 8.

SNAKE VENOMS

• Alirol E, Sharma SK, Bawaskar H, Kuch U, Chappuis F Snake bite in South Asia: a review. PLoS Negl Trop Dis 2010;4:1–9.

• Bush S, Lavonas E. Snake envenomation, moccasins. http://emedicine. medscape.com/article/ 771329-overview.

• Cetaruk E. Rattlesnakes and other crotalids. In: Brent J, Wallace K, Burkhart K, Phillips S, Donovan J. Critical care toxicology. New York: Mosby; 2005. p 1075–89.

• Chen C-C, Yang C-M, Hu F-R, Lee Y-C. Penetrating ocular injury caused by venomous snakebite. Am J Ophthalmol 2005;140:544–6.

• Messmer TA, Wiscomb GW. Nonvenomous snakes. Wildlife damage management series. Logan (UT): Utah State University Cooperative Extension; 1998. 4 p.

• Miller J. Venomoids: an overview. VenomousReptiles. org; 2001. http:// www.venomousreptiles.org/ articles/55

• Morita T. Structures and functions of snake venom CLPs (C-type lectin-like proteins) with anticoagulant-, procoagulant- and platelet-modulating activities. Toxicon 2005;45:1099–114.

• Paulchamy C. Pharmacological perspective of snake venoms from Viperidae Family. Internet J Pharmacol 2010;8:1–7.

• Qinghua L, Xiaowei Z, Wei Y, Chenji L, Yijun H, Pengxin Q, et al. A catalog for transcripts in the venom gland of the Agkistrodon acutus: identification of the toxins potentially involved in coagulopathy. Biochem Biophys Res Commun 2006;341:522–31.

• Wang YM, Wang SR, Tsai IH. Serine protease isoforms of Deinagkistrodon acutus venom: cloning, sequencing and phylogenetic analysis. Biochem J 2001;354:161– 8.

• White J. Overview of snake envenoming. In: Brent J, Wallace K, Burkhart K, Phillips S, Donovan J. Critical care toxicology. New York: Mosby; 2005. p 1051–74.

• WHO. Blood safety and laboratory technology: the clinical management of snake bites in the SouthEast Asian Region: annex 3— antivenoms for treating bites by South East Asian snakes—(listed by country of manufacture). http://www.searo.who.int/ en/Section10/Section17/ Section53/Section1024_3908. htm

SCORPION TOXINS

• Abdoon NA, Fatani AJ. Correlation between blood pressure, cytokines and nitric oxide in conscious rabbits injected with Leiurus quinquestriatus quinquestriatus scorpion venom. Toxicon 2009;54:471–80.

• Abroug F, Ouanes-Besbes L, Ouanes I, Dachraoui F, Hassen MF, Haguiga H, et al. Meta-analysis of controlled studies on immunotherapy in severe scorpion envenomation. Emerg Med J [Epub ahead of print 2011 May 11].

• Amitai, Y. Scorpions. In: Brent J, Wallace K, Burkhart K, Phillips S, Donovan J et al., eds, Critical care toxicology: diagnosis and management of the critically poisoned patient. Philadelphia (PA): Elsevier Mosby; 2005. p 1213–20.

• Bahloul M, Chaari A, Dammak H, Algia NB, Bouaziz M. Nosocomial scorpion envenomation: an unusual mode of scorpion sting. Clin Toxicol (Phila) 2010;48:962.

• Bawaskar HS, Bawaskar PH. Efficacy and safety of scorpion antivenom plūs prazosin compared with prazosin alone for venomous scorpion (Mesobuthus tamulus) sting: randomized open label clinical trial. BMJ 2010;341:c7136.

• Bosnak M, Ece A, Yobas I, Bosnak V, Kaplan M, Gurkan F. Scorpion sting envenomation in children in southeast Turkey. Wilderness Environ Med 2009;20:118–24.

• Bouaziz M, Bahloul M, Kallel H, Samet M, Ksibi H, Dammak H, et al. Epidemiological, clinical characteristics and outcome of severe scorpion envenomation in South Tunisia: multivariate analysis of 951 cases. Toxicon 2008;52:918–26.

• Chase P, Boyer-Hassen L, Mcnally J, Vazquez HL, Theodorou AA, Walter FG, Alagon A. Serum levels and urine detection of Centruroides sculpturatus venom in significantly envenomated patients. Clin Toxicol (Phila) 2009;47:24–8.

• Dehesa-Davila M, Alagon AC, Possani LD. Clinical toxicology of scorpion stings. In: Meier J, White J, eds. Handbook of clinical toxicology of animal venoms and poisons. Boca Raton: CRC Press; 1995. p 221–38.

• Fatani AJ, Ahmed A, Abdel-Halim RM, Abdoon NA, Darweesh AQ. Comparative study between the protective effects of Saudi and Egyptian antivenoms, alone or in combination with ion channel modulators, against deleterious actions of Leiurus quinquestriatus scorpion venom. Toxicon 2010;55:773–86.

• Jarrar BM, Al-Rowaily MA. Epidemiological aspects of scorpion stings in Al-Jouf Province, Saudi Arabia. Ann Saudi Med 2008;28:183–7.

• Lucas SM, Meier J. Biology and distribution of scorpions of medical importance. In: Meier J, White J, eds. Handbook of clinical toxicology of animal venoms and poisons. Boca Raton: CRC Press; 1995. p 205–19.

- Mills EJ, Ford N. Research into scorpion stings. BMJ 2011;342:c7369.

ABOUT THE AUTHOR

B arbarajean (BJ) Magnani, PhD, MD, FCAP, is internationally recognized for her expertise in clinical chemistry and toxicology, has been named a "Top Doctor" in *Boston* magazine and was named one of the Top 100 Most Influential Laboratory Medicine Professionals in the World by *The Pathologist*. She received her Master's and PhD from the State University of New York at Stony Brook, her medical degree from Boston University School of Medicine and completed her residency in Clinical Pathology at Tufts-New England Medical Center.

Dr. Magnani is currently Professor of Anatomic and Clinical Pathology (and Professor of Medicine) at Tufts University School of Medicine, Boston, MA, and serves as the Chair of the College of American Pathologists (CAP) Toxicology Committee. She is the author of *Lily Robinson and the Art of Secret Poisoning* (nVision Press), as well as one of the editors of *The Clinical Toxicology Laboratory: Contemporary Practice of Poisoning Evaluation, 2nd edition* (AACC Press) and *Clinical Toxicology Testing: A Guide for Laboratory Professionals* (CAP Press).

Made in United States
North Haven, CT
22 July 2024

55197995R00157